# MR. PENUMBRA'S
## 24-HOUR
## BOOKSTORE

**Center Point
Large Print**

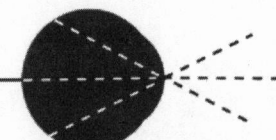

**This Large Print Book carries the
Seal of Approval of N.A.V.H.**

# MR. PENUMBRA'S
## 24-HOUR

## BOOKSTORE

# ROBIN SLOAN

CENTER POINT LARGE PRINT
THORNDIKE, MAINE

This Center Point Large Print edition
is published in the year 2012 by arrangement with
Farrar, Straus and Giroux.

This is a work of fiction.
All the characters, organizations, and events portrayed
in this novel are either products of the author's
imagination or are used fictitiously.

The text of this Large Print edition is unabridged.
In other aspects, this book may vary
from the original edition.
Printed in the United States of America
on permanent paper.
Set in 16-point Times New Roman type.

ISBN: 978-1-61173-609-0

Library of Congress Cataloging-in-Publication Data

Sloan, Robin, 1979–
    Mr. Penumbra's 24-hour bookstore / Robin Sloan.
    pages ; cm.
    ISBN 978-1-61173-609-0 (library binding : alk. paper)
    1. Bookstores—Employees—Fiction.
        2. Bookstores—California—San Francisco—Fiction.
        3. Large type books. I. Title.
        II. Title: Mister Penumbra's twenty-four hour bookstore.
    PS3619.L6278M77 2012b
    813′.6—dc23
                                                    2012033621

FOR BETTY ANN AND JIM

# CONTENTS

# THE BOOKSTORE

# HELP WANTED

LOST IN THE SHADOWS of the shelves, I almost fall off the ladder. I am exactly halfway up. The floor of the bookstore is far below me, the surface of a planet I've left behind. The tops of the shelves loom high above, and it's dark up there—the books are packed in close, and they don't let any light through. The air might be thinner, too. I think I see a bat.

I am holding on for dear life, one hand on the ladder, the other on the lip of a shelf, fingers pressed white. My eyes trace a line above my knuckles, searching the spines—and there, I spot it. The book I'm looking for.

But let me back up.

My name is Clay Jannon and those were the days when I rarely touched paper.

I'd sit at my kitchen table and start scanning help-wanted ads on my laptop, but then a browser tab would blink and I'd get distracted and follow a link to a long magazine article about genetically modified wine grapes. Too long, actually, so I'd add it to my reading list. Then I'd follow another link to a book review. I'd add the review to my reading list, too, then download the first chapter of the book—third in a series about vampire police. Then, help-wanted ads forgotten, I'd retreat to the living room, put my laptop on my belly, and read all day. I had a lot of free time.

I was unemployed, a result of the great food-chain contraction that swept through America in the early twenty-first century, leaving bankrupt burger chains and shuttered sushi empires in its wake.

The job I lost was at the corporate headquarters of NewBagel, which was based not in New York or anywhere else with a tradition of bagel-making but instead here in San Francisco. The company was very small and very new. It was founded by a pair of ex-Googlers who wrote software to design and bake the platonic bagel: smooth crunchy skin, soft doughy interior, all in a perfect circle. It was my first job out of art school, and I started as a designer, making marketing materials to explain and promote this tasty toroid: menus, coupons, diagrams, posters for store windows, and, once, an entire booth experience for a baked-goods trade show.

There was lots to do. First, one of the ex-Googlers asked me to take a crack at redesigning the company's logo. It had been big bouncy rainbow letters inside a pale brown circle; it looked pretty MS Paint. I redesigned it using a newish typeface with sharp black serifs that I thought sort of evoked the boxes and daggers of Hebrew letters. It gave NewBagel some gravitas and it won me an award from San Francisco's AIGA chapter.

Then, when I mentioned to the other ex-Googler that I knew how to code (sort of), she put me in charge of the website. So I redesigned that, too, and then managed a small marketing budget keyed to search terms like "bagel" and "breakfast" and "topology." I was also the voice of @NewBagel on Twitter and attracted a few hundred followers with a mix of breakfast trivia and digital coupons.

None of this represented the glorious next stage of human evolution, but I was learning things. I was moving up. But then the economy took a dip, and it turns out that in a recession, people want good old-fashioned bubbly oblong bagels, not smooth alien-spaceship bagels, not even if they're sprinkled with precision-milled rock salt.

The ex-Googlers were accustomed to success and they would not go quietly. They quickly rebranded to become the Old Jerusalem Bagel Company and abandoned the algorithm entirely so the bagels started coming out blackened and irregular. They instructed me to make the website look old-timey, a task that burdened my soul and earned me zero AIGA awards. The marketing budget dwindled, then disappeared. There was less and less to do. I wasn't learning anything and I wasn't moving anywhere.

Finally, the ex-Googlers threw in the towel and moved to Costa Rica. The ovens went cold and the website went dark. There was no money for severance, but I got to keep my company-issued MacBook and the Twitter account.

So then, after less than a year of employment, I was jobless. It turned out it was more than just the food chains that had contracted. People were living in motels and tent cities. The whole economy suddenly felt like a game of musical chairs, and I was convinced I needed to grab a seat, any seat, as fast as I could.

That was a depressing scenario when I considered the competition. I had friends who were designers like me, but they had already designed world-famous websites or advanced touch-screen interfaces, not just the logo for an upstart bagel shop. I had friends who worked at Apple. My best friend, Neel, ran his own company. Another year at NewBagel and I would have been in good shape, but I hadn't lasted long enough to build my portfolio, or even get particularly good at anything. I had an art-school thesis on Swiss typography (1957–1983) and I had a three-page website.

But I kept at it with the help-wanted ads. My standards were sliding swiftly. At first I had insisted I would only work at a company with a mission I believed in. Then I thought maybe it would be fine as long as I was learning something new. After that I decided it just couldn't be evil. Now I was carefully delineating my personal definition of evil.

It was paper that saved me. It turned out that I could stay focused on job hunting if I got myself away from the internet, so I would print out a ream of help-wanted ads, drop my phone in a drawer, and go for a walk. I'd crumple up the ads that required too much experience and deposit them in dented green trash cans along the way, and so by the time I'd exhausted myself and hopped on a bus back home, I'd have two or three promising prospectuses folded in my back pocket, ready for follow-up.

This routine did lead me to a job, though not in the way I'd expected.

San Francisco is a good place for walks if your legs are strong. The city is a tiny square punctuated by steep hills and bounded on three sides by water, and as a result, there are surprise vistas everywhere. You'll be walking along, minding your own business with a fistful of printouts, and suddenly the ground will fall away and you'll see straight down to the bay, with the buildings lit up orange and pink along the way. San Francisco's architectural style didn't really make inroads anywhere else in the country, and even when you live here and you're used to it, it lends the vistas a strangeness: all the tall narrow houses, the windows like eyes and teeth, the wedding-cake filigree. And looming behind it all, if you're facing the right direction, you'll see the rusty ghost of the Golden Gate Bridge.

I had followed one strange vista down a line of steep stairstepped sidewalks, then walked along the water, taking the very long way home. I had followed the line of old piers—carefully skirting the raucous chowder of Fisherman's Wharf—and watched seafood restaurants fade into nautical engineering firms and then social media startups. Finally, when my stomach rumbled, signaling its readiness for lunch, I had turned back in toward the city.

Whenever I walked the streets of San Francisco, I'd watch for HELP WANTED signs in windows—which is not something you really do, right? I should probably be more suspicious of those. Legitimate employers use Craigslist.

Sure enough, the 24-hour bookstore did not have the look of a legitimate employer:

HELP WANTED
Late Shift
Specific Requirements
Good Benefits

Now: I was pretty sure "24-hour bookstore" was a euphemism for something. It was on Broadway, in a euphemistic part of town. My help-wanted hike had taken me far from home; the place next door was called Booty's and it had a sign with neon legs that crossed and uncrossed.

I pushed the bookstore's glass door. It made a

bell tinkle brightly up above, and I stepped slowly through. I did not realize at the time what an important threshold I had just crossed.

Inside: imagine the shape and volume of a normal bookstore turned up on its side. This place was absurdly narrow and dizzyingly tall, and the shelves went all the way up—three stories of books, maybe more. I craned my neck back (why do bookstores always make you do uncomfortable things with your neck?) and the shelves faded smoothly into the shadows in a way that suggested they might just go on forever.

The shelves were packed close together, and it felt like I was standing at the border of a forest—not a friendly California forest, either, but an old Transylvanian forest, a forest full of wolves and witches and dagger-wielding bandits all waiting just beyond moonlight's reach. There were ladders that clung to the shelves and rolled side to side. Usually those seem charming, but here, stretching up into the gloom, they were ominous. They whispered rumors of accidents in the dark.

So I stuck to the front half of the store, where bright midday light pressed in and presumably kept the wolves at bay. The wall around and above the door was glass, thick square panes set into a grid of black iron, and arched across them, in tall golden letters, it said (in reverse):

MR. PENUMBRA'S 24-HOUR BOOKSTORE

Below that, set in the hollow of the arch, there was a symbol—two hands, perfectly flat, rising out of an open book.

So who was Mr. Penumbra?

"Hello, there," a quiet voice called from the stacks. A figure emerged—a man, tall and skinny like one of the ladders, draped in a light gray button-down and a blue cardigan. He tottered as he walked, running a long hand along the shelves for support. When he came out of the shadows, I saw that his sweater matched his eyes, which were also blue, riding low in nests of wrinkles. He was very old.

He nodded at me and gave a weak wave. "What do you seek in these shelves?"

That was a good line, and for some reason, it made me feel comfortable. I asked, "Am I speaking to Mr. Penumbra?"

"I am Penumbra"—he nodded—"and I am the custodian of this place."

I didn't quite realize I was going to say it until I did: "I'm looking for a job."

Penumbra blinked once, then nodded and tottered over to the desk set beside the front door. It was a massive block of dark-whorled wood, a solid fortress on the forest's edge. You could probably defend it for days in the event of a siege from the shelves.

"Employment." Penumbra nodded again. He slid up onto the chair behind the desk and regarded me across its bulk. "Have you ever worked at a bookstore before?"

"Well," I said, "when I was in school I waited tables at a seafood restaurant, and the owner sold his own cookbook." It was called *The Secret Cod* and it detailed thirty-one different ways to—You get it. "That probably doesn't count."

"No, it does not, but no matter," Penumbra said. "Prior experience in the book trade is of little use to you here."

Wait—maybe this place really was all erotica. I glanced down and around, but glimpsed no bodices, ripped or otherwise. In fact, just next to me there was a stack of dusty Dashiell Hammetts on a low table. That was a good sign.

"Tell me," Penumbra said, "about a book you love."

I knew my answer immediately. No competition. I told him, "Mr. Penumbra, it's not one book, but a series. It's not the best writing and it's probably too long and the ending is terrible, but I've read it three times, and I met my best friend because we were both obsessed with it back in sixth grade." I took a breath. "I love *The Dragon-Song Chronicles*."

Penumbra cocked an eyebrow, then smiled. "That is good, very good," he said, and his smile grew, showing jostling white teeth. Then he squinted at me, and his gaze went up and down. "But can you climb a ladder?"

• • •

And that is how I find myself on this ladder, up on the third floor, minus the floor, of Mr. Penumbra's 24-Hour Bookstore. The book I've been sent up to retrieve is called AL-ASMARI and it's about 150 percent of one arm-length to my left. Obviously, I need to return to the floor and scoot the ladder over. But down below, Penumbra is shouting, "Lean, my boy! Lean!"

And wow, do I ever want this job.

# COAT BUTTONS

SO THAT WAS A MONTH AGO. Now I'm the night clerk at Penumbra's, and I go up and down that ladder like a monkey. There's a real technique to it. You roll the ladder into place, lock its wheels, then bend your knees and leap directly to the third or fourth rung. You pull with your arms to keep your momentum going, and in a moment you're already five feet in the air. As you're climbing, you look straight ahead, not up or down; you keep your eyes focused about a foot in front of your face and you let the books zoom by in a blur of colorful spines. You count the rungs in your head, and finally, when you're at the right level, reaching for the book you've come up to retrieve . . . why, of course, you lean.

As a professional capability, this might not be as marketable as web design, but it's probably more fun, and at this point I'll take anything I can get.

I only wish I had to use my new skill more often. Mr. Penumbra's 24-Hour Bookstore does not operate around the clock due to an overwhelming number of customers. In fact, there are hardly any, and sometimes I feel more like a night watchman than a clerk.

Penumbra sells used books, and they are in such uniformly excellent condition that they might as well be new. He buys them during the day—you can only sell to the man with his name on the windows—and he must be a tough customer. He doesn't seem to pay much attention to the bestseller lists. His inventory is eclectic; there's no evidence of pattern or purpose other than, I suppose, his own personal taste. So, no teenage wizards or vampire police here. That's a shame, because this is exactly the kind of store that makes you want to buy a book about a teenage wizard. This is the kind of store that makes you want to *be* a teenage wizard.

I've told my friends about Penumbra's, and a few of them have stopped in to ogle the shelves and watch me climb into the dusty heights. I'll usually cajole them into buying something: a Steinbeck novel, some Borges stories, a thick Tolkien tome—all of those authors evidently of interest to Penumbra, because he stocks the complete works of each. At the minimum, I'll send my friends packing with a postcard. There's a pile of them on the front desk. They show the front of the store in pen and ink—a fine-lined design so old and uncool that it's become cool again—and Penumbra sells them for a dollar each.

But a buck every few hours doesn't pay my salary. I can't figure out what does pay my salary. I can't figure out what keeps this bookstore in business at all.

There's a customer I've seen twice now, a

woman who I am fairly certain works next door at Booty's. I am fairly certain about this because both times her eyes were ringed raccoon-like with mascara and she smelled like smoke. She has a bright smile and dusty blond-brown hair. I can't tell how old she is—she could be a tough twenty-three or a remarkable thirty-one—and I don't know her name, but I do know she likes biographies.

On her first visit, she browsed the front shelves in a slow circle, scuffing her feet and doing absentminded stretches, then came up to the front desk. "D'you have the one about Steve Jobs?" she asked. She was wearing a puffy North Face jacket over a pink tank top and jeans, and her voice had a little twang in it.

I frowned and said, "Probably not. But let's check."

Penumbra has a database that runs on a decrepit beige Mac Plus. I pecked its creator's name into the keyboard and the Mac made a low chime—the sound of success. She was in luck.

We tilted our heads to scan the BIOGRAPHY section and there it was: a single copy, shiny like new. Maybe it had been a Christmas present to a tech-executive dad who didn't actually read books. Or maybe Tech Dad wanted to read it on his Kindle instead. In any case, somebody sold it here, and it passed Penumbra's muster. Miraculous.

"He was so handsome," North Face said, holding the book at arm's length. Steve Jobs peered out of the white cover, hand on his chin, wearing round glasses that looked a bit like Penumbra's.

A week later, she came hopping through the front door, grinning and silently clapping her hands—it made her seem more twenty-three than thirty-one—and said, "Oh, it was just great! Now listen"—here she got serious—"he wrote another one, about Einstein." She held out her phone, which showed an Amazon product page for Walter Isaacson's biography of Einstein. "I saw it on the internet but I thought maybe I could buy it here?"

Let's be clear: This was incredible. This was a bookseller's dream. This was a stripper standing athwart history, yelling, *Stop!*—and then we discovered, heads tilted hopefully, that Penumbra's BIOGRAPHY section did not contain *Einstein: His Life and Universe.* There were five different books about Richard Feynman, but nothing at all about Albert Einstein. Thus spoke Penumbra.

"Really?" North Face pouted. "Shoot. Well, I guess I'll buy it online. Thanks." She wandered back out into the night, and so far she hasn't returned.

Let me be candid. If I had to rank book-acquisition experiences in order of comfort, ease, and satisfaction, the list would go like this:

1. The perfect independent bookstore, like Pygmalion in Berkeley.
2. A big, bright Barnes & Noble. I know they're corporate, but let's face it—those stores are nice. Especially the ones with big couches.
3. The book aisle at Walmart. (It's next to the potting soil.)
4. The lending library aboard the U.S.S. *West Virginia*, a nuclear submarine deep beneath the surface of the Pacific.
5. Mr. Penumbra's 24-Hour Bookstore.

So I set myself to righting the ship. No, I do not know anything about bookstore management. No, I do not have my finger on the pulse of the post-strip-club shopping crowd. No, I have never really righted any ships, unless you count the time I saved the Rhode Island School of Design fencing club from bankruptcy by organizing a twenty-four-hour Errol Flynn movie marathon. But I do know there are things that Penumbra is obviously doing wrong—things he isn't doing at all.

Like marketing.

I have a plan: First I'll prove myself with some small successes, then ask for a budget to place some print ads, put a few signs in the window, maybe even go big with a banner on the bus shelter just up the street: WAITING FOR YOUR BUS? COME WAIT WITH US! Then I'll keep the bus schedule open on my laptop so I can give customers a five-minute warning when the next one is coming. It will be brilliant.

But I have to start small, and with no customers to distract me, I work hard. First, I connect to the unprotected Wi-Fi network next door called *bootynet*. Then I go one by one through the local review sites, writing glowing reports of this hidden gem. I send friendly emails with winking emoticons to local blogs. I create a Facebook group with one member. I sign up for Google's hyper-targeted local advertising program—the same one we used at NewBagel—which allows you to identify your quarry with absurd precision. I choose characteristics from Google's long form:

- lives in San Francisco
- likes books
- night owl
- carries cash
- not allergic to dust
- enjoys Wes Anderson movies
- recent GPS ping within five blocks of here

I only have ten dollars to spend on this, so I have to be specific.

That's all the demand side. There's also supply to think about, and Penumbra's supply is capricious to say the least—but that's only part of the story. Mr. Penumbra's 24-Hour Bookstore is, I have learned, really two stores in one.

There's the more-or-less normal bookstore, which is up front, packed in tight around the desk. There are short shelves marked HISTORY and BIOGRAPHY and POETRY. There's Aristotle's *Nicomachean Ethics* and Trevanian's *Shibumi*. This more-or-less normal bookstore is spotty and frustrating, but at least it's stocked with titles that you could find in a library or on the internet.

The other bookstore is stacked behind and above all that, on the tall laddered shelves, and it is comprised of volumes that, as far as Google knows, don't exist. Trust me, I've searched. Many of these have the look of antiquity—cracked leather, gold-leaf titles—but others are freshly bound with bright crisp covers. So they're not all ancient. They're just all . . . unique.

I think of this as the Waybacklist.

When I started working here, I assumed they were just all from tiny presses. Tiny Amish presses with no taste for digital record-keeping. Or I thought maybe it was all self-published work—a whole collection of hand-bound one-offs that never made it to the Library of Congress or anywhere else. Maybe Penumbra's was a kind of orphanage.

But now, a month into my clerkship, I'm starting to think it's more complicated than that. You see, to go with the second store, there's a second set of customers—a small community of people who orbit the store like strange moons. They are nothing like North Face. They are older. They arrive with algorithmic regularity. They never browse. They come wide awake, completely sober, and vibrating with need. For example:

The bell above the door will tinkle, and before it's done, Mr. Tyndall will be shouting, breathless, "Kingslake! I need Kingslake!" He'll take his hands off his head (has he really been running down the street with his hands on his head?) and clamp them down on the front desk. He will repeat it, as if he's already told me once that my shirt is on fire, and why am I not taking swift action:

"Kingslake! Quickly!"

The database on the Mac Plus encompasses the regular books and the Waybacklist alike. The latter aren't shelved according to title or subject (do they even have subjects?), so the computer assist is crucial. Now I will type K-I-N-G-S-L-A-K-E and the Mac will churn slowly—Tyndall bouncing on his heels—and then chime and show its cryptic response. Not BIOGRAPHY or HISTORY or SCIENCE FICTION AND FANTASY, but: 3-13. That's the Waybacklist, aisle 3, shelf 13, which is only about ten feet up.

"Oh, thank goodness, thank you, yes, thank goodness," Tyndall will say, ecstatic. "Here is my book"—he will produce a very large book from somewhere, possibly his pants; it will be the one

28

he's returning, exchanging for KINGSLAKE— "and here is my card." He will slide a prim laminated card across the table, marked with the same symbol that graces the front windows. It will bear a cryptic code, stamped hard into the heavy paper, which I will record. Tyndall will be, as always, lucky number 6WNJHY. I will mistype it twice.

After I do my monkey business on the ladder, I will wrap KINGSLAKE in brown paper. I will try to make small talk: "How's your night going, Mr. Tyndall?"

"Oh, very good, better now," he will breathe, taking the package with shaking hands. "Making progress, slow, steady, sure! *Festina lente*, thank you, thank you!" Then the bell will tinkle again as he hurries back out into the street. It will be three in the morning.

Is this a book club? How do they join? Do they ever pay?

These are the things I ask myself when I sit here alone, after Tyndall or Lapin or Fedorov has left. Tyndall is probably the weirdest, but they're all pretty weird: all graying, single-minded, seemingly imported from some other time or place. There are no iPhones. There's no mention of current events or pop culture or anything, really, other than the books. I definitely think of them as a club, though I have no evidence that they know one another. Each comes in alone and never says a word about anything other than the object of his or her current, frantic fascination.

I don't know what's inside those books—and it's part of my job not to know. After the ladder test, back on the day I was hired, Penumbra stood behind the front desk, gazed at me with bright blue eyes, and said:

"This job has three requirements, each very strict. Do not agree to them lightly. Clerks in this store have followed these rules for nearly a century, and I will not have them broken now. One: You must always be here from ten p.m. to six a.m. exactly. You must not be late. You cannot leave early. Two: You may not browse, read, or otherwise inspect the shelved volumes. Retrieve them for members. That is all."

I know what you're thinking: dozens of nights alone, and you've never cracked a cover? No, I haven't. For all I know, Penumbra has a camera somewhere. If I sneak a peek and he finds out, I'm fired. My friends are dropping like flies out there; whole industries, whole parts of the country, are shutting down. I don't want to live in a tent. I need this job.

And besides, the third rule makes up for the second:

"You must keep precise records of all trans-actions. The time. The customer's appearance. His state of mind. How he asks for the book. How he receives it. Does he appear to be injured. Is he wearing a sprig of rosemary on his hat. And so on."

I guess under normal circumstances this would feel like a creepy job requirement. Under the actual circumstances—lending strange books to stranger scholars in the middle of the night—it feels perfectly appropriate. So, rather than spend my time staring at the forbidden shelves, I spend it writing about the customers.

On my first night, Penumbra showed me a low shelf inside the front desk where, lined up, there was a set of oversized leather-bound tomes, all identical except for bright Roman numerals on their spines. "Our logbooks," he said, running his finger down the line, "going back nearly a century." He hauled up the rightmost tome and laid it on the desk with a heavy *whump*. "You will help to keep them now." The logbook's cover bore the word NARRATIO, deeply embossed, and a symbol—the symbol from the front windows. Two hands, open like a book.

"Open it," Penumbra said.

Inside, the pages were wide and gray, filled with dark handwriting. There were sketches, too: thumbnail portraits of bearded men, tight geometric doodles. Penumbra gave the pages a heave and found the place about halfway through, marked with an ivory bookmark, where the writing ran out. "You will note names, times, and

31

titles," he said, tapping the page, "but also, as I said, manner and appearance. We keep a record for every member, and for every customer who might yet become a member, in order to track their work." He paused, then added, "Some of them are working very hard indeed."

"What are they doing?"

"My boy!" he said, eyebrows raised. As if nothing could be more obvious: "They are reading."

So, on the pages of the book labeled NARRATIO, numbered IX, I do my best to keep a clear, accurate record of what transpires during my shift, with only an occasional literary flourish. I guess you could say rule number two isn't quite absolute. There's one weird book I'm allowed to touch in Penumbra's. It's the one I'm writing.

When I see Penumbra in the morning, if there's been a customer, he will ask me about it. I'll read a bit out of the logbook, and he will nod at my record-keeping. But then he will probe even deeper: "A respectable rendering of Mr. Tyndall," he'll say. "But tell me, do you remember, were the buttons on his coat made of mother-of-pearl? Or were they horn? Some kind of metal? Copper?"

Yes, okay: it does seem strange that Penumbra keeps this dossier. I can't imagine a purpose for it, not even a nefarious one. But when people are past a certain age, you sort of stop asking them why they do things. It feels dangerous. What if you say, *So, Mr. Penumbra, why do you want to know about Mr. Tyndall's coat buttons?* and he pauses, and scratches his chin, and there's an uncomfortable silence—and we both realize he can't remember?

Or what if he fires me on the spot?

Penumbra keeps his own counsel, and the message is clear: do your job, and don't ask questions. My friend Aaron just got laid off last week and now he's going to move back in with his parents in Sacramento. In this economic environment, I prefer not to test Penumbra's boundaries. I need this chair.

Mr. Tyndall's coat buttons were jade.

# MATROPOLIS

T O RUN MR. PENUMBRA'S 24-Hour Bookstore around the clock, one owner and two
clerks divide the circle of the sun into thirds, and
I get the darkest slice. Penumbra himself takes
the mornings—I guess you'd call it prime time,
except that this store doesn't really have one of
those. I mean, a single customer is a major event,
and a single customer is as likely to show up at
midnight as at half-past noon.

So I pass the bookstore baton to Penumbra, but
I receive it from Oliver Grone, the quiet soul who
carries it through the evening.

Oliver is tall and solid, with thick limbs and
huge feet. He has curly, coppery hair and ears that
stick out perpendicular to his head. In another life,
he might have played football or rowed crew or
kept low-class gentlemen out of the club next
door. In this life, Oliver is a graduate student at
Berkeley, studying archaeology. Oliver is training
to be a museum curator.

He's quiet—too quiet for his size. He speaks in
short, simple sentences and always seems to be
thinking about something else, something long
ago and/or far away. Oliver daydreams about
Ionian columns.

His knowledge runs deep. One night I quizzed
him using a book called *The Stuff of Legend*,

snagged from the bottom of Penumbra's tiny HISTORY section. I covered the headings with my hand and showed him the photos alone:

"Minoan bull totem, 1700 B.C.," he called out. Correct.

"Basse Yutz flagon, 450 B.C. Maybe 500." Yes.

"Roof tile, A.D. 600. Gotta be Korean." Also yes.

At the end of the quiz, Oliver was ten for ten. I'm convinced his brain simply works on a different time scale. I can barely remember what I ate for lunch yesterday; Oliver, on the other hand, is casually aware of what was happening in 1000 B.C. and what it all looked like.

This makes me jealous. Right now, Oliver Grone and I are peers: we have exactly the same job and sit in exactly the same chair. But soon, very soon, he will advance by one very significant degree and accelerate away from me. He will find a place in the real world, because he's good at something—something other than climbing ladders in a lonely bookstore.

Every night I show up at 10:00 p.m. and find Oliver behind the front desk, always reading a book, always with a title like *The Care and Feeding of Terra-Cotta* or *Arrowhead Atlas of Pre-Columbian America*. Every night I rap my fingers on the dark wood. He looks up and says, "Hey, Clay." Every night I take his place, and we nod farewell like soldiers—like men who uniquely understand each other's circumstances.

• • •

When I'm done with my shift, it's six in the morning, which is an awkward time to be set loose in the world. Generally I go home and read or play video games. I'd say it was to unwind except that the night shift at Penumbra's doesn't really wind a person up. So mostly I'm just killing time until my roommates rise to meet me.

Mathew Mittelbrand is our artist-in-residence. He's rail-thin, pale-skinned, and keeps strange hours—even stranger than mine, because they're less predictable. Many mornings I don't have to wait for Mat; instead, I come home to discover that he's been up all night toiling on his latest project.

During the day (more or less) Mat works on special effects at Industrial Light and Magic in the Presidio, making props and sets for movies. He gets paid to design and build laser rifles and haunted castles. But—I find this very impressive—he doesn't use computers. Mat is part of the dwindling tribe of special-effects artists who still make things with knives and glue.

Whenever he's not at ILM, Mat is working on some project of his own. He works with crazy intensity, feeding hours like dry twigs into the fire, just absolutely consuming them, burning them up. He sleeps lightly and briefly, often sitting up straight in a chair or lying pharaoh-like on the couch. He's like a storybook spirit, a little djinn or something, except instead of air or water his element is imagination.

Mat's latest project is his biggest yet, and soon there won't be room for me or the couch anymore. Mat's latest project is taking over the living room.

He calls it Matropolis, and it's made out of boxes and cans, paper and foam. It's a model railroad with no railroad. The underlying topography is all steep hills made from packing peanuts held in place with wire mesh. It started on one card table, but Mat has added two more, both at different levels, like tectonic plates. Spreading across the tabletop terrain there's a city.

It's a scaled-down dreamscape, a bright glittering hyper-city made with scraps of the familiar. There are Gehry-esque curves made from smooth tinfoil. There are Gothic spikes and crenellations made from dry macaroni. There is an Empire State Building made from shards of green glass.

Taped to the wall behind the card tables there are Mat's photo references: printed-out images of museums, cathedrals, office towers, and row houses. Some are skyline shots, but more are close-ups: zoomed-in photos of surfaces and textures taken by Mat himself. Often he stands and stares at them, rubbing his chin, processing the grit and glint, breaking it down and reassembling it with his own bespoke LEGO set. Mat uses everyday materials so ingeniously that their original provenance fades away and you can only see them as the tiny buildings they've become.

On the couch there's a black plastic radio remote; I pick it up and click one of the knobs. A toy-sized airship dozing near the doorway buzzes to life and scoots toward Matropolis. Its master can maneuver it so it docks at the top of the Empire State Building, but I can only make it bump against the windows.

Just up the hall from Matropolis is my bedroom. There are three rooms here for three roommates. Mine is the smallest, just a little white cube with Edwardian filigree in the ceiling. Mat's room is the biggest by far, but it's drafty—it's up in the attic, at the top of a steep narrow staircase. And the third room, a perfect balance between size and comfort, belongs to our third roommate, Ashley Adams. She's currently asleep but will not be for long. Ashley rises at precisely six forty-five every morning.

Ashley is beautiful. Probably too beautiful—too shiny and clean-lined, like a 3-D model. Her hair is blond and straight, cropped clean at her shoulders. Her arms are toned from twice-weekly rock-climbing sessions. Her skin is perpetually sun-kissed. Ashley is an account executive at a PR agency, and in that capacity she ran PR for NewBagel, which is how we met. She liked my logo. At first I thought I had a crush on her, but then I realized she's an android.

I don't mean that in a bad way! I mean, when we figure them out, androids are going to be totally great, right? Smart and strong and organized and thoughtful. Ashley is all of those things. And she's our patron: the apartment is hers. She's been living here for years, and our low rent reflects her long tenure.

I for one welcome our new android overlords.

After I'd been here for about nine months, our then-roommate Vanessa moved to Canada to get an eco-MBA, and it was me who found Mat to replace her. He was a friend of a friend from art school; I'd seen his show at a tiny white-walled gallery, all miniature neighborhoods built inside wine bottles and lightbulbs. When it came to pass that we were looking for a roommate and he was looking for an apartment, I was excited about living side by side with an artist, but I wasn't sure Ashley would go for it.

Mat came to visit, wearing a snug blue blazer over sharp-creased slacks. We sat in the living room (then dominated by a flat-screen TV, with no tabletop cities even dreamt of) and he told us about his current task at ILM: the design and construction of a bloodthirsty demon with blue-denim skin. It was part of a horror movie set inside an Abercrombie & Fitch.

"I'm learning how to sew," he explained. Then

he pointed to one of Ashley's cuffs: "Those are really good seams."

Later, after Mat left, Ashley told me she appreciated his neatness. "So if you think he'll be a good fit, I'm fine with him," she said.

This is the key to our harmonious cohabitation: although their objectives are different, Mat and Ashley share a deep appreciation for details. For Mat, it's a tiny graffiti tag on a tiny subway stop. For Ashley, it's underwear that matches her twinset.

But the true test came early, with Mat's first project. It happened in the kitchen.

The kitchen: Ashley's sanctum sanctorum. I tread lightly in the kitchen; I prepare meals that are easy to clean up, like pasta and Pop-Tarts. I do not use her fancy Microplane or her complicated garlic press. I know how to turn the burners on and off, but not how to activate the oven's convection chamber, which I suspect requires two keys, like the launch mechanism on a nuclear missile.

Ashley loves the kitchen. She's a foodie, an epicurean, and she's never prettier, or more android-perfect, than on weekends, cooking a fragrant risotto in a color-coordinated apron with her hair tied in a blond knot on top of her head.

Mat could have done his first project up in the attic, or in the small scrubby backyard. But no. He chose the kitchen.

This was during my post-NewBagel period of

unemployment, so I was there to watch it happen. In fact, I was leaning in close, inspecting Mat's handiwork, when Ashley appeared. She was just home from work, still dressed in J.Crew carbon and cream. She gasped.

Mat had a huge Pyrex cauldron set up on the stove, and inside there was a slow-churning mixture of oil and dye. It was heavy and highly viscous, and with the slow application of heat from below, it was curling and blooming in slow motion. The kitchen lights were all turned off, and Mat had two bright arc lamps set up behind the cauldron; they shone through and cast red and purple shadows that spun across the granite and travertine.

I straightened and stood, silent. The last time I'd been caught like this, I was nine, making vinegar-and-baking-soda volcanoes on the kitchen table after school. My mom wore pants just like Ashley's.

Mat's eyes rose slowly. His sleeves were rolled up around his elbows. His dark leather shoes were shiny in the gloom, and so were the tips of his fingers, coated in oil.

"It's a simulation of the Horsehead Nebula," he said. Obviously.

Ashley was silent, staring. Her mouth hung open a little bit. Her keys were dangling on her finger, arrested in midflight toward the tidy peg where they lived, just above the chore checklist.

Mat had been living with us for three days.

Ashley took two steps forward and leaned in close, just as I had, and peered into the cosmic depths. A saffron blob was pushing its way up through a roiling layer of green and gold.

"Holy shit, Mat," she breathed. "That's beautiful."

So Mat's astrophysical stew simmered on, and his other projects continued in sequence, getting bigger and messier and taking up more space. Ashley took an interest in his progress; she'd wander into the room, put a hand on one hip, scrunch her nose, and make a deftly constructive comment. She moved the TV herself.

This is Mat's secret weapon, his passport, his get-out-of-jail-free card: Mat makes things that are beautiful.

So of course I told Mat he should come visit the bookstore, and tonight he does, at half-past two. The bell over the door tinkles to announce his arrival, and before he says a word, his neck bends back to follow the shelves up into the shadowy reaches. He turns toward me, points a plaid-jacketed arm straight to the ceiling, and says: "I want to go up there."

I've only been working here for a month and don't quite have the confidence for mischief yet, but Mat's curiosity is infectious. He stalks straight over to the Waybacklist and stands between the shelves, leaning in close, examining the grain of the wood, the texture of the spines.

I concede: "Okay, but you have to hold on tight. And don't touch any of the books."

"Don't touch them?" he says, testing the ladder. "What if I want to buy one?"

"You can't buy them—they're for borrowing. You have to be a member of the club."

"Rare books? First editions?" He's already in midair. He moves fast.

"More like only editions," I say. No ISBNs here.

"What are they about?"

"I don't know," I say quietly.

"What?"

Saying it louder, I realize how lame it sounds: "I don't know."

"You've never looked at one?" He's paused on the ladder, looking back down. Incredulous.

Now I'm getting nervous. I know where this is going.

"Seriously, never?" He's reaching for the shelves.

I consider shaking the ladder to signal my displeasure, but the only thing more problematic than Mat looking at one of the books would be Mat plunging to his death. Probably. He has one in his hands, a fat black-bound volume that threatens to unbalance him. He teeters on the ladder and I grit my teeth.

44

"Hey, Mat," I say, my voice suddenly high-pitched and whiny, "why don't you just leave it—"

"This is amazing."

"You should—"

"Seriously amazing, Jannon. You've never seen this?" He clutches the book to his chest and takes a step back down.

"Wait!" Somehow it feels less transgressive to keep it closer to the place where it belongs. "I'll come up." I pull another ladder into position opposite his and leap up the rungs. In a moment, Mat and I are level, having a hushed conference at thirty feet.

The truth, of course, is that I am desperately curious. I'm annoyed at Mat, but also grateful that he's playing the part of the devil on my shoulder. He balances the thick volume against his chest and tilts it my way. It's dark up here, so I lean across the space between the shelves to see the pages clearly.

For this, Tyndall and the rest come running in the middle of the night?

"I was hoping it would be an encyclopedia of dark rituals," Mat says.

The two-page spread shows a solid matrix of letters, a blanket of glyphs with hardly a trace of white space. The letters are big and bold, punched onto the paper in a sharp serif. I recognize the alphabet—it's roman, which is to say, normal—but not the words. Actually, there aren't really words at all. The pages are just long runs of letters—an undifferentiated jumble.

"Then again," Mat says, "we have no way of knowing it's *not* an encyclopedia of dark rituals . . ."

I pull another book from the shelf, this one tall and flat with a bright green cover and a brown spine that says KRESIMIR. Inside, it's just the same.

"Maybe they're recreational puzzles," Mat says. "Like, super-advanced sudoku."

Penumbra's customers are, in fact, exactly the kind of people you'd see in coffee shops, working through one-sided chess problems or solving Saturday crosswords with blue ballpoints pressed perilously hard into the newsprint.

Down below, the bell tinkles. A jangle of cold fear makes a quick round-trip from my brain to my fingertips and back. From the front of the store, a low voice calls out, "Is anyone der?"

I hiss at Mat: "Put it back." Then I hustle down the ladder.

When I step wheezing from the stacks, it is Fedorov at the door. Of all the customers I've met, he's the oldest—his beard is snowy white and the skin on his hands is papery-thin—but also probably the most clear-eyed. He seems a lot like Penumbra, actually. Now he slides a book across the desk—he's returning CLOVTIER—then taps two fingers sharply and says, "I vill need Murao next."

Here we go. I find MVRAO in the database and send Mat back up the ladder. Fedorov eyes him curiously. "Anudder clerk?"

"A friend," I say. "Just helping out."

Fedorov nods. It occurs to me that Mat could pass muster as a very young member of this club. He and Fedorov are both wearing brown corduroys tonight.

"You hev been here, vat, tirty-seven days?"

I couldn't have told you that, but yes, I'm sure it's thirty-seven days exactly. These guys tend to be very precise. "That's right, Mr. Fedorov," I say cheerily.

"End vat do you tink?"

"I like it," I say. "It's better than working in an office."

Fedorov nods at that and passes over his card. He's 6KZVCY, naturally. "I vorked at HP"—he says it *Heych-Pee*—"for tirty years. Now, det vas an office." Then he ventures: "You hev used a HP celculator?"

Mat returns with MVRAO. It's a big one, thick and wide, bound in mottled leather.

"Oh, yeah, definitely," I say, wrapping the book in brown paper. "I had one of the graphing calculators all through high school. It was an HP-38."

Fedorov beams like a proud grandparent. "I vorked on de tventy-eight, vhich vas de precursor!"

That makes me smile. "I probably still have it somewhere," I tell him, and pass MVRAO across the front desk.

Fedorov scoops it up in both hands. "Tenk you," he says. "You know, de tirty-eight did not hev Reverse Polish Notation"—he gives his book (of dark rituals?) a meaningful tap—"end I should tell you, RPN is hendy for dis kind of work."

I think Mat's right: sudoku. "I'll keep that in mind," I say.

"Okay, tenk you again." The bell tinkles and we watch Fedorov go slowly up the sidewalk toward the bus stop.

"I looked at his book," Mat says. "Same as the others."

What seemed strange before now seems even stranger.

"Jannon," Mat says, turning to face me squarely. "There's something I have to ask you."

"Let me guess," I say. "Why haven't I ever looked at the—"

"Do you have a thing for Ashley?"

Well, that's not what I expected. "What? No."

"Okay, good. Because I do."

I blink and stare blankly at Mat Mittelbrand standing there in his tiny, perfectly tailored suit jacket. It's like Jimmy Olsen confessing that he has a thing for Wonder Woman. The contrast is just too much. And yet—

"I'm going to put the moves on her," he says gravely. "Things might get weird." He says it like a commando setting up a midnight raid. Like: *Sure, this is going to be extraordinarily dangerous, but don't worry. I've done it before.*

My vision shifts. Maybe Mat isn't Jimmy Olsen but Clark Kent, and underneath there's a Superman. He would have to be a five-foot-four Superman, but still.

"I mean, technically, we already made out once."

Wait, what—

"Two weeks ago. You weren't home. You were here. We drank a bunch of wine."

My head spins a little, not with the dissonance of Mat and Ashley together, but with the realization that this thread of attraction has been twisting under my nose and I had no idea. I hate it when that happens.

Mat nods, as if that's all settled now. "Okay, Jannon. This place is awesome. But I gotta go."

"Back to the apartment?"

"No, the office. Pulling an all-nighter. Jungle monster."

"Jungle monster."

"Made from living plants. We have to keep the studio really hot. I might come back for another break. This place is cool and dry."

Mat leaves. Later, in the logbook, I write:

A cool night with no clouds. The bookstore is visited by the youngest customer it has seen in (this clerk believes) many years. He wears corduroys, a tailored suit jacket, and, under it, a sweater-vest stitched with tiny tigers. The customer purchases one postcard (under duress), then makes his exit to resume work on a jungle monster.

It's very quiet. I set my chin in my palm and count my friends and wonder what else is hiding in plain sight.

# THE DRAGON-SONG
# CHRONICLES, VOLUME I

T HE NEXT NIGHT, another friend visits the
store, and not just any friend: my oldest.
Neel Shah and I have been best friends since
sixth grade. In the unpredictable fluid dynamics
of middle school, I found myself somehow
floating near the top, an inoffensive everyman
who was just good enough at basketball and not
cripplingly afraid of girls. Neel, by contrast, sank
straight to the bottom, shunned by jock and nerd
alike. My cafeteria tablemates snorted that he
looked funny, talked funny, smelled funny.

But we bonded that spring over a shared
obsession with books about singing dragons, and
we ended up best friends. I stood up for him,
defended him, expended prepubescent political
capital on his behalf. I got him invited to pizza
parties and lured members of the basketball team
into our Rockets & Warlocks role-playing group.
(They didn't last long. Neel was always the
dungeon master, and he always sent single-minded
droids and undead orcs after them.) In seventh
grade, I suggested to Amy Torgensen, a pretty
straw-haired girl who loved horses, that Neel's
father was an exiled prince, rich beyond measure,
and that Neel might therefore make an excellent
escort to the winter formal. It was his first date.

So I guess you could say Neel owes me a few favors, except that so many favors have passed between us now that they are no longer distinguishable as individual acts, just a bright haze of loyalty. Our friendship is a nebula.

Now Neel Shah appears framed in the front door, tall and solid, wearing a snug black track jacket, and he ignores the tall dusty Waybacklist completely. Instead he zeroes in on the short shelf labeled SCIENCE FICTION AND FANTASY.

"Dude, you've got Moffat!" he says, holding up a fat paperback. It's *The Dragon-Song Chronicles, Volume I*—the very book we bonded over back in sixth grade, and still our mutual favorite. I've read it three times. Neel has probably read it six.

"This is like an old copy, too," he says, riffling the pages. He's right. The newest edition of the trilogy, published after Clark Moffat died, features stark geometric covers that make a single continuous pattern when you line all three books up on the shelf. This one has an airbrushed rendering of a fat blue dragon wreathed in sea foam.

I tell Neel he ought to buy it, because it's a collector's edition and it's probably worth more than whatever Penumbra is charging. And because I haven't sold more than a postcard in six days. Normally I'd feel bad pressuring one of my friends to buy a book, but Neel Shah is now, if not quite rich beyond measure, then definitely competitive with some low-level princes. At

52

around the same time I was struggling to make minimum wage at Oh My Cod! in Providence, Neel was starting his own company. Fast-forward five years and see the magic of compound effort: Neel has, to my best approximation, a few hundred thousand dollars in the bank, and his company is worth millions more. By contrast, I have exactly $2,357 in the bank and the company I work for—if you can call it a company—exists in the extrafinancial space inhabited by money launderers and fringe churches.

Anyway, I figure Neel can spring for an old paperback, even if he doesn't really have time to read anymore. While I'm digging for change in the front desk's dark drawers, his attention turns, at last, to the shadowy shelves dominating the back half of the store.

"What's all that?" he says. He's not sure if he's interested or not. As a rule, Neel prefers the new and shiny to the old and dusty.

"That," I say, "is the real store."

Mat's intervention has made me a bit bolder with the Waybacklist.

"What if I told you," I say, leading Neel back toward the shelves, "that this bookstore was frequented by a group of strange scholars?"

"Awesome," Neel says, nodding. He smells warlocks.

"And what if I told you"—I pick a black-bound book from a low shelf—"that every one of these

53

books is written in code?" I open it wide to show a field of jumbled letters.

"That's crazy," Neel says. He traces a finger down the page, through the maze of serifs. "I've got a guy from Belarus who breaks codes. Copy protection, stuff like that."

Embedded in that sentence is the difference between Neel's life, post–middle school, and mine: Neel has guys—guys who do things for him. I don't have guys. I barely have a laptop.

"I could have him take a look at this," Neel continues.

"Well, I don't know for sure that they're in code," I admit. I close the book and slide it back onto the shelf. "And even if they are, I'm not sure it's, like, worth cracking. The guys who borrow these books are pretty weird."

"That's always how it starts!" Neel says, thumping my shoulder. "Think of *The Dragon-Song Chronicles*. Do you meet Telemach Half-Blood on the first page? No, dude. You meet Fernwen."

The main character of *The Dragon-Song Chronicles* is Fernwen the scholarly dwarf, who is small even by dwarven standards. He was cast out of his warrior clan at an early age and—anyway, yes, maybe Neel has a point.

"We gotta figure this out," he says. "How much?"

I explain how it works, how the members all have cards—but now it's not just idle talk.

Whatever the cost to join Penumbra's lending club, Neel can pay it.

"Find out how much it costs," Neel says. "You're sitting on a Rockets & Warlocks scenario here, I swear." He's grinning. He switches to his low dungeon-master voice: "Do not wuss out now, Claymore Redhands."

Oof. He's deployed my Rockets & Warlocks name against me. It is a spell with ancient power. I concede. I'll ask Penumbra.

We return to the short shelves and the airbrushed covers. Neel flips through another of our old favorites, a story about a huge cylindrical spaceship slowly approaching the earth. I tell him about Mat's plan to woo Ashley. Then I ask him how his company is doing. He unzips his track jacket and points proudly to the gunmetal-gray T-shirt underneath.

"We made these," he says. "Rented a 3-D body scanner, custom-tailored each shirt. They fit perfectly. Like, *perfectly*."

Neel is in amazing shape. Every time I see him, I cannot help but superimpose my memory of the chubby sixth-grader, because he has now somehow attained the preposterous V-shape of a comic book superhero.

"It's good branding, you know?" he says.

The snug T-shirt has the logo of Neel's company printed across the chest. In tall electric-blue letters it says: ANATOMIX.

• • •

In the morning, when Penumbra arrives, I broach the subject of a friend buying entry into the Waybacklist. He shrugs out of his peacoat—it is an epic peacoat, finely made, with wool from the blackest of sheep—and sets himself up on the chair behind the front desk.

"Oh, it is not a matter of purchase," he says, steepling his fingers, "but rather of intention."

"Well, my friend is just curious," I say. "He's a total bibliophile." This is not actually true. Neel prefers the movie adaptations of books. He is continuously indignant that no one has ever made movies out of *The Dragon-Song Chronicles*.

"Well," Penumbra says, considering, "he will find the contents of these books . . . challenging. And to gain access to them, he must agree to a contract."

"So, wait—it does cost money?"

"No, no. Your friend must simply promise to read deeply. These are special books"—he waves a long hand at the Waybacklist—"with special contents that reward close attention. Your friend will find that they lead him to something remarkable, but only if he is willing to work very hard indeed."

"Like philosophy?" I say. "Math?"

"Nothing so abstract," Penumbra says, shaking his head. "The books present a puzzle"—he cocks his head at me—"but you know this, my boy, do you not?"

I grimace and admit it: "Yeah. I've looked."

"Good." Penumbra nods sharply. "There is nothing worse than an incurious clerk." His eyes twinkle at that. "The puzzle can be solved with time and care. I cannot speak of what waits with the solution, but suffice it to say, many have devoted their lives to it. Now, whether it is something your . . . friend will find rewarding, I cannot say. But I suspect he might."

He smiles a crooked smile. I realize that Penumbra thinks we're using the friend-hypothetical here; that is, he thinks we're talking about me. Well, maybe we are, at least a little bit.

"Of course, the relationship between book and reader is private," he says, "so we go on trust. If you tell me that your friend will read these books deeply, in a way that honors their authors, I will believe you."

I know that Neel definitely will not read them that way, and I'm not sure this is something I want to sign up for, either. Not yet. I am intrigued and creeped out in equal measure. So I simply say: "Okay. I'll tell him."

Penumbra nods. "There is no shame in it if your friend is not yet ready for the task. Perhaps it will grow more interesting to him with time."

# STRANGER IN A STRANGE LAND

THE NIGHTS FALL one into the other, and the bookstore grows quieter and quieter. A week goes by without a single customer. On my laptop, I summon up the dashboard for my hyper-targeted ad campaign, and discover that it has delivered, so far, exactly zero impressions. There's a bright yellow message from Google in the corner of the screen suggesting that my criteria might be too narrow and I might have specified a customer base that does not exist.

I wonder what it's like in here during the day, during Penumbra's sun-dappled shift. I wonder if Oliver gets a rush of customers in the evening, after everybody leaves work. I wonder if this silence and solitude might actually be damaging my brain. Don't get me wrong: I'm grateful to have a job, to sit in this chair, to quietly accrue dollars (not that many) that I can use to pay my rent, to buy pizza slices and iPhone apps. But I used to work in an office; I used to work on a team. Here it's just me and bats. (Oh, I know there are bats up there.)

Lately, even the Waybacklist borrowers seem to be missing. Have they been seduced by some other book club on the other side of town? Have they all bought Kindles?

I have one, and I use it most nights. I always

imagine the books staring and whispering, *Traitor!*—but come on, I have a lot of free first chapters to get through. My Kindle is a hand-me-down from my dad, one of the original models, a slanted, asymmetrical plate with a tiny gray screen and a bed of angled keys. It looks like a prop from *2001: A Space Odyssey*. There are newer Kindles with bigger screens and subtler industrial design, but this one is like Penumbra's postcards: so uncool it's cool again.

Halfway through the first chapter of *Cannery Row*, the screen flashes black, freezes, then fades. This happens most nights. The Kindle's battery is supposed to last, like, two months, but I left mine out on the beach too long and now it only goes for about an hour unplugged.

So I switch to my MacBook and make my rounds: news sites, blogs, tweets. I scroll back to find the conversations that happened without me during the day. When every single piece of media you consume is time-shifted, does that mean it's actually *you* that's time-shifted?

Finally, I click over to my new favorite: Grumble.

Grumble is a person, probably a human male, a secretive programmer who operates at the intersection of literature and code—part *Hacker News*, part *Paris Review*. Mat emailed me a link after he visited the store, guessing that Grumble's work might resonate here. He was correct.

Grumble manages a bustling pirate library. He writes complicated code to break the DRM on e-books; he builds complicated machines to copy the words out of real books. If he worked for Amazon, he'd probably be rich. But instead he cracked the supposedly uncrackable Harry Potter series and posted all seven e-books on his site, free to download—with a few changes. Now, if you want to read Potter without paying, you suffer fleeting references to a young wizard named Grumblegrits who studies at Hogwarts alongside Harry. It's not so bad; Grumblegrits gets a few good lines.

But it's Grumble's newest project that has me mesmerized. It's a map of the locations of every science fiction story published in the twentieth century. He's plucked them out with code and plotted them in 3-D space, so year by year you see humankind's collective imagination reaching farther: to the moon, to Mars, Jupiter, Pluto, to Alpha Centauri and beyond. You can zoom and rotate the whole universe, and you can also jump into a little polygonal spaceship and cruise around in the cockpit. You can rendezvous with Rama or find the Foundation worlds.

So, two things:

1. Neel is going to love this.
2. I want to be like Grumble. I mean, what if I could make something this cool? That

would be a real skill. I could join a startup. I could go work at Apple. I could see and interact with other human beings under the warm glow of the daystar.

Lucky for me, Grumble has, in customary hacker-hero fashion, released the code that powers the map. It's a whole 3-D graphics engine written in a programming language called Ruby—the same one we used to run the website at NewBagel—and it's completely free.

So now I'm going to use Grumble's code to make something of my own. Looking around, I realize my project is standing right in front of me: I'll learn 3-D graphics by making a model of Mr. Penumbra's 24-Hour Bookstore. I mean, it's a tall, skinny box full of smaller boxes—how hard can that be?

To begin, I had to copy the database from Penumbra's old Mac Plus onto my laptop, which was actually not a trivial task, since the Mac Plus uses plastic floppy disks and there's no way to get one of those into a MacBook. I had to buy an old USB floppy drive on eBay. It cost three dollars, plus five for shipping, and it felt strange to plug it into my laptop.

But now, with the data in hand, I'm building my model of the store. It's crude—just a bunch of gray blocks slotted together like virtual LEGOs— but it's starting to look familiar. The space is appropriately shoe-boxy and all the shelves are there. I've set them up with a coordinate system, so my program can find aisle 3, shelf 13 all by itself. Simulated light from the simulated windows casts sharp-edged shadows through the simulated store. If this sounds impressive to you, you're over thirty.

It's taken three nights of trial and error, but now I'm stringing out long lines of code, learning as I go. It feels good to be making something: a fairly persuasive polygonal approximation of Penumbra's store is spinning slowly on my screen, and I'm happier than I've been since the fall of NewBagel. I've got the new album from a peppy local band called Moon Suicide piping through my laptop speakers, and I'm just about to load the database into—

The bell tinkles and I clack the mute key on my laptop. Moon Suicide goes silent, and when I look up, I see an unfamiliar face. Usually I can detect instantly whether I'm dealing with a member of the world's weirdest book club or a normal late-night browser. But now my spider-sense is jammed.

The customer is short but sturdy, in some thickening limbo of middle age. He's wearing a slate-gray suit with a white button-down open at the collar. All of that would signal normality if it weren't for his face: he has a ghostly pallor, a stubbly black beard, and eyes like dark pencil-points. Also, there's a parcel under his arm, neatly wrapped in brown paper.

His eyes go immediately to the short shelves up front, not the Waybacklist, so maybe he's a normal customer. Maybe he's coming from Booty's next door. I ask, "Can I help you?"

"What is all this? What is the meaning of this?" he sputters, glaring at the short shelves.

"Yeah, I know it doesn't look like much," I say. In the next breath, I intend to point out a few of the surprising highlights of Penumbra's tiny inventory, but he cuts me off:

"Are you joking? Not much?" He throws his parcel down on the desk—*whap*—and stalks over to the SCIENCE FICTION AND FANTASY shelf. "What is this doing here?" He holds up Penumbra's single copy of *The Hitchhiker's Guide to the Galaxy*. "And this? Are you kidding me?" He holds up *Stranger in a Strange Land*.

I'm not sure what to say, because I'm not sure what's going on.

He stalks back up to the front desk, still holding both books. He slaps them down on the wood. "Who are you, anyway?" His dark eyes are flashing, challenging.

"I'm the guy who runs the store," I say, as evenly as I can muster. "Do you want to buy those or what?"

His nostrils flare. "You don't run this store. You're not even a novice."

64

Ouch. Sure, I've only been working here a little over a month, but still, there's not much to it—

"And you don't have any idea who really does run this store, do you?" he continues. "Has Penumbra told you?"

I'm silent. This is definitely not a normal customer.

"No." He sniffs. "I guess he hasn't. Well, more than a year ago, we told your boss to get rid of this junk." He taps the *Hitchhiker's Guide* with each word for emphasis. The cuffs of his suit jacket are open at the last button. "And not for the first time."

"Listen, I really don't know what you're talking about." I will remain calm. I will remain civil. "So, seriously, do you want to buy those?"

He surprises me by digging a crumpled twenty-dollar bill out of his pants pocket. "Oh, absolutely," he says, and tosses the money onto the desk. I hate it when people do that. "I want evidence of Penumbra's disobedience." Pause. His dark eyes glitter. "Your boss is in trouble."

What, for peddling science fiction? Why does this guy hate Douglas Adams so much?

"And what's that?" he says sharply, pointing to the MacBook. The model of the store is stretched across the screen, rotating slowly.

"None of your business," I say, tilting it away.

"None of my business?" he sputters. "Do you

even know—You don't." He rolls his eyes as if he is suffering through the worst customer service experience in the history of the universe. Then he shakes his head and composes himself. "Listen carefully. This is important." He pushes the parcel across the desk with two fingers. It's wide and flat and familiar. His eyes level on me and he says, "This place is a shit show, but I need to know I can trust you to give this to Penumbra. Put it in his hands. Don't put it on a shelf. Don't leave it for him. Put it in his hands."

"Okay," I say. "Fine. No problem."

He nods. "Good. Thank you." He scoops up his purchases and pushes the front door open. Then, on his way out, he turns. "And tell your boss that Corvina sends his regards."

In the morning, Penumbra has barely made it through the front door before I am recounting what happened, saying it too fast and out of order, I mean, what was that guy's problem, and who is Corvina, and what's this package, and seriously, what was his *problem*—

"Calm yourself, my boy," Penumbra says, lifting his voice and his long hands to quiet me. "Calm yourself. Slow down."

"There," I say. I point at the parcel like it's a dead animal. For all I know, it is a dead animal, or maybe just the bones of one, laid out in a neat pentagram.

"Ahhh," Penumbra breathes. He wraps his long fingers around the parcel and lifts it lightly from the desk. "How wonderful."

But of course it's not a box of bones. I know exactly what it is, and I've known since the pale-faced visitor stepped into the store, and somehow the truth of it is freaking me out even more, because it means that whatever's happening here is more than just one old man's eccentricity.

Penumbra peels back the brown paper. Inside, there's a book.

"A new addition to the shelves," he says. *"Festina lente."*

The book is very slim but very beautiful. It's bound in brilliant gray, some kind of mottled material that shimmers silver in the light. The spine is black, and in pearly letters it says ERDOS. So the Waybacklist grows by one.

"It has been quite some time since one of these arrived," Penumbra says. "This requires a celebration. Wait here, my boy, wait here."

He retreats through the shelves into the back room. I hear his shoes on the steps that lead up to his office, on the other side of the door marked PRIVATE through which I have never ventured. When he returns, he carries two foam cups stacked one inside the other and a bottle of scotch, half-empty. The label says FITZGERALD'S and it looks about as old as Penumbra. He pours a half inch of gold into each cup and hands one to me.

"Now," he says, "describe him. The visitor. Read it from your logbook."

"I didn't write anything down," I confess. In fact, I haven't done anything at all. I've just been pacing the store all night, keeping my distance from the front desk, afraid to touch the parcel or look at it or even think about it too hard.

"Ah, but it must go into the logbook, my boy. Here, write it as you tell it. Tell me."

I tell him, and I write it down as I go. It makes me feel better, as if the weirdness is flowing out of my blood and onto the page, through the dark point of the pen:

"The store was visited by a presumptuous jackass—"

"Er—perhaps it would be wisest not to write that," Penumbra says lightly. "Say perhaps that he had the aspect of . . . an urgent courier."

Okay, then: "The store was visited by an urgent courier named Corvina, who—"

"No, no," Penumbra interrupts. He closes his eyes and pinches the bridge of his nose. "Stop. Before you write, I will explain. He was extremely pale, weasel-eyed, forty-one years old, with a thick build and an ill-advised beard, wearing a suit of smooth wool, single-breasted, with functioning buttons at the cuffs, and black leather shoes that came to sharp points—correct?"

Exactly. I didn't catch the shoes, but Penumbra has got this one nailed.

"Yes, of course. His name is Eric, and his gift is a treasure." He swirls his scotch. "Even if he is too enthusiastic in the playing of his part. He gets that from Corvina."

"So who's Corvina?" I feel funny saying it, but: "He sends his regards."

"Of course he does," Penumbra says, rolling his eyes. "Eric admires him. Many of the young ones do." He's avoiding the question. He's quiet for a moment, and then he lifts his eyes to meet mine. "This is more than a bookstore, as you have no doubt surmised. It is also a kind of library, one of many around the world. There is another in London, another in Paris—a dozen, altogether. No two are alike, but their function is the same, and Corvina oversees them all."

"So he's your boss."

Penumbra's face darkens at that. "I prefer to think of him as *our patron,*" he says, pausing a little on each word. The *our* is not lost on me, and it makes me smile. "But I suspect Corvina would agree wholeheartedly with your characterization."

I explain what Eric said about the books on the short shelves—about Penumbra's disobedience.

"Yes, yes," he says with a sigh. "I have been through this before. It is foolishness. The genius of the libraries is that they are all different. Koster in Berlin with his music, Griboyedov in Saint Petersburg with his great samovar. And here in San Francisco, the most striking difference of all."

"What's that?"

"Why, we have books that people might actually want to read!" Penumbra guffaws at this, and shows a toothy grin. I laugh, too.

"So it's no big deal?"

Penumbra shrugs. "That depends," he says. "It depends how seriously one takes a rigid old taskmaster who believes that everything must be exactly the same everywhere and always." He pauses. "As it happens, I do not take him very seriously at all."

"Does he ever visit?"

"Never," Penumbra says sharply, shaking his head. "He has not been to San Francisco in many years . . . more than a decade. No, he is busy with his other duties. And thank goodness for that."

Penumbra lifts his hands and waves them at me, shooing me away from the desk. "Go home now. You have witnessed something rare, and more meaningful than you know. Be grateful for it. And drink your scotch, my boy! Drink!"

I swing my bag up onto my shoulder and empty my cup in two stiff gulps.

"That," Penumbra says, "is a toast to Evelyn Erdos." He holds the sparkling gray book aloft, and speaks as though addressing her: "Welcome, my friend, and well done. Well done!"

# THE PROTOTYPE

THE NEXT NIGHT, I enter as usual and wave hello to Oliver Grone. I want to ask him about Eric, but I don't quite have the language for it. Oliver and I have never talked directly about the weirdness of the store. So I start like this:

"Oliver, I have a question. You know how there are normal customers?"

"Not many."

"Right. And there are members who borrow books."

"Like Maurice Tyndall."

"Right." I didn't know his name was Maurice. "Have you ever seen somebody deliver a *new* book?"

He pauses and thinks. Then he says simply: "Nope."

As soon as he leaves I am a mess of new theories. Maybe Oliver's in on it, too. Maybe he's a spy for Corvina. The quiet watcher. Perfect. Or maybe he's part of some deeper conspiracy. Maybe I've only scratched the surface. I know there are more bookstores—libraries?—like this, but I still don't know what "like this" means. I don't know what the Waybacklist is *for*.

I flip through the logbook from front to back, looking for something, anything. A message from the past, maybe: *Beware, good clerk, the wrath of Corvina.* But no. My predecessors played it just as straight as I have.

The words they wrote are plain and factual, just descriptions of the members as they come and go. Some of them I recognize: Tyndall, Lapin, and the rest. Others are mysteries to me—members who visit only during the day, or members who stopped visiting long ago. Judging by the dates sprinkled through the pages, the book covers a little over five years. It's only half-full. Am I going to fill it for another five? Am I going to write dutifully for years with no idea what I'm writing *about?*

My brain is going to melt into a puddle if I keep this up all night. I need a distraction—a big, challenging distraction. So I lift my laptop's lid and resume work on the 3-D bookstore.

Every few minutes I glance up at the front windows, out into the street beyond. I'm watching for shadows, the flash of a gray suit or the glint of a dark eye. But there's nothing. The work smooths away the strangeness, and finally I'm in the zone.

If a 3-D model of this store is actually going to be useful, it probably needs to show you not only where the books are located but also which are currently loaned out, and to whom. So I've somewhat sketchily transcribed my last few weeks of logbook entries and taught my model to tell time.

Now the books glow like lamps in the blocky

3-D shelves, and they're color-coded, so the books borrowed by Tyndall light up blue, Lapin's green, Fedorov's yellow, and so on. That's pretty cool. But my new feature also introduced a bug, and now the shelves are all blinking out of existence when I rotate the store too far around. I'm sitting hunched over the code, trying in vain to figure it out, when the bell tinkles brightly.

I make an involuntary chirp of surprise. Is it Eric, back to yell at me again? Or is it Corvina, the CEO himself, come at last to visit his wrath upon—

It's a girl. She's leaning halfway into the store, and she's looking at me, and she's saying, "Are you open?"

Why, *yes,* girl with chestnut hair cropped to your chin and a red T-shirt with the word BAM! printed in mustard yellow—yes, as a matter of fact, we are.

"Absolutely," I say. "You can come in. We're always open."

"I was just waiting for the bus and my phone buzzed—I think I have a coupon?"

She walks straight up to the front desk, pushes her phone out toward me, and there, on the little screen, is my Google ad. The hyper-targeted local campaign—I'd forgotten about it, but it's still running, and it found someone. The digital coupon I designed is right there, peeking out of her scratched-up smartphone. Her nails are shiny.

"Yes!" I say. "That's a great coupon. The best!" I'm talking too loud. She's going to turn around and leave. Google's astonishing advertising algorithms have delivered to me a supercute girl, and I have no idea what to do with her. She swivels her head to take in the store. She looks dubious.

History hinges on such small things. A difference of thirty degrees, and this story would end here. But my laptop is angled just so, and on my screen, the 3-D bookstore is spinning wildly on two axes, like a spaceship tumbling through a blank cosmos, and the girl glances down, and—

"What's that?" she says, one eyebrow raised. One dark lovely eyebrow.

Okay, I have to play this right. Don't make it sound too nerdy: "Well, it's a model of this store, except you can see which books are available . . ."

The girl's eyes light up: "Data visualization!" She's no longer dubious. Suddenly she's delighted.

"That's right," I say. "That's it exactly. Here, take a look."

We meet halfway, at the end of the desk, and I show her the 3-D bookstore, which is still disappearing whenever it spins too far around. She leans in close.

"Can I see the source code?"

If Eric's malevolence was surprising, this girl's curiosity is astonishing. "Sure, of course," I say, toggling through dark windows until raw Ruby fills the screen, all color-coded red and gold and green.

"This is what I do for work," she says, hunching down low, peering at the code. "Data viz. Do you mind?" She gestures at the keyboard. Uh, no, beautiful late-night hacker girl, I do not mind.

My limbic system has grown accustomed to a certain (very low) level of human (female) contact. With her standing right next to me, her elbow poking me just the tiniest bit, I basically feel drunk. I'm trying to formulate my next steps. I'll recommend Edward Tufte, *The Visual Display of Quantitative Information*. Penumbra has a copy—I've seen it on the shelf. It's huge.

She's scrolling fast through my code, which is a little embarrassing, because my code is full of comments like *Hell, yeah!* and *Now, computer, it is time for you to do my bidding.*

"This is great," she says, smiling. "And you must be Clay?"

It's in the code—there's a method called *clay_is_awesome*. I assume every programmer writes one of those.

"I'm Kat," she says. "I think I found the problem. Want to see?"

I've been struggling for hours, but this girl— Kat—has found the bug in my bookstore in five minutes flat. She's a genius. She talks me through the debugging process and explains her reasoning, which is quick and confident. And then, *tap tap,* she fixes the bug.

"Sorry, I'm hogging it," she says, swiveling the laptop back to me. She pushes a lock of hair back behind her ear, stands up straight, and says, with mock composure, "So, Clay, why are you making a model of this bookstore?" As she says it, her eyes follow the shelves up to the ceiling.

I'm not sure if I want to be completely honest about the deep strangeness of this place. *Hello, nice to meet you, I sell unreadable books to weird old people—want to get dinner?* (And suddenly I am gripped with the certainty that one of those people is going to come careening through the front door. Please, Tyndall, Fedorov, all of you: Stay home tonight. Keep reading.)

I play up a different angle: "It's sort of a history thing," I say. "The store's been open for almost a century. I think it's the oldest bookstore in the city—maybe the whole West Coast."

"That's amazing," she says. "Google's like a baby compared to that." That explains it: this girl is a Googler. So she really is a genius. Also, one of her teeth is chipped in a cute way.

"I love data like this," she says, nodding her chin toward my laptop. "Real-world data. Old data."

This girl has the spark of life. This is my primary filter for new friends (girl- and otherwise) and the highest compliment I can pay. I've tried

76

many times to figure out exactly what ignites it—what cocktail of characteristics comes together in the cold, dark cosmos to form a star. I know it's mostly in the face—not just the eyes but the brow, the cheeks, the mouth, and the micromuscles that connect them all.

Kat's micromuscles are very attractive.

She says, "Have you tried doing a time-series visualization?"

"Not yet, not exactly, no." I do not, in fact, even know what that is.

"At Google, we do them for search logs," she says. "It's cool—you'll see some new idea flash across the world, like a little epidemic. Then it burns out in a week."

This sounds very interesting to me, but mostly because this girl is very interesting to me.

Kat's phone makes a bright *ping* and she glances down. "Oh," she says, "that's my bus." I curse the city's public transit system for its occasional punctuality. "I can show you what I mean about the time-series stuff," she ventures. "Want to meet up sometime?"

Why, yes, as a matter of fact I do. Maybe I'll just go ahead and buy her the Tufte book. I'll bring it wrapped in brown paper. Wait—is that weird? It's an expensive book. Maybe there's a low-key paperback edition. I could buy it on Amazon. That's stupid, I work at a bookstore. (Could Amazon ship it fast enough?)

Kat is still waiting for me to answer. "Sure," I squeak.

She scribbles her email address on one of Penumbra's postcards: *katpotente@*—of course—*gmail.com*. "I'll save my coupon for another time," she says, waving her phone. "See you later."

As soon as she leaves, I log in to check my hyper-targeted ad campaign. Did I accidentally check the box that said "beautiful"? (What about "single"?) Can I afford this introduction? In pure marketing terms, this was a failure: I did not sell any books, expensive or otherwise. Actually, I'm a dollar in the hole, thanks to the scribbled-on postcard. But there's no reason to worry: from my original budget of eleven dollars, Google has subtracted just seventeen cents. In return, I have received a single ad impression—a single, perfect ad impression—delivered exactly twenty-three minutes ago.

Later, after an hour of late-night isolation and lignin inhalation have sobered me up, I do two things.

First: I email Kat and ask her if she wants to get lunch tomorrow, which is a Saturday. I might sometimes be faint of heart, but I do believe in striking while the iron is hot.

Then: I google "time-series visualization" and start work on a new version of my model, thinking that maybe I can impress her with a prototype. I am really into the kind of girl you can impress with a prototype.

The idea is to animate through the borrowed books over time instead of just seeing them all at once. First, I transcribe more names, titles, and times from the logbook into my laptop. Then I start hacking.

Programming is not all the same. Normal written languages have different rhythms and idioms, right? Well, so do programming languages. The language called C is all harsh imperatives, almost raw computer-speak. The language called Lisp is like one long, looping sentence, full of subclauses, so long in fact that you usually forget what it was even about in the first place. The language called Erlang is just like it sounds: eccentric and Scandinavian. I cannot program in any of these languages, because they're all too hard.

But Ruby, my language of choice since NewBagel, was invented by a cheerful Japanese programmer, and it reads like friendly, accessible poetry. Billy Collins by way of Bill Gates.

But, of course, the point of a programming language is that you don't just read it; you write it, too. You make it do things for you. And this, I think, is where Ruby shines:

Imagine that you're cooking. But instead of following the recipe step-by-step and hoping for the best, you can actually take ingredients in and out of the pot whenever you want. You can add salt, taste it, shake your head, and pull the salt back out. You can take a perfectly crisp crust, isolate it, and then add whatever you want to the inside. It's no longer just a linear process ending in success or (mostly, for me) frustrating failure. Instead, it's a loop or a curlicue or a little scribble. It's play.

So I add some salt and a little butter and I get a prototype of the new visualization working by two in the morning. Immediately I notice something strange: the lights are following one another.

On my screen, Tyndall will borrow a book from the top of aisle two. Then, in another month, Lapin will ask for one from the same shelf. Five weeks later, Imbert will follow—exactly the same shelf—but meanwhile, Tyndall has already returned and gotten something new from the bottom of aisle one. He's a step ahead.

I hadn't noticed the pattern because it's so spread out in space and time, like a piece of music with three hours between each note, all played in different octaves. But here, condensed and accelerated on my screen, it's obvious. They're all playing the same song, or dancing the same dance, or—yes—solving the same puzzle.

The bell tinkles. It's Imbert: short and solid, with his bristly black beard and sloping newsboy cap. He hoists his current book (a monstrous red-bound volume) and pushes it across the desk. I quickly scrub through the visualization to find his place in the pattern. An orange light bounces across my screen, and before he says a word, I know he's going to ask for a book right in the middle of aisle two. It's going to be—

"Prokhorov," Imbert wheezes. "Prokhorov must be next."

Halfway up the ladder, I feel dizzy. What's going on? No daredevil maneuvers this time; it's all I can do to keep my balance as I pull slim, black-bound PROKHOROV off the shelf.

Imbert presents his card—6MXH2I—and takes his book. The bell tinkles, and I am alone again.

In the logbook, I record the transaction, noting Imbert's cap and the smell of garlic on his breath. And then I write, for the benefit of some future clerk, and perhaps also to prove to myself that this is real:

Strange things are afoot at Mr. Penumbra's 24-Hour Bookstore.

# MAXIMUM HAPPY IMAGINATION

. . . CALLED SINGULARITY SINGLES," Kat Potente is saying. She's wearing the same red and yellow BAM! T-shirt from before, which means (a) she slept in it, (b) she owns several identical T-shirts, or (c) she's a cartoon character—all of which are appealing alternatives.

Singularity Singles. Let's see. I know (thanks to the internet) that the Singularity is the hypothetical point in the future where technology's growth curve goes vertical and civilization just sort of reboots itself. Computers get smarter than people, so we let them run the show. Or maybe they let themselves . . .

Kat nods. "More or less."

"But Singularity Singles . . . ?"

"Speed-dating for nerds," she says. "They have one every month at Google. The male-to-female ratio is really good, or really bad. Depends who—"

"You went to this."

"Yeah. I met a guy who programmed bots for a hedge fund. We dated for a while. He was really into rock-climbing. He had nice shoulders."

Hmm.

"But a cruel heart."

We are in the Gourmet Grotto, part of San Francisco's gleaming six-floor shopping mall. It's downtown, right next to the cable-car terminus, but I don't think tourists realize it's a mall; there's no parking lot. The Gourmet Grotto is its food court, probably the best in the world: all locally grown spinach salads and pork belly tacos and sushi sans mercury. Also, it's belowground, and it connects directly to the train station, so you never have to walk outside. Whenever I come here, I pretend I'm living in the future and the atmosphere is irradiated and wild bands of biodiesel bikers rule the dusty surface. Hey, just like the Singularity, right?

Kat frowns. "That's the twentieth-century future. After the Singularity, we'll be able to solve those problems." She cracks a falafel in two and offers me half. "And we'll live forever."

"Come on," I say. "This is just the old dream of immortality—"

"It *is* the dream of immortality. So?" She pauses, chews. "Let me put it a different way. This is going to sound strange, especially because we just met. But, I know I'm smart."

That's definitely true—

"And I think you're smart, too. So why does that have to end? We could accomplish so much if we just had more time. You know?"

I chew my falafel and nod. This is an interesting girl. Kat's utter directness suggests home-schooling, yet she is also completely charming. It helps, I guess, that she's beautiful. I glance down at her T-shirt. You know, I think she owns a bunch that are identical.

"You have to be an optimist to believe in the Singularity," she says, "and that's harder than it seems. Have you ever played Maximum Happy Imagination?"

"Sounds like a Japanese game show."

Kat straightens her shoulders. "Okay, we're going to play. To start, imagine the future. The good future. No nuclear bombs. Pretend you're a science fiction writer."

Okay: "World government . . . no cancer . . . hover-boards."

"Go further. What's the good future after that?"

"Spaceships. Party on Mars."

"Further."

"*Star Trek*. Transporters. You can go anywhere."

"Further."

I pause a moment, then realize: "I can't."

Kat shakes her head. "It's really hard. And that's, what, a thousand years? What comes after that? What could possibly come after that? Imagination runs out. But it makes sense, right? We probably just imagine things based on what we already know, and we run out of analogies in the thirty-first century."

I'm trying hard to imagine an average day in the year 3012. I can't even come up with a half-decent scene. Will people live in buildings? Will they wear clothes? My imagination is almost physically straining. Fingers of thought are raking the space behind the cushions, looking for loose ideas, finding nothing.

"Personally, I think the big change is going to be our brains," Kat says, tapping just above her ear, which is pink and cute. "I think we're going to find different ways to think, thanks to computers. You expect me to say that"—yes—"but it's happened before. It's not like we have the same brains as people a thousand years ago."

Wait: "Yes we do."

"We have the same hardware, but not the same software. Did you know that the concept of privacy is, like, totally recent? And so is the idea of romance, of course."

Yes, as a matter of fact, I think the idea of romance just occurred to me last night. (I don't say that out loud.)

"Each big idea like that is an operating system upgrade," she says, smiling. Comfortable territory. "Writers are responsible for some of it. They say Shakespeare invented the internal monologue."

Oh, I am very familiar with the internal monologue.

"But I think the writers had their turn," she says, "and now it's programmers who get to upgrade the human operating system."

I am definitely talking to a girl from Google. "So what's the next upgrade?"

"It's already happening," she says. "There are

all these things you can do, and it's like you're in more than one place at one time, and it's totally normal. I mean, look around."

I swivel my head, and I see what she wants me to see: dozens of people sitting at tiny tables, all leaning into phones showing them places that don't exist and yet are somehow more interesting than the Gourmet Grotto.

"And it's not weird, it's not science fiction at all, it's . . ." She slows down a little and her eyes dim. I think she thinks she's getting too intense. (How do I know that? Does my brain have an app for that?) Her cheeks are flushed and she looks great with all her blood right there at the surface of her skin.

"Well," she says finally, "it's just that I think the Singularity is totally reasonable to imagine."

Her sincerity makes me smile, and I feel lucky to have this bright optimistic girl sitting with me here in the irradiated future, deep beneath the surface of the earth.

I decide it's time to show her the souped-up 3-D bookstore, now with amazing new time-series capability. You know: just a prototype.

"You did this last night?" she says, and cocks an eyebrow. "Very impressive."

I don't say that it took me all night and part of this morning. Kat probably could have cooked it up in fifteen minutes.

We watch the colored lights curl around one

another. I rewind it, and we watch again. I explain what happened with Imbert—the prototype's predictive power.

"Could have been luck," Kat says, shaking her head. "We'd need to look at more data to see if there's really a pattern. I mean, you might just be projecting. Like the face on Mars."

Or like when you're absolutely sure a girl likes you, but it turns out she doesn't. (I don't say that out loud, either.)

"Is there more data we can add to the visualization? This only covers a few months, right?"

"Well, there are other logbooks," I say. "But they're not really data—just description. And it would take forever to type it into the computer. It's all handwriting, and I can barely read my own . . ."

Kat's eyes light up: "A natural language corpus! I've been looking for an excuse to use the book scanner." She grins and slaps the table. "Bring it to Google. We have a machine for this. You *have* to bring it to Google."

She's bouncing in her seat a little, and her lips make a pretty shape when she says the word *corpus*.

# THE SMELL OF BOOKS

MY CHALLENGE: get a book out of a bookstore. If I am successful, I might learn something interesting about this place and its purpose. More important: I might impress Kat.

I can't just take the logbook, because Penumbra and Oliver use it, too. The logbook is part of the store. If I ask to take it home, I'll need a good reason, and I can't really imagine a good reason. *Hey, Mr. Penumbra, I want to go over my sketch of Tyndall in watercolors?* Yeah, right.

There's another possibility. I could take a different logbook, an older one—not IX but VIII or even II or I. That feels risky. Some of those logbooks are older than Penumbra himself, and I'm afraid they might fall apart if I touch them. So the most recently retired logbook, VIII, is the safest and sturdiest bet . . . but it's also the closest at hand. You see VIII every time you slide the current logbook back onto the shelf, and I'm very sure Penumbra would notice its absence. Now, maybe VII or VI . . .

I'm crouching down behind the front desk, poking logbook spines with one finger to test their structural integrity, when the bell above the door tinkles. I spring up straight—it's Penumbra.

He unwinds the thin gray scarf around his neck and makes an odd circuit around the front of the store, rapping his knuckles on the front desk, casting his eyes across the short shelves and then up to the Waybacklist. He makes a quiet sigh. Something is up.

"Today is the day, my boy," he finally says, "that I took over this bookstore, thirty-one years ago."

Thirty-one years. Penumbra's been sitting at this desk for longer than I've been alive. It makes me realize how new I am to this place—what a fleeting addition.

"But it wasn't until eleven years later," he adds, "that I changed the name on the front."

"Whose name was up there before?"

"Al-Asmari. He was my mentor and, for many years, my employer. Mohammad Al-Asmari. I always thought his name looked better on the glass. I still do."

"Penumbra looks good," I say. "It's mysterious."

He smiles at that. "When I changed the name, I thought I would change the store, too. But it hasn't changed that much at all."

"Why not?"

"Oh, many reasons. Some good, some bad. It has a bit to do with our funding . . . and I have been lazy. In the early days, I read more. I sought out new books. But now, it seems, I've settled on my favorites."

Well, now that you mention it . . . "Maybe you should think about getting some more popular stuff," I venture. "There's a market for independent bookstores, and a lot of people don't even know this place is here, but when they discover it, there's not a lot to choose from. I mean, some of my friends have come to check it out, and . . . we just don't have anything they want to buy."

"I did not know people your age still read books," Penumbra says. He raises an eyebrow. "I was under the impression they read everything on their mobile phones."

"Not everyone. There are plenty of people who, you know—people who still like the smell of books."

"The smell!" Penumbra repeats. "You know you are finished when people start talking about the smell." He smiles at that—then something occurs to him, and he narrows his eyes. "I do not suppose you have a . . . Kindle?"

Uh-oh. It feels like it's the principal asking me if I have weed in my backpack. But in a friendly way, like maybe he wants to share it. As it happens, I do have my Kindle. I pull it out of my messenger bag. It's a bit battered, with wide scratches across the back and stray pen marks near the bottom of the screen.

Penumbra holds it aloft and frowns. It's blank. I reach up and pinch the corner and it comes to life. He sucks in a sharp breath, and the pale gray rectangle reflects in his bright blue eyes.

"Remarkable," he says. "And to think I was still

impressed by this species"—he nods to the Mac Plus—"of magic mirror."

I open the Kindle's settings and make the text a little bigger for him.

"The typography is beautiful," Penumbra says, peering in close, holding his glasses up to the Kindle's screen. "I know that typeface."

"Yeah," I say, "it's the default." I like it, too.

"It is a classic. Gerritszoon." He pauses at that. "We use it on the front of the store. Does this machine ever run out of electricity?" He gives the Kindle a little shake.

"The battery's supposed to last a couple of months. Mine doesn't."

"I suppose that is a relief." Penumbra sighs and passes it back to me. "Our books still do not require batteries. But I am no fool. It is a slender advantage. So I suppose it is a good thing we have"—and here he winks at me—"such a generous patron."

I stuff the Kindle back into my bag. I'm not consoled. "Honestly, Mr. Penumbra, if we just got some more popular books, people would love this place. It would be . . ." I trail off, then decide to speak the truth: "It would be more fun."

He rubs his chin, and his eyes have a far-off look. "Perhaps," he says at last. "Perhaps it is time to muster some of the energy I had thirty-one years ago. I will think on it, my boy."

• • •

I haven't given up on getting one of those old logbooks to Google. Back at the apartment, in the shadow of Matropolis, sprawled out on the couch, sipping an Anchor Steam even though it's seven in the morning, I tell my tale to Mat, who is poking tiny bullet holes in the skin of a fortresslike building with pale marbled skin. Immediately he formulates a plan. I was counting on this.

"I can make a perfect replica," he says. "Not a problem, Jannon. Just bring me reference images."

"But you can't copy every page, can you?"

"Just the outside. The covers, the spine."

"What happens when Penumbra opens the perfect replica?"

"He won't. You said this is, like, from the archives, right?"

"Right—"

"So it's the surface that matters. People want things to be real. If you give them an excuse, they'll believe you." Coming from the special-effects wizard, this is not unconvincing.

"Okay, so all you need is pictures?"

"Good pictures." Mat nods. "Lots of them. Every angle. Bright, even light. Do you know what I mean when I say bright, even light?"

"No shadows?"

"No shadows," he agrees, "which is, of course, going to be impossible in that place. It's basically a twenty-four-hour shadow store."

93

"Yep. Shadows and book smell, we've got it all."

"I could bring over some lights."

"I think that might give me away."

"Right. Maybe a few shadows will be okay."

So the scheme is set. "Speaking of dark deeds," I say, "how's it going with Ashley?"

Mat sniffs. "I am wooing her in the traditional way," he says. "Also, I am not allowed to talk about it in the apartment. But she's having dinner with me on Friday."

"Impressive compartmentalization."

"Our roommate is nothing but compartments."

"Does she . . . I mean . . . what do you guys talk about?"

"We talk about everything, Jannon. And do you realize"—he points down to the pale marbled fortress—"she found this box? She picked it out of the trash at her office."

Amazing. Rock-climbing, risotto-cooking PR professional Ashley Adams is contributing to the construction of Matropolis. Maybe she's not such an android after all.

"That's progress," I say, raising my beer bottle.

Mat nods. "That's progress."

# THE PEACOCK FEATHER

**I** 'M MAKING PROGRESS of my own: Kat invites me to a house party. Unfortunately, I can't go. I can never go to any parties, because my shift at the store starts at precisely party o'clock. Disappointment twists in my heart; the ball is in her court, she's bouncing me a nice easy pass, and my hands are tied.

**too bad,** she types. We are chatting in Gmail.

Yes, too bad. Although, wait: **Kat, you believe that we humans will one day outgrow these bodies and exist in a sort of dimensionless digital sublime, right?**

**right!!**

**I'll bet you wouldn't actually put that to the test.**

**what do you mean?**

This is what I mean: **I'll come to your party, but I'll come via laptop—*via video chat.* You'll have to be my chaperone: carry me around, introduce me to people.** She'll never go for this.

**omg brilliant! yes let's do it! you have to dress up, though. and you have to drink.**

She goes for it. But: **Wait, I'm going to be at work, I can't drink—**

**you have to. or it will hardly be a party now will it?**

I sense an incompatibility between Kat's belief

in a disembodied human future and her insistence on alcohol consumption, but I let it slide, because I'm going to a party.

It is 10:00 p.m. and I am behind the front desk at Penumbra's, wearing a light gray sweater over a blue striped shirt and, in a joke I hope I will be able to triumphantly reveal at some point later in the evening, pants of crazy purple paisley. Get it? Because no one will be able to see me below the waist—okay, yes, you get it.

Kat comes online at 10:13 p.m. and I press the green button in the shape of a camera. She appears on my screen, wearing her red BAM! T-shirt as always. "You look cute," she says.

"You're not dressed up," I say. No one else is dressed up.

"Yeah, but you're just a floating head," she says. "You have to look extra-good."

The store melts away and I fall headfirst into the view of Kat's apartment—a place, I remind you, that I have never visited in person. It's a wide-open left, and Kat pans her laptop around like a camera to show me what's what. "This is the kitchen," she says. Gleaming glass-faced cupboards; an industrial stove; a stick-figure *xkcd* comic on the refrigerator. "The living room," she says, sweeping me around. My view blurs into dark pixelated streaks, then re-forms itself into a sprawling space with a wide TV and long low couches. There are movie posters in neat narrow frames: *Blade Runner*, *Planet of the Apes*, *WALL·E*. People are sitting in a circle—half on the couches, half on the carpet—playing a game.

"Who's that?" a voice chirps. My view swivels and I am looking at a round-faced girl with dark curls and chunky black glasses.

"This is an experimental simulated intelligence," Kat says, "designed to produce engaging party banter. Here, test it." She sets the laptop down on the granite countertop.

Dark Curls leans in close—eek, really close—and squints. "Wait, really? Are you real?"

Kat doesn't abandon me. It would be easy to do: set the laptop down, get called away, don't come back. But no: for a whole hour she shepherds me around the party, introducing me to her roommates (Dark Curls is one of them) and her friends from Google.

She brings me over to the living room and we play the game in the circle. It's called Traitor, and a skinny dude with a wispy mustache leans in to explain that it was invented at the KGB and all the secret agents used to play it back in the sixties. It's a game about lying. You're given a particular role, but you have to convince the group that you're someone else entirely. The roles are assigned with playing cards, and Kat holds mine up to the camera for me.

"It's not fair," says a girl across the circle. She

has hair so pale it's almost white. "He has an advantage. We can't see any of his tells."

"You're totally right," Kat says, frowning. "And I know for a fact that he wears paisley pants when he's lying."

On cue, I tip my laptop down to give them a view, and the laughter is so loud it crackles and fuzzes out in the speakers. I laugh, too, and pour myself another beer. I'm drinking from a red party cup here in the store. Every few minutes I glance up at the door and a dagger of fear dances across my heart, but the buffer of adrenaline and alcohol eases the prick. There won't be any customers. There are never any customers.

We get into a conversation with Kat's friend Trevor, who also works at Google, and a different kind of dagger slips through my defenses then. Trevor is reeling out a long story about a trip to Antarctica (who goes to Antarctica?) and Kat is leaning in toward him. It looks almost gravitational, but maybe her laptop is just sitting at an angle. Slowly, other people peel away and Trevor's focus narrows to Kat alone. Her eyes are shining back, and she's nodding along.

No, come on. There's nothing to it. It's just a good story. She's a little drunk. I'm a little drunk. However, I do not know if Trevor is drunk, or—

The bell tinkles. My gaze snaps up. Shit. It's not a lonely late-night browser or anyone I can safely ignore. It's one of the club: Ms. Lapin. She's the only woman (that I know of) who borrows books from the Waybacklist, and now she is edging into the store, clutching her ponderous purse like a shield. She has a peacock feather stuck into her hat. That's new.

I try to focus my eyeballs independently, one on the laptop and one on Lapin. It doesn't work.

"Hello, good evening," she says. Lapin has a voice that sounds like an old tape stretched out of shape, always wavering and changing pitch. She lifts a black-gloved hand to straighten the peacock feather or maybe just to check that it's still there. Then she slides a book out of her purse. She's returning BVRNES.

"Hello, Ms. Lapin!" I say too loud and too fast. "What can I get for you?" I consider using my spooky prototype to predict the name of her next book without waiting for her, but my screen is currently occupied by—

"What did you say?" Kat's voice burbles. I mute the laptop.

Lapin doesn't notice. "Well," she says, gliding up to the front desk, "I'm not sure how to pronounce it, but, I think it might be Par-zee-bee, or perhaps, perhaps Pra-zinky-blink—"

You have got to be kidding me. I try my best to transliterate what she's saying, but the database comes up empty. I try again with a different set of phonetic assumptions. Nope, nothing. "Ms. Lapin," I say, "how do you spell it?"

"Oh, it's *P, B,* that's a *B, Z, B,* no, sorry, *Y* . . ."

You—have got—to be kidding—me.

"*B* again, that's just one *B, Y,* no, I mean, yes, *Y* . . ."

The database says: Przybylowicz. That's just ridiculous.

I race up the ladder, pull PRZYBYLOWICZ so violently from the shelf that I almost make its neighbor PRYOR pop out and drop to the floor, and return to Lapin, my face set in a mask of steely annoyance. Kat is moving silently on the screen, waving to someone.

I have the book wrapped up, and Lapin has her card out—6YTP5T—but then she glides over to one of the short shelves up front, the ones with the normal books. Oh, no.

Long seconds pass. She works her way across the shelf marked ROMANCE, the peacock feather bobbing when she tilts her head to read the spines.

"Oh, I think I'll get this, too," she says finally, returning with a bright red Danielle Steel hardcover. Then it takes her approximately three days to find her checkbook.

"So," she wavers, "that's thirteen, let's see, thirteen dollars and how many cents?"

"Thirty-seven."

"Thirteen . . . dollars . . ." She writes with agonizing slowness, but I have to admit, her script is beautiful. It's dark and looping, almost calligraphic. She presses the check flat and signs it slowly: *Rosemary Lapin.*

She hands it to me, finished, and at the very bottom there's a line of tiny type that informs me she's been a member of the Telegraph Hill Credit Union since—oh, wow—since 1951.

Jeez. Why am I punishing this old woman for my own weird ways? Something softens inside of me. My mask melts and I give her a smile—a real one.

"Have a good night, Ms. Lapin," I say. "Come again soon."

"Oh, I'm working as fast as I can," she says, and smiles a sweet smile of her own that makes her cheeks puff out like pale plums. "*Festina lente.*" She slips her Waybacklist treasure and her guilty pleasure into her purse together. They poke out at the top: matte brown and shiny red. The door tinkles, and she and her peacock feather are gone.

The customers say that sometimes. They say: *Festina lente.*

I lunge back down toward the screen. When I unmute the speaker, Kat and Trevor are still chatting happily. He's telling another story, this one about an expedition to cheer up some depressed penguins, and it is apparently hilarious. Kat is laughing. There is so much bubbly laughter coming out of my laptop speakers. Trevor is apparently the cleverest, most interesting man in the whole city of San Francisco. Neither of them is on camera, so I assume she is touching his arm.

"Hey, guys," I say. *"Hey, guys."*

I realize they've muted me, too.

All at once I feel stupid, and I am sure this whole thing has been a terrible idea. The point of a party at Kat's apartment is that *I* tell a funny story and Kat touches *my* arm. This exercise in telepresence, on the other hand, does not have a point, and everyone is probably laughing at me and making faces at the laptop just off-camera. My face is burning. Can they tell? Am I turning a strange shade of red on the screen?

I stand and step away from the camera's gaze. Exhaustion floods into my brain. I've been performing hard for the past two hours, I realize— a grinning puppet in an aluminum proscenium. What a mistake.

I put my palms on the bookstore's broad front windows and look out through the cage of tall golden type. It's Gerritszoon, all right, and it's a scrap of familiar grace in this lonely place. The curve of the *P* is beautiful. My breath fogs the glass. Be normal, I tell myself. Just go back and be normal.

"Hello?" a voice pipes out of my laptop. Kat.

I slide back into place behind the desk. "Hi."

Trevor is gone. Kat is alone. In fact, she's somewhere completely different now.

"This is my room," she says softly. "Like it?"

It's spartan, not much more than a bed and a desk and a heavy black trunk. It looks like a cabin on an ocean liner. No: a pod on a spaceship. In the corner of the room, there's a white plastic laundry basket, and scattered around it—near-misses—I see a dozen identical red T-shirts.

"That was my theory," I say.

"Yeah," Kat says, "I decided I didn't want to waste brain cycles"—she yawns—"figuring out what to wear every morning."

The laptop rocks and there's a blur and then we are on her bed, and her head is propped up on her hand, and I can see the curve of her chest. My heart is suddenly beating very fast, as if I'm there with her, stretched out and expectant—as if I am not sitting here alone in the dim light of this bookstore, still wearing paisley pants.

"This was pretty fun," she says quietly, "but I wish you could have come for real."

She stretches and presses her eyes shut like a cat. I can't think of a single thing to say, so I just put my chin on my palm and look into the camera.

"It would be nice if you were here," she murmurs. Then she falls asleep. I am alone in the bookstore, looking across the city at her sleeping form, lit only by the gray light of her laptop. In time it, too, falls asleep, and the screen goes dark.

Alone in the store after the party, I do my homework. I've made my selection: I gently pull logbook VII (old but not too old) off the shelf and get Mat his reference images: wide shots and close-ups, snapped with my phone from a dozen angles, all showing the same wide, flat rectangle of battered brown. I snap detail shots of the bookmark, the binding, the pale gray pages, and the deeply embossed NARRATIO on the cover above the store's symbol, and when Penumbra arrives in the morning, my phone is back in my pocket and the images are on their way to Mat's inbox. There's a little *whoosh* as each of them goes.

I've left the current logbook up on the desk. I'll do that from now on. I mean, why put it on the shelf all the time? Sounds like a recipe for back strain if you ask me. With luck, this choice will catch on and cast a new shadow of normalcy in which I can crouch and hide. That's what spies do, right? They walk to the bakery and buy a loaf of bread every day—perfectly normal—until one day they buy a loaf of uranium instead.

# MAKE AND MODEL

IN THE DAYS THAT FOLLOW, I spend more time with Kat. I see her apartment unmediated by screens. We play video games. We make out.

One night we try to cook dinner on her industrial stove, but halfway through we judge the steaming sludge of kale a failure, so instead she pulls a neat plastic tub out of the refrigerator, full of spicy couscous salad. Kat can't find any spoons, so she serves it up with an ice-cream scoop.

"Did you make this?" I ask, because I don't think she did. It's perfect.

She shakes her head. "It's from work. I bring food home most days. It's free."

Kat spends most of her time at Google. Most of her friends work at Google. Most of her conversations revolve around Google. Now I am learning that most of her calories come from Google. I think it's impressive: she's smart and enthusiastic about her work. But it's also intimidating, because my workplace is not a gleaming crystal castle full of smiling savants. (That's how I imagine Google. Also, lots of funny hats.)

There's a real limit to the relationship I can build with Kat in her non-Google hours, simply because there aren't that many of them, and I think I want more than that. I want to earn entrance into Kat's world. I want to see the princess in her castle.

My ticket to Google is logbook VII.

Over the course of the next three weeks, Mat and I painstakingly construct the logbook's body double. The surface is Mat's specialty. He starts with a sheet of new leather and stains it with coffee. Then he brings a pair of vintage golf cleats down from his attic aerie; I squeeze my feet into them and march back and forth across the leather for two hours.

The logbook's guts require more research. In the living room late at night, Mat works on his miniature city while I sit on the couch with my laptop, googling widely, reading detailed book-making tutorials out loud. We learn about binding. We track down vellum wholesalers. We find dusky ivory cloth and thick black thread. We buy a book block on eBay.

"You're good at this, Jannon," Mat tells me when we set the blank pages into glue.

"What, book-making?" (We do this on the kitchen table.)

"No, learning things on the fly," he says. "It's what we do at work. Not like the computer guys, you know? They just do the same thing every time. It's always just pixels. For us, every project is different. New tools, new materials. Every-thing's always new."

"Like the jungle monster."

"Exactly. I had forty-eight hours to become a bonsai master."

Mat Mittelbrand hasn't met Kat Potente, but I think they would get along: Kat, who believes so deeply in the human brain's potential, and Mat, who can learn anything in a day. Thinking about that, I feel suddenly sympathetic to Kat's point of view. If we could keep Mat going for a thousand years, he could probably build us a whole new world.

The fake logbook's crowning detail, and the toughest challenge, is the embossing on the cover. The original has the word NARRATIO pressed deep into the leather, and after zoomed-in scrutiny of the reference images, I discover that this text, too, is set in good old Gerritszoon. That's bad news.

"Why?" Mat asks. "I think I have that font on my computer."

"You have Gerritszoon," I cluck, "suitable for emails, book reports, and résumés. This"—I point to the blown-up NARRATIO on my laptop screen—"is Gerritszoon Display, suitable for billboards, magazine spreads, and, apparently, occult book covers. See, it has pointier serifs."

Mat nods gravely. "The serifs are pointy indeed."

Back at NewBagel, when I designed menus and posters and (may I remind you) an award-winning logo, I learned all about the digital font marketplace. Nowhere else is the bucks-to-bytes ratio so severe. Here's what I mean: An e-book costs about ten dollars, right? And it's usually about a megabyte's worth of text. (For the record, you download more data than that every time you look at Facebook.) With an e-book, you can see what you paid for: the words, the paragraphs, the possibly boring expositions of digital marketplaces. Well, it turns out a digital font is also about a megabyte, but a digital font costs not tens of dollars but hundreds, sometimes thousands, and it's abstract, basically invisible—a thin envelope of math describing tiny letterforms. The whole arrangement offends most people's consumer instincts.

So of course people try to pirate fonts. I am not one of those people. I took a typography course in school and for our final project, everyone had to design their own typeface. I had grand aspirations for mine—it was called Telemach—but there were just too many letters to draw. I couldn't finish it in time. It ended up capitals-only, suitable for shouty posters and stone tablets. So trust me, I know how much sweat goes into those shapes. Typographers are designers; designers are my people; I am committed to supporting them. But now FontShop.com tells me that Gerritszoon Display, distributed by FLC Type Foundry of New York City, costs $3,989.

So of course I will try to pirate this font.

A connection zigzags through my brain. I close the tab for FontShop and go instead to Grumble's library. It's not only pirated e-books here. There are fonts, too—illegal letters of every shape and size. I page through the listings: Metro and Gotham and Soho, all free for the taking. Myriad and Minion and Mrs Eaves. And there, too, is Gerritszoon Display.

I feel a pang of remorse as I download it, but really just a tiny pang. FLC Type Foundry is probably somehow a subsidiary of Time Warner. Gerritszoon is an old font, its eponymous creator long dead. What does he care how his typeface is used, and by whom?

Mat sets the word above a carefully traced outline of the bookstore's symbol—two hands, open like a book—and with that, we have our design. The next day at ILM, he carves the whole thing out of scrap metal using a plasma cutter—in Mat's world, a plasma cutter is as customary as a pair of scissors—and finally we press it into the false-weathered leather with a fat C-clamp. It sits silently embossing on the kitchen table for three days and three nights, and when Mat releases the clamp, the cover is perfect.

So finally, it is time. Night falls. I take Oliver Grone's place at the front desk and begin my shift.

Tonight I will claim my ticket to adventure in Kat's world. Tonight I will make the switch.

But it turns out I would make a terrible spy—I can't seem to calm myself down. I've tried everything: reading long works of investigative journalism; playing the computer version of Rockets & Warlocks; pacing the Waybacklist. I can't stay focused on anything for more than three minutes.

Now I've resigned myself to sitting at the front desk, but I can't stop squirming. If fidgets were Wikipedia edits, I would have completely revamped the entry on guilt by now, and translated it into five new languages.

Finally, it's quarter to six. The thinnest tendrils of dawn are creeping in from the east. People in New York are softly starting to tweet. I'm completely exhausted because I've spent the whole night vibrating.

The real logbook VII is stuffed into my messenger bag but way too big for it, so it bulges out and looks, to my eye, like the most ludicrously incriminating thing in the world. It's like when one of those huge African snakes swallows an animal whole and you can see it wiggling around in there, all the way down.

The fake logbook is standing with its stepsiblings. When I slid it into place, I realized it left a telltale streak in the dust on the shelf's edge. First I panicked. Then I ventured deep into the Waybacklist, scooped dust off the shelves there, and sprinkled it in front of the fake logbook until the depth and grade of the dust matched perfectly.

I have a dozen explanations (with branching subplots) if Penumbra spots the difference. But I have to admit: the fake logbook looks great. My touch-up dust is ILM-caliber. It looks real and I don't think I'd give it a second glance and, whoa, the bell tinkles over the front door—

"Good morning," Penumbra says. "How was the night?"

"Fine good great," I say. Too fast. Slow down. Remember: the shadow of normalcy. Crouch there.

"You know," Penumbra says, peeling off his peacoat, "I have been thinking. We should retire this fellow"—he taps the Mac Plus on the head with two fingers, a gentle *thwack thwack*—"and acquire something more up-to-date. Nothing too expensive. Perhaps you can recommend a make and model?"

Make and model. I've never heard anyone talk about computers that way. You can have a MacBook in any color you want, as long as it's bare metal. "Yeah that's great," I say. "Sure I'll do some research Mr. Penumbra maybe a refurbished iMac I think they're just as good as the new ones." I say it all in one breath, already heading for the door. I feel sick.

"And," he says gingerly, "perhaps you could use it to construct a website."

My heart is bursting.

"The store should have one. It is past time."

It's done, my heart has exploded, and a few other small organs may have ruptured, too, but I am committed to this course—I am committed to Kat Potente's corpus:

"Wow that's awesome we should totally do that I love websites but I've really got to go Mr. Penumbra see you later."

He pauses, then smiles a lopsided smile. "Very well. Have a good day."

Twenty minutes later, I'm on the train to Mountain View, clutching my bulging bag to my chest. It's strange—my transgression is so slight. Who cares about the whereabouts of an old logbook from an obscure used bookstore for sixteen measly hours? But it doesn't feel that way. It feels like I'm one of the two people in the world Penumbra is supposed to be able to count on, and it turns out I can't be trusted.

All of this, just to impress a girl. The train's rumble and sway put me to sleep.

# THE SPIDER

T HE RAINBOW SIGN next to the train station that points the way to Google's campus has faded a bit in the Silicon Valley sun. I follow the pale arrow down a curving sidewalk flanked by eucalyptus trees and bike racks. Around the bend, I see wide lawns and low buildings and, between the trees, flashes of branding: red, green, yellow, blue.

The buzz about Google these days is that it's like America itself: still the biggest game in town, but inevitably and irrevocably on the decline. Both are superpowers with unmatched resources, but both are faced with fast-growing rivals, and both will eventually be eclipsed. For America, that rival is China. For Google, it's Facebook. (This is all from tech-gossip blogs, so take it with a grain of salt. They also say a startup called MonkeyMoney is going to be huge next year.) But here's the difference: staring down the inevitable, America pays defense contractors to build aircraft carriers. Google pays brilliant programmers to do whatever the hell they want.

Kat meets me at a blue security checkpoint, requests and receives a visitor badge with my name and affiliation printed in red, and leads me into her domain. We cut through a broad parking lot, the blacktop baking in the sun. There are no cars here; instead, the lot is packed full of white shipping containers set up on short stilts.

"These are pieces of the Big Box," Kat says, pointing. A semi truck is arriving at the far end of the lot, roaring and hissing. Its carriage is painted bright red-green-blue, and it's towing one of the white containers.

"They're like LEGO blocks," she continues, "except each one has disk space, tons of it, and CPUs and everything else, and connections for water and power and internet. We build them in Vietnam, then ship them wherever. They all hook up automatically, no matter where they are. All together, they're the Big Box."

"Which does . . . ?"

"Everything," she says. "Everything at Google runs in the Big Box." She points a brown arm toward a container with WWW stenciled across the side in tall green letters. "There's a copy of the web in there." YT: "Every video on YouTube." MX: "All your email. Everybody's email."

Penumbra's shelves don't seem so tall anymore.

Wide walkways curve through the main campus. There's a bike lane, and Googlers whiz by on carbon-fiber racers and fixed gears with battery packs. There's a pair of graybeards on recumbents and a tall dude with blue dreadlocks pedaling a unicycle.

"I reserved some time on the book scanner at twelve-thirty," Kat says. "Lunch first?"

The Google mess hall comes into view, wide and low, a white pavilion staked out like a garden party. The front is open, tarp pulled up above the entryways, and short lines of Googlers poke out onto the lawn.

Kat pauses, squinting. Calculating. "This one," she says finally, and tugs me over to the leftmost line. "I'm a pretty good queue strategist. But it's not easy here—"

"Because everyone at Google is a queue strategist," I suggest.

"Exactly. So sometimes there's bluffing. This guy's a bluffer," she says, jabbing the Googler just ahead of us in line with her elbow. He's tall and sandy-haired and he looks like a surfer.

"Hey, I am Finn," he says, holding out a blocky, long-fingered hand. "Your first visit to Google?" He says it *Gew-gell,* with a little pause in the middle.

It is indeed, my ambiguously European friend. I make small talk: "How's the food?"

"Oh, fantastic. The chef is famous . . ." He pauses. Something clicks. "Kat, he must use the other line."

"Right. I always forget," Kat says. She explains, "Our food is personalized. It has vitamins, some natural stimulants."

Finn nods vigorously. "I am experimenting with my potassium level. Now I am up to eleven bananas every day. Body hacking!" His face splits into a wide grin. Wait, did the couscous salad have stimulants?

"Sorry," Kat says, frowning. "The visitor line is over there." She points across the lawn, and I leave her with the body-hacking Euro-surfer.

So now I'm waiting next to a sign that says EXTERNAL DEPENDENCIES alongside three dudes in khakis and blue button-downs with leather phone holsters. Across the grass, the Googlers all wear snug jeans and bright T-shirts.

Kat is talking to someone else now, a slender brown-skinned boy who's joined the line just behind her. He's dressed like a skater, so I assume he has a PhD in artificial intelligence. A lance of jealousy spikes down behind my eyes, but I'm prepared for it; I knew it would come, here in the crystal castle where Kat knows everyone and everyone knows her. So I just let it pass, and I remind myself that she brought me here. This is the trump card in these situations: Yes, everyone else is smart, everyone else is cool, everyone else is healthy and attractive—but she brought you. You have to wear that like a pin, like a badge.

I look down and realize my visitor badge actually says that—

NAME: Clay Jannon
COMPANY: Mr. Penumbra's 24-Hour Bookstore
HOST: Kat Potente

—so I peel it off and stick it a little higher up on my shirt.

The food is, as promised, fantastic. I get two scoops of lentil salad and a thick pink stripe of fish, seven sturdy green lines of asparagus, and a single chocolate-chip cookie that has been optimized for crispiness.

Kat waves me over to a table near the pavilion's perimeter, where a quick breeze is rustling the white tarp. Little slices of light dance across the table, which has a paper covering marked out with a pale blue grid. At Google, they eat lunch on graph paper.

"This is Raj," she says, waving a forkful of lentil salad (which looks just like mine) at the skater PhD. "We went to school together." Kat studied symbolic systems at Stanford. Did everybody here go to Stanford? Do they just give you a job at Google when you graduate?

When Raj speaks, he seems suddenly ten years older. His voice is clipped and direct: "So what do you do?"

I hoped that question would be outlawed here, replaced by some quirky Google equivalent, like: *What's your favorite prime number?* I point at my badge and concede that I work at the opposite of Google.

"Ah, books." Raj pauses a moment, chewing. Then his brain slots into a groove: "You know, old books are a big problem for us. Old knowledge in

117

general. We call it OK. Old knowledge, OK. Did you know that ninety-five percent of the internet was only created in the last five years? But we know that when it comes to all human knowledge, the ratio is just the opposite—in fact, OK accounts for most things that most people know, and have ever known."

Raj is not blinking, and possibly not breathing.

"So where is it, right? Where's the OK? Well, it's in old books, for one thing"—he uncaps a thin-tipped marker (where did that come from?) and starts drawing on the graph-paper tablecloth—"and it's also in people's heads, a lot of traditional knowledge, that's what we call TK. OK and TK." He's drawing little overlapping blobs, labeling them with acronyms. "Imagine if we could make all that OK/TK available all the time, to everyone. On the web, on your phone. No question would go unanswered ever again."

I wonder what Raj has in his lunch.

"Vitamin D, omega-3s, fermented tea leaves," he says, still scribbling. He makes a single dot off to the side of the blobs and smooshes the marker down, making the black ink bleed. "That's what we've got stored in the Big Box right now," he says, pointing to the dot, "and just think how valuable it is. If we could add all this"—he sweeps his hand across the OK/TK blobs like a general planning conquest—"then we could really get serious."

• • •

"Raj has been at Google a long time," Kat says. We're wandering away from the mess hall. I snagged an extra cookie on the way out, and I'm nibbling on it now. "He's pre-IPO and he was PM for ages."

The acronyms at this place! But I think I know this one. "Wait"—I'm confused—"Google has a prime minister?"

"Ha, no," she says. "Product Management. It's a committee. It used to be two people, then it was four, now it's bigger. Sixty-four. The PM runs the company. They approve new projects, assign engineers, allocate resources."

"So these are all the top executives."

"No, that's the thing. It's a lottery. Your name gets drawn and you serve on the PM for twelve months. Anybody could be chosen. Raj, Finn, me. Pepper."

"Pepper?"

"The chef."

Wow—it's so egalitarian it's beyond democracy. I realize: "It's jury duty."

"You're not eligible until you've worked here for a year," Kat explains. "And you can get out of it if you're working on something super-super-important. But people take it really seriously."

I wonder if Kat Potente has been summoned.

She shakes her head. "Not yet," she says. "But I'd love to do it. I mean, the odds aren't great.

119

Thirty thousand people work here, there are sixty-four on the PM. You do the math. But it's growing all the time. People say they might expand it again."

Now I'm wondering what it would be like if we ran the whole country like this.

"That's totally what Raj wants to do!" Kat laughs. "After he finds all the OK and TK, of course." She shakes her head at that; she's making fun of him a little. "He has a whole plan to pass a constitutional amendment. If anybody could do it . . ." Pursed lips again. "Actually, it probably wouldn't be Raj." She laughs, and I do, too. Yeah, Raj is a little too intense for Middle America.

So I ask, "Who could pull it off?"

"Maybe I could," Kat says, puffing her chest out.

Maybe you could.

We walk past Kat's domain: data viz. It's perched on a low hill, a cluster of prefab boxes set around a small amphitheater where stone steps lead down to a bank of giant screens. We peek down. There's a pair of engineers sitting on the amphitheater steps, laptops on their knees, watching a cluster of bubbles bounce around on one screen, all connected with wavy lines. Every few seconds the bubbles freeze and the lines snap straight, like the hair sticking up on the back of your neck. Then the screen flashes solid red. One of the engineers mutters a quiet curse and leans in to her laptop.

Kat shrugs. "Work in progress."

"What's it for?"

"Not sure. Probably something internal. Most of the stuff we do is internal." She sighs. "Google's so big, it's an audience all by itself. I mostly make visualizations that get used by other engineers, or ad sales, or the PM . . ." She trails off. "To tell you the truth, I'd love to make something everybody could see!" She laughs as if relieved to say it out loud.

We pass through a glade of tall cypress on the edge of campus—it makes a nice golden dapple on the sidewalk—and come to a low brick building with no marking other than a handwritten sign taped to the dark glass door:

BOOK SCANNER

Inside, the building feels like a field hospital. It's dark and a little warm. Harsh floodlights glare down on an operating table ringed with long, many-jointed metal arms. The air stings like bleach. The table is also surrounded by books: stacks and stacks of them, piled high on metal carts. There are big books and little books; there are bestsellers and old books that look like they would fit in at Penumbra's. I spy Dashiell Hammett.

A tall Googler named Jad runs the book scanner. He has a perfectly triangular nose over a fuzzy brown beard. He looks like a Greek philosopher. Maybe it's just because he's wearing sandals.

"Hey, welcome," he says, smiling, shaking Kat's hand, then mine. "Nice to have somebody from data viz in here. And you . . . ?" He looks at me, eyebrows raised.

"Not a Googler," I confess. "I work at an old bookstore."

"Oh, cool," Jad says. Then he darkens: "Except, I mean. Sorry."

"Sorry for what?"

"Well. For putting you guys out of business." He says it very matter-of-factly.

"Wait, which guys?"

"Book . . . stores?"

Right. I don't actually think of myself as part of the book business; Penumbra's store feels like something else entirely. But . . . I do sell books. I am the manager of a Google ad campaign designed to reach potential book buyers. Somehow it snuck up on me: I am a bookseller.

Jad continues, "I mean, once we've got everything scanned, and cheap reading devices are ubiquitous . . . nobody's going to need bookstores, right?"

"Is that the business model for this?" I say, nodding at the scanner. "Selling e-books?"

"We don't really have a business model." Jad

shrugs. "We don't need one. The ads make so much money, it kinda takes care of everything." He turns to Kat: "Don't you think that's right? Even if we made, like, five . . . million . . . dollars?" (He's not sure if that sounds like a lot of money or not. For the record: it does.) "Yeah, nobody would even notice. Over there"—he waves a long arm vaguely back toward the center of campus—"they make that much, like, every twenty minutes."

That is super-depressing. If I made five million dollars selling books, I'd want people to carry me around in a palanquin constructed from first editions of *The Dragon-Song Chronicles*.

"Yeah, that's more or less right"—Kat nods—"but it's a good thing. It gives us freedom. We can think long-term. We can invest in stuff like this." She steps closer to the scanner's bright table with its long metal arms. Her eyes are wide and glinting in the light. "Just look at it."

"Anyway, sorry," Jad says to me quietly.

"We'll be fine," I say. "People still like the smell of books." And besides, Jad's book scanner isn't the only project with far-off funding. Penumbra's has a patron of its own.

I dig the logbook out of my bag and hand it over. "Here's the patient."

Jad holds it under the floodlights. "This is a beautiful book," he says. He runs long fingers across the embossing on the cover. "What is it?"

"Just a personal diary." I pause. "Very personal."

He gently opens the logbook and clips the front and back of the cover into a right-angled metal frame. No spines broken here. Then he places the frame on the table and locks it down with four clicky brackets. Finally, he gives it a test wiggle; the frame and its passenger are secure. The logbook is strapped in like a test pilot, or a crash-test dummy.

Jad scoots us back away from the scanner. "Stay behind this," he says, pointing to a yellow line on the floor. "The arms are sharp."

His long fingers go *tap-tap* behind a bank of flat monitors. There's a low, gut-rumbling hum, then a high warning chime, and then the book scanner leaps into action. The floodlights start strobing, turning everything in the chamber into a stop-motion movie. Frame by frame, the scanner's spidery arms reach down, grasp page corners, peel them back. It's mesmerizing. I've never seen anything at once so fast and so delicate. The arms stroke the pages, caress them, smooth them down. This thing loves books.

At each flash of the lights, two giant cameras set above the table swivel and snap images in tandem. I sidle up next to Jad, where I can see the pages of the logbook stacking up on his monitors. The two cameras are like two eyes, so the images are in 3-D, and I watch his computer lift the words right up off the pale gray pages. It looks like an exorcism.

I walk back over to Kat. Her toes are on the yellow line and she's leaning in close to the book scanner. I'm afraid she's going to get stabbed in the eye.

"This is awesome," she breathes.

It really is. I feel a pang of pity for the logbook, its secrets all plucked out in minutes by this whirlwind of light and metal. Books used to be pretty high-tech, back in the day. Not anymore.

# THE FOUNDER'S PUZZLE

I T'S LATER, around eight, and we are in Kat's spaceship-pod bedroom, at her white spaceship-console desk. She's sitting on my lap, leaning in to her MacBook. She's explaining OCR, the process by which a computer transforms swoops of ink and streaks of graphite into characters it can comprehend, like *K* and *A* and *T*.

"It's not trivial," she says. "That was a big book." Also, my predecessors had handwriting almost as bad as mine. But Kat has a plan. "It would take my computer all night to process these pages," she says. "But we're impatient, right?" She's typing at warp ten, composing long commands I do not understand. Yes, we are definitely impatient.

"So we'll get hundreds of machines to do it all at once. We'll use Hadoop."

"Hadoop."

"Everybody uses it. Google, Facebook, the NSA. It's software—it breaks a big job into lots of tiny pieces and spreads them out to lots of different computers at the same time."

Hadoop! I love the sound of it. Kat Potente, you and I will have a son, and we will name him Hadoop, and he will be a great warrior, a king!

She stretches forward, her palms planted on the desk. "I love this." Her eyes are set firmly on the screen, where a diagram is blossoming: a skeletal flower with a blinking center and dozens—no, hundreds—of petals. It's growing fast, transforming from a daisy to a dandelion to a giant sunflower. "A thousand computers are doing exactly what I want right now. My mind is not just here," she says, tapping her head, "it's out there. I love it—the feeling."

She moves against me. I can smell everything sharply all of a sudden; her hair, shampooed recently, is up against my face. Her earlobes stick out a little, round and pink, and her back is strong from the Google climbing wall. I trace my thumbs down her shoulder blades, across the bumps of her bra straps. She moves again, rocking. I push up her T-shirt and the letters, squished, reflect in the laptop screen: BAM!

Later, Kat's laptop makes a low chime. She slides away from me, hops off the bed, and climbs back onto her black desk chair. Perched there on her toes, her spine curving down into the screen, she looks like a gargoyle. A beautiful naked-girl-shaped gargoyle.

"It worked," she says. She turns to me, flushed, her hair dark and wild. Grinning. "It worked!"

It's way past midnight, and I'm back at the bookstore. The real logbook is safely on its shelf. The fake logbook is tucked into my bag. Everything has gone exactly according to plan. I'm alert, I'm feeling good, and I'm ready to visualize. I pull the scanned data out of the Big Box; it takes less than a minute over *bootynet*. All the little tales anyone has ever scratched into that logbook stream back into my laptop, perfectly processed.

Now, computer, it is time for you to do my bidding.

This sort of thing never works perfectly at first. I pipe the raw text into the visualization and it looks like Jackson Pollock got his hands on my prototype. There are splotches of data everywhere, blobs of pink and green and yellow, all harsh arcade-game hues.

The first thing I do is change the palette. Earth tones, please.

Now: I'm dealing with too much information here. I only want to see who borrowed what. Kat's analysis was smart enough to tag names and titles and times in the text, and the visualization knows how to plot those, so I link data to display and I see something familiar: a swarm of colored lights bouncing through the shelves, each one representing a customer. These, though, are customers from years ago.

It doesn't look like much—just a colorful mess migrating through the Waybacklist. Then, on a hunch, I connect the dots, so it's not a swarm but a set of constellations. Every customer leaves a trail, a drunken zigzag through the shelves. The shortest constellation, rendered in red clay, makes a tiny Z, just four data points. The longest, in dark moss, curves around the whole width of the store in a long jagged oval.

It still doesn't look like much. I give the 3-D bookstore a push with the trackpad and set it spinning on its axes. I stand up to stretch my legs. On the other side of the desk, I pick up one of the Dashiell Hammetts, untouched by anyone since I noticed them that first day in the store. That's sad. I mean, seriously: shelves full of gibberish get all the attention while *The Maltese Falcon* gathers dust? It's beyond sad. It's stupid. I should start looking for a different job. This place will drive me nuts.

When I come back to the desk, the bookstore is still spinning, whirling like a carousel . . . and something strange is happening. Once every rotation, the dark moss constellation snaps into focus. For just a moment, it makes a picture and— it can't be. I smack my hand on the trackpad, slow the model to a halt, and bring it back around. The dark moss constellation makes a clear picture. The other constellations fit, too. None of them are as complete as the dark moss, but they follow the curve of a chin, the slope of an eye. When the model is lined up straight, as if I were peering in from the front door—very close to where I'm sitting right now—the constellations come to life. They make a face.

It's Penumbra.

• • •

The bell tinkles and he walks into the store trailed by a long coil of fog. I'm tongue-tied, with no idea how to begin. I'm faced with two Penumbras at once: one, a mute staring wire-frame on my laptop screen, and the other, an old man in the doorway just starting to smile.

"Good morning, my boy," he says cheerily. "Did anything of note transpire in the night?"

For a moment, I strongly consider closing my laptop's lid and never speaking of this again. But no: I'm too curious. I can't just sit at my desk and let this web of weirdness spin out around me. (That describes a lot of jobs, I realize, but this is potentially a special kind of magick-with-a-*k* weirdness.)

"What do you have there?" he asks. "Have you begun work on our website?"

I swivel my laptop around to show him. "Not exactly."

Half-smiling, he holds his glasses at an angle and peers down at the screen. His face goes slack, and then he says, quietly: "The Founder." He turns to me. "You solved it." He claps a hand to his forehead and his face splits into a giddy smile. "You solved it already! Look at him! Right there on the screen!"

Look at *him?* Isn't this—Oh. I realize now, with Penumbra leaning in close, that I have made the common mistake of assuming that all old people look the same. The wire-frame portrait on the screen has Penumbra's nose, but its mouth is a tiny curving bow. Penumbra's is flat and wide, built for grinning.

"How did you do it?" he continues. He's so proud, like I'm his grandson and I just hit a home run, or cured cancer. "I must see your notes! Did you use Euler's method? Or the Brito inversion? There is no shame in that, it clears away much of the confusion early on . . ."

"Mr. Penumbra," I say, triumph in my voice, "I scanned an old logbook—" Then I realize this carries a larger implication, so I stutter and confess, "Well, I took an old logbook. Borrowed it. Temporarily."

Penumbra crinkles his eyes. "Oh, I know, my boy," he says, not unkindly. He pauses. "Your simulacrum smelled strongly of coffee."

Right, so: "I borrowed an old logbook, and we scanned it"—his face changes and suddenly he's concerned, like instead of curing cancer, maybe I have it—"because Google has this machine, it's superfast, and Hadoop, it just goes—I mean, a thousand computers, like that!" I snap for emphasis. I don't think he has any idea what I'm talking about. "Anyway, the point is, we just pulled out the data. Automatically."

There's a tremor in Penumbra's micromuscles. Close-up like this, I'm reminded that he is, in fact, very old.

"Google," he breathes. There's a long pause. "How curious." He straightens. He has the strangest expression on his face—the emotive equivalent of 404 PAGE NOT FOUND. Talking mostly to himself, he says, "I will have to make a report."

Wait, what kind of report? Are we talking about a police report? Grand theft codex? "Mr. Penumbra, is there a problem? I don't understand why—"

"Oh, yes, I know," he says sharply, and his eyes flash at me. "I see it now. You cheated—would that be fair to say? And as a result, you have no idea what you have accomplished."

I look down at the desk. That would be fair to say.

When I look back up at Penumbra, his gaze has softened. "And yet . . . you did it all the same." He turns and wanders into the Waybacklist. "How curious."

"Who is it?" I ask suddenly. "Whose face?"

"It is the Founder," Penumbra says, running a long hand up along one of the shelves. "The one who waits, hiding. He vexes novices for years. Years! And yet you revealed him in—what? A single month?"

Not quite: "Just one day."

Penumbra takes a sharp breath. His eyes flash again. They are pulled wide and, reflecting the light from the windows, they crackle electric blue

in a way I've never seen. He gasps, "Incredible."
He takes a breath, a deeper one. He looks rattled
and exhilarated; actually, he looks a little crazy. "I
have work to do," he says. "I must make plans. Go
home, my boy."

"But—"

"Go home. Whether you understand it or not,
you have done something important today."

He turns and walks deeper into the dark and
dusty shelves, talking quietly to himself. I gather
up my laptop and my messenger bag and I slip out
the front door. The bell makes just the barest
tinkle. I glance back through the tall windows,
and, behind the curving golden type, Penumbra
has disappeared.

# WHY DO YOU LOVE BOOKS SO MUCH?

WHEN I RETURN THE NEXT NIGHT, I see something I've never seen before, something that makes me gasp and stop in my tracks:

Mr. Penumbra's 24-Hour Bookstore is dark.

It looks all wrong. The store is always open, always awake, like a little lighthouse on this seedy stretch of Broadway. But now the lamps are doused and there is a tidy square of paper stuck to the inside of the front door. In Penumbra's spidery script, it says:

*CLOSED (AD LIBRIS)*

I don't have a key to the store, because I've never needed one. It's always been a handoff— Penumbra to Oliver, Oliver to me, me to Penumbra. For a moment I am furious, full of selfish rage. What the hell? When will it open again? Wasn't I supposed to get an email or something? This is a pretty irresponsible thing for an employer to do.

But then I get worried. This morning's encounter was well beyond the pale. What if it got Penumbra so worked up that he suffered a tiny heart attack? Or a massive heart attack? What if he's dead? Or what if he's weeping to himself in a lonely apartment somewhere, where his family never visits him because Grandpa Penumbra is weird and smells like books? A flood of shame washes through my blood and mixes with the anger and they swirl together into a heavy soup that makes me feel sick.

I walk to the liquor store on the corner to get some chips.

For the next twenty minutes, I stand on the curb, dumbly munching Fritos and wiping my hand on my pants leg, not sure what to do next. Should I go home and come back tomorrow? Should I look Penumbra up in the phone book and try to call him? Scratch that. I know without checking that Penumbra will not be in the phone book, and besides, I don't actually know where to find one of those.

I'm standing there, trying to imagine some clever course of action, when I see a familiar figure come gliding up the street. It's not Penumbra; he doesn't glide. This is—it's Ms. Lapin. I duck behind a trash can (why did I just duck behind a trash can?) and watch her scoot toward the store, gasp when she reaches a range at which she can detect its dereliction, then swoop in close to the front door, where she stretches up on tiptoe to inspect the CLOSED (AD LIBRIS) sign, nose pressed to the glass, no doubt auguring deep meaning in those three words.

Then she glances furtively up and down the street, and when the pale oval of her face swivels this way, I see a look of tight-drawn fear. She turns and glides back the way she came.

I drop my Fritos in the trash can and follow her.

Lapin breaks away from Broadway and picks a path toward Telegraph Hill. Her velocity is steady, even as the landscape rises underneath her; she's the little eccentric that could. I'm huffing and puffing, quick-stepping a block behind her, struggling to keep up. The nozzle head of Coit Tower rises on the hill high above us, a spindly gray cutout against the deeper darkness of the sky. Midway along a narrow street that curves up around the contour of the hill, Lapin disappears.

I sprint to the spot where she last stood and there I find a skinny stone staircase set into the hillside, running like an alleyway between the houses, cutting steeply upward under a scrim of branches. Lapin is somehow already halfway up.

I try to call out after her—"Ms. Lapin!"—but I'm too winded and it comes out as a wheeze. So I cough and grunt and lean into the hill and follow her up.

It's quiet on the staircase. The only light comes from tiny windows set high in the houses on either side; it spills out into the branches above, heavy with dark plums. Up ahead, there's a loud rustle and a chorus of squawks. In another moment a flock of wild parrots, roused from their perches, comes barnstorming down the tree-lined tube into the open night air. Wingtips brush the top of my head.

Up ahead, there's a sharp click and a creak and then a crack of light widens into a square. My quarry's shadow passes through it, and then it closes tight. Rosemary Lapin is home.

I make it to the landing and sit on a step to catch my breath. This lady has serious stamina. Maybe she's light, with bones like a bird. Maybe she's slightly buoyant. I look back down the way we came, and through the lace of black branches I can see the lights of the city far below.

Dishes clink and clatter inside. I knock on Ms. Lapin's door.

There's a long conspicuous silence. "Ms. Lapin?" I call. "It's Clay, from, uh, from the bookstore. The clerk. I just wanted to ask you about something." Or maybe about everything.

The silence stretches out. "Ms. Lapin?"

I watch a shadow break the bar of light below the door. It hovers there—then the lock rattles and Ms. Lapin peeks out. "Hello," she says sweetly.

Her home is the burrow of a bibliophile hobbit—low-ceilinged, close-walled, and brimming over with books. It is small but not uncomfortable; the air smells strongly of cinnamon and weakly of pot. There is a high-backed chair that faces a tidy fireplace.

Lapin is not sitting in the chair. She is instead backed into the corner of her ship's-galley kitchen, as far as she can get from me while still being in the same room. I think she would climb out the window if she could reach it.

"Ms. Lapin," I say, "I need to get in touch with Mr. Penumbra."

"How about some tea?" she says. "Yes, some tea, and then you'll be on your way." She fiddles with a heavy brass teapot. "Busy night for a young one, I suppose, plenty of places to go, people to see—"

"Actually, I'm supposed to be working."

Her hands shake on the stovetop. "Of course, well, plenty of jobs to be had, don't fret—"

"I don't need a job!" More gently, I say, "Ms. Lapin, really. I just need to get in touch with Mr. Penumbra."

Lapin pauses, but only barely. "There are so many professions. You could be a baker, a taxidermist, a ferryboat captain . . ." Then she turns, and I think it's the first time she's ever looked straight at me. Her eyes are gray-green. "Mr. Penumbra has gone away."

"So when is he coming back?"

Lapin says nothing, just looks at me, then slowly turns to tend the teapot, which has started to shudder and hiss on top of her tiny stove. A glittering compound of curiosity and dread oozes into my brain. Time to go for broke.

I pull out my laptop, which is probably the most advanced piece of technology that has ever crossed the threshold of Lapin's lair, and set it up on a stack of heavy books, all from the Waybacklist. The shiny MacBook looks like a hapless alien trying to blend in with the quiet stalwarts of human civilization. I crack it open—glowing alien guts revealed!—and cue the visualization as Lapin crosses the room with two cups in two saucers.

When her eye catches the screen and she recognizes the bookstore in 3-D, she crash-lands the saucers onto the table with a clatter. Clasping her hands together beneath her chin, she bends in low and watches the wire-frame face take shape.

She squeaks, "You found him!"

Lapin spreads a wide scroll of thin, almost translucent paper on the table, now cleared of books. It's my turn to gape: it is a view of the bookstore, rendered in gray pencil, and it, too, shows a web of lines connecting spaces on the shelves. But it's incomplete; in fact, it's barely started. You can see the curve of a chin and the hook of a nose, but nothing else. Those lines, dark and sure, are surrounded by the fuzz of eraser marks—a layered history of ghost lines that have been drawn and removed many times.

How long, I wonder, has Lapin been working on this?

Her face tells the tale. Her cheeks are trembling, like she's on the verge of tears. "That is why," she says, glancing back at my laptop. "That is why Mr. Penumbra went. Oh, what have you done? How did you do that?"

"Computers," I tell her. "Big ones."

Lapin makes a sigh and finally surrenders to her chair. "This is terrible," she says. "After all that work."

"Ms. Lapin," I say, "what were you working on? What is this all about?"

Lapin closes her eyes and says, "I am forbidden to speak of it." She sneaks a peek with one eye. I am quiet, open-faced, trying to look as harmless as possible. She sighs again. "But Mr. Penumbra did like you. He liked you a great deal."

I don't like the sound of the past tense here. Lapin stretches for her tea but can't quite reach it, so I lift the cup and saucer and hand them to her.

"And it feels good to talk about it," she continues, "after so many years of reading, reading, reading." She pauses and sips her tea. "You will speak of this to no one?"

I shake my head. No one.

"Very well," she says. She takes a deep breath. "I am a novice in a fellowship known as the Unbroken Spine. It is more than five hundred years old." Then, primly: "As old as books themselves."

Wow. Lapin, just a novice? She must be eighty years old.

"How did you get started?" I venture.

"I was one of his customers," she says. "I had been going to the store for, oh, six or seven years. I was paying for a book one day—I remember this so clearly—when Mr. Penumbra looked me in the eye and said, 'Rosemary'"—she does a good Penumbra impression—"'Rosemary, why do you love books so much?'

"And I said, 'Well, I don't know.'" She's animated, almost girlish now: "'I suppose I love them because they're quiet, and I can take them to the park.'" She narrows her eyes. "He watched me, and he didn't say a word. So then I said, 'Well, actually, I love books because books are my best friends.' Then he smiled—he has a wonderful smile—and he walked over and got on that ladder, and climbed higher than I'd ever seen him climb."

Of course. I get it: "He gave you a book from the Waybacklist."

"What did you call it?"

"Oh, the—you know, the shelves in back. The code books."

"They are *codex vitae*," she says, pronouncing it precisely. "Yes, Mr. Penumbra gave me one, and he gave me the key to decode it. But he said it was the only key he would ever give me. I would have to find the next on my own, and the next after that." Lapin frowns a little. "He said it wouldn't take long to become one of the unbound, but it's been very difficult for me."

Wait: "The unbound?"

"There are three orders," Lapin says, and ticks them off on thin fingers: "Novice, unbound, and bound. To become one of the unbound, you solve the Founder's Puzzle. It's the store, you see. You go from one book to another, decoding each one, finding the key to the next. They're all shelved in a particular way. It's like a tangle of string."

I get it: "That's the puzzle I solved."

She nods once, frowns, and sips her tea. Then, as if suddenly remembering: "You know, I was a computer programmer once."

No way.

"Back when they were big and gray, like elephants. Oh, it was hard work. We were the first to do it."

Amazing. "Where was this?"

"Pacific Bell, just down on Sutter Street"—she waves a finger toward downtown—"back when the telephone was still very high-tech." She grins and flutters her eyelashes theatrically. "I was a very modern young woman, you know."

Oh, I believe it.

"But it's been such a long time since I used a machine like that. It never even crossed my mind to do what you did. Oh, even though this"—she

waves a hand at the heap of books and papers—
"has been such a chore. Struggling from one book
to the next. Some of the stories are good, but
others . . ." She sighs.

There's a clatter of footfalls outside, a bright
chorus of squawks, and then a fast knocking at the
door. Lapin's eyes go wide. The knocking doesn't
stop. The door is vibrating.

Lapin pushes herself up out of her chair and
turns the knob and there is Tyndall, eyes wide,
hair wild, standing with one hand on his head, the
other poised in mid-knock.

"He's gone!" he cries, careening into the room.
"Called to the library! How can it be?" He's
pacing in quick circles, repeating himself, a coil of
nervous energy coming unspun. His eyes glance
over to me, but he doesn't stop or slow down.
"He's gone! Penumbra is gone!"

"Maurice, Maurice, calm down," Lapin says.
She steers him into her chair, where he collapses,
squirming and fidgeting.

"What will we do? What can we do? What must
we do? With Penumbra gone . . ." Tyndall trails
off, then cocks his head toward me: "Can you run
the store?"

"Wait, hold on," I say. "He's not dead. He's
just—didn't you just say he's visiting a library?"

The look on Tyndall's face tells a different tale.
"He's not coming back," he says, shaking his
head. "Not coming back, not coming back."

That compound—more dread than curiosity now—is spreading into my stomach. It's a bad feeling.

"Heard it from Imbert, who heard it from Monsef. Corvina is angry. Penumbra will be burned. Burned! This is the end for me! The end for you!" He waves a finger at Rosemary Lapin. Now her cheeks are trembling.

I don't understand this at all. "What do you mean, Mr. Penumbra will be *burned?*"

Tyndall says, "Not the man, the book—his book! Just as bad, even worse. Better flesh than page. They will burn his book, just like Saunders, Moffat, Don Alejandro, the enemies of the Unbroken Spine. He, him, Glencoe, the worst—he had a dozen novices! All of them abandoned, lost." He looks at me with damp, desperate eyes, and blurts, "I was almost finished!"

I really have gotten myself involved in a cult.

"Mr. Tyndall," I say flatly, "where is it? Where is this library?"

Tyndall shakes his head. "Don't know. Just a novice. Now never will, never will . . . unless." He looks up. There's a glimmer of hope in his eyes, and he says it again: "Can you run the store?"

I cannot run the store, but I can use it. Thanks to Tyndall, I know Penumbra is in trouble somewhere, and I know it's my fault. I don't understand how or why, but it was undeniably me that sent

Penumbra packing, and now I'm truly worried about him. This cult seems like it might have been designed specifically to prey on bookish old people—Scientology for scholarly seniors. If that's true, then Penumbra is already deep in its clutches. So, enough poking around and gently guessing: I am going to raid Mr. Penumbra's 24-Hour Bookstore for the answers I need.

But first I have to get inside.

It's the middle of the next day, and I am standing on Broadway, shivering, contemplating the plate-glass windows, when Oliver Grone is suddenly standing beside me. Jeez, he's quiet for such a big dude.

"What's going on?" he asks.

I eye him carefully. What if Oliver has already been inducted into this cult?

"Why are you standing out here?" he asks. "It's cold."

No. He's like me; he's an outsider. But maybe he's an outsider with a key.

He shakes his head. "The door's never been locked. I always just walk in and take Mr. Penumbra's place, you know?"

Right, and I take Oliver's. But now Penumbra is missing. "Now we're stuck out here."

"Well. We could try the fire escape."

Twenty minutes later, Oliver and I are using climbing muscles honed in Penumbra's shadowy stacks. We have a utility ladder purchased at a hardware store five blocks away, and it's set up in the narrow alley between the bookstore and the strip club.

A skinny bartender from Booty's is back here, too, sitting on an upturned plastic bucket, sucking on a cigarette. He eyes us once, then returns to his phone. He appears to be playing Fruit Ninja.

Oliver goes first while I hold the ladder, and then I climb up after him on my own. This is all foreign territory. I had abstractly understood that this alley existed, and that there was a fire escape in it, but I still don't understand where the fire escape connects to the store. There's a whole back part of Penumbra's where I do not often tread. Beyond the bright front shelves and the dark reaches of the Waybacklist, there's a tiny break room with a tiny table and a tiny bathroom, and beyond that, the door marked PRIVATE that leads to Penumbra's office. I take this injunction seriously, just as I took rule number two (regarding the sanctitude of the Waybacklist) seriously, at least until Mat got involved.

"Yeah, the door leads to a flight of stairs," Oliver says. "They go up." We are both standing on the fire escape, which makes a high metallic whine when either of us shifts our weight. There's a wide window, old glass set into scratched and pitted wood. I pull and it doesn't budge. Oliver bends down, makes a quiet grad-student grunt, and it flies open with a *pop* and a shriek. I glance down at the bartender in the alley. He's ignoring us with the discipline of one whose job often requires it.

We hop through the window frame and into the darkness of Penumbra's second-floor study.

There is grunting and shuffling and a loud whispered *ouch,* and then Oliver finds a switch. Orange light blooms from a lamp set on a long desk, revealing the space around us.

Penumbra is a much bigger nerd than he lets on.

The desk is loaded down with computers, none of them manufactured later than 1987. There's an old TRS-80 connected to a squat brown TV. There's an oblong Atari and an IBM PC with a bright blue plastic case. There are long boxes full of floppy disks and stacks of thick manuals, their titles printed in boxy letters:

**TAKING A BITE OUT OF YOUR APPLE**
**BASIC PROGRAMS FOR FUN AND PROFIT**
**VISICALC MASTER CLASS**

Next to the PC there is a long metal box topped with two rubber cups. Next to the box is an old rotary phone with a long, curving handset. I think the box is a modem, possibly the world's most ancient; when you're ready to go online, you plug the handset into those rubber cups, as if the computer is literally making a phone call. I've never seen one in person, only in snarky can-you-believe-this-is-how-it-used-to-work blog posts. I'm floored, because this means Penumbra has, at some point in his life, tiptoed into cyberspace.

On the wall behind the desk there's a world map, very big and very old. On this map there is no Kenya, no Zimbabwe, no India. Alaska is a blank expanse. There are gleaming pins pushed into the paper. Pins poke London, Paris, and Berlin. Pins poke Saint Petersburg, Cairo, and Tehran. There are more—and these must be the bookstores, the little libraries.

While Oliver rummages through a stack of papers, I power up the PC. The switch flips over with a loud *thwack* and the computer rumbles to life. It sounds like an airplane taking off; there's a loud roar, then a screech, then a staccato sequence of beeps. Oliver jerks around.

"What are you doing?" he whispers.

"Looking for clues, same as you." I don't know why he's whispering.

"But what if there's weird stuff on there?" he says, still whispering. "Like porn."

The computer musters a command-line prompt. This is okay; I can figure this out. When you work on websites, you interact with far-off servers in ways that have not really changed much since

1987, so I think back to NewBagel and tap in a few exploratory instructions.

"Oliver," I say absently, "have you done any digital archaeology?"

"No," he says, doubled over a set of drawers. "I don't really mess with anything newer than the twelfth century."

The PC's tiny disk is full of text files, inscrutably named. When I inspect one, it's a jumble of characters. So that either means it's raw data, or it's encrypted, or . . . yes. This is one of the books from the Waybacklist, one of the books that Lapin called a *codex vitae*. I think Penumbra transcribed it into his PC.

There's a program called EULERMETHOD. I key it in, take a deep breath, press return . . . and the PC beeps in protest. In bright green text, it tells me there are errors in the code—lots of them. The program won't run. Maybe it never ran.

"Look at this," Oliver says from across the room.

He's leaning over a thick book on top of a filing cabinet. The cover is leather, embossed just like the logbooks, and it says PECUNIA. Maybe it's a private logbook for all the really juicy details of the book business. But no: when Oliver flips it open, the book's purpose is revealed. It's a ledger, each page cut into two wide columns and dozens of narrow rows, each row carrying an entry in Penumbra's spidery script:

*FESTINA LENTE CO.* *$10,847.00*

*FESTINA LENTE CO.* *$10,853.00*

*FESTINA LENTE CO.* *$10,859.00*

Oliver flips through the pages of the ledger. The entries go month by month, and they go back decades. So there's our patron: the Festina Lente Company must connect to Corvina somehow.

Oliver Grone is a trained excavator. While I was playing hacker, he's been finding something useful. I follow his lead, moving around the room step-by-step, looking for clues.

There's another low cabinet. On top: a dictionary, a thesaurus, a wrinkled *Publishers Weekly* from 1993, a Burmese take-out menu. Inside: paper, pencils, rubber bands, a stapler.

There's a coatrack, empty except for a thin gray scarf. I've seen Penumbra wear it before.

There are photos in black frames on the far wall, next to the stairs that lead down. One shows the store itself, but it must be decades old: it's black-and-white, and the street looks different. Instead of Booty's next door, there's a restaurant called Arigoni's, with candles and checkered tablecloths. Another photo, this one in Kodachrome color, shows a pretty middle-aged woman with bobbed blond hair hugging a redwood tree, one heel kicked up, beaming at the camera.

The last photo shows three men posing in front of the Golden Gate Bridge. One is older, with the look of a professor: a sharp hook of a nose and a wry, winning grin. The other two are much younger. One is broad-chested and thick-armed, like an old-school bodybuilder. He has a black mustache and a steeply receding hairline, and with one arm he's giving the camera a thumbs-up. His other arm is draped around the shoulders of the third man, who's tall and skinny, with—

Wait. The third man is Penumbra. Yes, he is long-ago Penumbra, with a halo of brown hair and flesh on his cheeks. He's smiling. He looks so young.

I crack open the frame and pull out the photo. On the back, in Penumbra's script, there's a caption:

*Two novices & a great teacher*
*Penumbra, Corvina, Al-Asmari*

Amazing. The older man must be Al-Asmari, and that makes the one with the mustache Corvina, who is now Penumbra's boss, CEO of Weird Bookstores Worldwide, which might be the Festina Lente Company. It's got to be this Corvina who summoned Penumbra back to the library to be punished or fired or burned or worse. He's hale and hearty in this photo, but he must be as old as Penumbra now. He must be a cruel skeleton.

"Look at this!" Oliver calls again from across the room. He is definitely better at detective work than I am. First the ledger, and now this: he holds up an Amtrak timetable, freshly printed. He spreads it out on the desk, and there it is, boxed by four sharp strokes—our employer's destination.

Penn Station.

Penumbra is going to New York City.

# EMPIRES

THE SCENARIO as I see it goes like this:

The bookstore is closed. Penumbra is gone, recalled by his boss, Corvina, to the secret library that is actually the headquarters of the bibliophile cult known as the Unbroken Spine. Something is going to be burned. The library is in New York City, but nobody knows where—not yet.

Oliver Grone is going to climb in through the fire escape and run the store for at least a few hours every day to keep Tyndall and the rest all satisfied. Maybe Oliver can learn a little more about the Unbroken Spine along the way.

As for me: I have my quest. The arrival time on the other end of Penumbra's train—of course he would take the train—is still two days in the future. Right now he's chugging through the middle of the country, and if I work fast, I can head him off at the pass. Yes: I can intercept him and rescue him. I can set things right and get my job back. I can find out what exactly is going on.

I tell Kat about all of it, as I am becoming accustomed to doing. It feels like loading a really hard math problem into a computer. I just key in all the variables, push return, and:

"It won't work," she says. "Penumbra is an old

155

man. I get the feeling this thing has been part of his life for a long time. I mean, it basically *is* his life, right?"

"Right, so—"

"So I don't think you'll get him to just . . . quit. Like, I've been at Google for, what, three years? That's hardly a lifetime. But even now you couldn't just meet me at the train station and tell me to turn around. This company is the most important part of my life. It's the most important part of me. I'd walk right past you."

She's right, and it's disconcerting, both because it means I'll need a new plan and because, while I can recognize the truth in what she's saying, it doesn't actually make any sense to me. I've never felt that way about a job (or a cult). You could stop me at the train station and talk me into anything.

"But I think you should absolutely go to New York," Kat says.

"Okay, now I'm confused."

"This is too interesting not to pursue. What's the alternative? Find another job and spend forever wondering what happened to your old boss?"

"Well, that's definitely plan B—"

"Your first instinct was right. You've just got to be more"—she pauses and purses her lips— "strategic. And you've got to take me with you." She grins. Obviously. How can I say no?

"Google has a big New York office," Kat says, "and I've never been there, so I'll just say I want to go meet the team. My manager will be fine with that. What about you?"

What about me? I have a quest and I have an ally. Now all I need is a patron.

Let me give you some advice: make friends with a millionaire when he's a friendless sixth-grader. Neel Shah has plenty of friends—investors, employees, other entrepreneurs—but on some level they know, and he knows, that they are friends with Neel Shah, CEO. By contrast, I am, and always will be, friends with Neel Shah, dungeon master.

It is Neel who will be my patron.

His home serves double duty as his company's headquarters. Back when San Francisco was young, Neel's place was a wide brick firehouse; today, it's a wide brick techno-loft with fancy speakers and superfast internet. Neel's company spreads out on the firehouse floor, where nineteenth-century firemen used to eat nineteenth-century chili and tell nineteenth-century jokes. They've been replaced by a squad of skinny young men who are their opposite: men who wear delicate neon sneakers, not heavy black boots, and when they shake your hand, it's not a meaty squash but a limp slither. Most of them have accents—maybe that hasn't changed?

Neel finds programming prodigies, brings them to San Francisco, and assimilates them. These are

Neel's guys, and the greatest of them is Igor, who is nineteen and comes from Belarus. To hear Neel tell it, Igor taught himself matrix math on the back of a shovel, ruled the Minsk hacker scene as a sixteen-year-old, and would have proceeded directly to a perilous career in software piracy if Neel hadn't spotted his 3-D handiwork in a demo video posted on YouTube. Neel got him a visa, bought him a plane ticket, and had a desk waiting at the firehouse when he arrived. Next to the desk there was a sleeping bag.

Igor offers me his chair and goes in search of his employer.

The walls, all thick timber and exposed brick, are covered with giant posters of classic women: Rita Hayworth, Jane Russell, Lana Turner, all printed in shimmering black-and-white. Monitors continue the theme. On some screens, the women are blown up and pixelated; on others, they're repeated a dozen times. Igor's monitor shows Elizabeth Taylor as Cleopatra, except half of her is a sketchy 3-D model, a green wire-frame that slinks across the screen in sync with the film.

Neel made his millions in middleware. That is to say, he makes software that's used by other people who make software, mostly video games. He sells tools that they need the same way a painter needs a palette or a filmmaker needs a camera. He sells tools they cannot do without—tools they will pay top dollar for.

I'll cut to the chase: Neel Shah is the world's leading expert on boob physics.

He developed the first version of his break-through boob-simulation software while he was still a sophomore at Berkeley, and shortly after that he licensed it to a Korean company that was developing a 3-D beach volleyball game. The game was terrible but the boobs were phenomenal.

Today, that software—now called Anatomix—is the de facto tool for the simulation and representation of breasts in digital media. It's a sprawling package that lets you create and model, with breathtaking realism, the entire universe of human boobs. One module provides variables for size, shape, authenticity. (Breasts aren't spheres, Neel will tell you, and they're not water balloons. They're complicated structures, almost architectural.) Another module renders the breasts—paints them with pixels. It's a particular kind of skin, with a quality that's luminous and very hard to achieve. Something called subsurface scattering is involved.

If you are in the business of simulating a boob, Neel's software is the only serious option. It does more than that—thanks to Igor's exertions, Anatomix can now render the entire human body, with perfectly calibrated jiggle and luminosity in places you didn't realize you had either—but boobs are still the company's bread and butter.

Really, I think Igor and the rest of Neel's guys

are just in the translation business. The inputs—pinned to the walls, glowing on every screen—are specific world-historic movie babes. The outputs are generalized models and algorithms. And it's gone full circle: Neel will tell you, in strictest secrecy, that his software is now being used in movie postproduction.

Neel comes quick-stepping down the spiral staircase, waving and grinning. Below his molecule-tight gray T-shirt, he's wearing deeply uncool stonewashed jeans and bright New Balances with puffy white tongues. You can never escape the sixth grade entirely.

"Neel," I explain when he pulls up a chair, "I need to go to New York tomorrow."

"What's up? A job?"

No, the opposite of a job: "My elderly employer has disappeared and I'm trying to track him down."

"I am *so* not surprised," Neel says, eyes narrowing.

"You were right," I say. Warlocks.

"Let's hear it." He settles in.

Igor reappears and I relinquish his chair, standing to make my case. I tell Neel what has emerged. I explain it like the setup for a Rockets & Warlocks adventure: the backstory, the characters, the quest before us. The party is forming, I say: I have a rogue (that's me) and a wizard (that's Kat). Now I need a warrior. (Why does the typical adventuring group consist of a wizard, a warrior, and a rogue, anyway? It should really be a wizard, a warrior, and a rich guy. Otherwise who's going to pay for all the swords and spells and hotel rooms?)

Neel's eyes light up. I knew this would be the right rhetorical strategy. Next, I show him the 3-D bookstore, with the wrinkled and mysterious Founder angling into view.

He lifts his eyebrows. He's impressed. "I didn't know you could code," he says. His eyes narrow and his biceps pulse. He's thinking. Finally, he says, "You want to give this to one of my guys here? Igor, take a look—"

"Neel, no. The graphics don't matter."

Igor leans over anyway. "I tink it looks nice," he says good-naturedly. On the screen behind him, Cleopatra bats wire-frame eyelashes.

"Neel, I just need to fly to New York. Tomorrow." I give him the knowing eye of friendship. "And Neel . . . I need a warrior."

He scrunches up his face. "I don't think so . . . I have a lot of work to do here."

"But this is a Rockets & Warlocks scenario. You called it. How many times did we invent something like this? Now it's real."

"I know, but we have a big release coming up, and—"

I make my voice low: "Do not wuss out now, Nilric Quarter-Blood."

That's a stab in the belly with a rogue's poison dagger and we both know it.

"Neel . . . reek?" Igor repeats wonderingly. Neel glowers at me.

"The plane has Wi-Fi," I say. "These guys won't miss you." I turn to Igor: "Will they?"

The Babbage of Belarus grins and shakes his head.

When I was a kid reading fantasy novels, I daydreamed about hot girl wizards. I never thought I'd actually meet one, but that's only because I didn't realize wizards were going to walk among us and we'd just call them Googlers. Now I'm in a hot girl wizard's bedroom and we're sitting on her bed, trying to solve an impossible problem.

Kat has convinced me that we'll never be able to catch Penumbra at Penn Station. There's too much surface area, she says—too many ways Penumbra can get off the train and up to the street. She has math to prove this. There's an 11 percent chance we'll spot him, and if we fail, he'll be lost for good. What we need instead is a bottleneck.

The best bottleneck, of course, would be the library itself. But where does the Unbroken Spine make its home? Tyndall doesn't know. Lapin doesn't know. Nobody knows.

Intensive googling reveals no website and no

address for the Festina Lente Company. There are no mentions in newspapers, magazines, or classified ads going back a century. These guys don't just fly under the radar; they're subterranean.

But it has to be a real place, right?—a place with a front door. Is it marked? I'm thinking about the bookstore. On the front windows, there's Penumbra's name, and there's that symbol, the same one that's on the logbook and ledger. Two hands, open like a book. I have a picture of it on my phone.

"Good idea," Kat says. "If a building has that symbol anywhere—on a window, carved into stone—we can find it."

"What, by conducting a complete sidewalk survey of Manhattan? That would take, like, five years."

"Twenty-three, actually," Kat says. "If we did it the old-fashioned way."

She pulls her laptop across the sheets and shakes it to life. "But guess what we have in Google Street View? Pictures of every building in Manhattan."

"So subtract the walking time, and now it'll only take us—thirteen years?"

"You've got to start thinking differently," Kat clucks, shaking her head. "This is one of the things you learn at Google. Stuff that used to be hard . . . just isn't hard anymore."

I still don't understand how computers can help us with this particular species of problem.

"Well, what about hu-mans-and-com-pu-ters," Kat says, her voice pitched like a cartoon robot, "work-ing-to-ge-ther?" Her fingers fly across the keyboard and there are commands I recognize: King Hadoop's army is on the march again. She switches her voice back to normal: "We can use Hadoop to read pages in a book, right? So we can use it to read signs on buildings, too."

Of course.

"But it will make mistakes," she says. "Hadoop will probably get us from a hundred thousand buildings down to, like, five thousand."

"So we're down to five days instead of five years."

"Wrong!" Kat says. "Because guess what—we have ten thousand friends. It's called"—she clicks a tab triumphantly and fat yellow letters appear on the screen—"Mechanical Turk. Instead of sending jobs to computers, like Hadoop, it sends jobs to real people. Lots of them. Mostly Estonians."

She commands King Hadoop *and* ten thousand Estonian footmen. She is unstoppable.

"What do I keep telling you?" Kat says. "We have these new capabilities now—nobody gets it." She shakes her head and says it again: "Nobody gets it."

Now I make my voice into a cartoon robot, too: "The-Sin-gu-la-ri-ty-is-near!"

Kat laughs and moves symbols around on her screen. A big red number in the corner tells us that 30,347 workers are waiting to do our bidding.

"Hu-man-girl-very-beau-ti-ful!" I tickle Kat's ribs and make her click the wrong box; she shoves me with her elbow and keeps working. While I watch, she queues up thousands of photos of Manhattan addresses. There are brownstones, skyscrapers, parking structures, public schools, storefronts—all captured by the Google Street View trucks, all flagged by a computer as maybe, possibly, containing a book made from two hands, although in most cases (actually, in all but one) it's just something that the computer has mistaken for the Unbroken Spine's symbol: two hands in prayer, an ornate Gothic letter, a cartoon drawing of a twisty brown pretzel.

Then she sends the images off to Mechanical Turk—a whole army of eager souls lined up at laptops around the world—along with my reference photo and a simple question: Do these match? Yes or no?

On her screen, a little yellow timer says the task will take twenty-three minutes.

I can see what Kat is talking about: this really is intoxicating. I mean, King Hadoop's computer army was one thing, but this is real people. Lots of them. Mostly Estonians.

"Oh, hey, guess what?" Kat says suddenly, a jolt

of excitement animating her face. "They're going to announce the new Product Management soon."

"Wow. Good luck?"

"Well, you know, it's not completely random. I mean, it's partially random. But there's also, like—it's an algorithm. And I asked Raj to put in a good word for me. With the algorithm."

Of course. So this means two things: (1) Pepper the chef will, in fact, never be chosen to lead the company; and (2) if Google doesn't put this girl in charge, I'm going to switch to some other search engine.

We stretch out side by side on Kat's squishy spaceship bed, our legs interlaced, commanding more people now than there are in the town where I was born. She is Queen Kat Potente with her instant empire and I am her loyal consort. We won't command them all for long, but hey: nothing lasts long. We all come to life and gather allies and build empires and die, all in a single moment—maybe a single pulse of some giant processor somewhere.

The laptop makes a low chime, and Kat rolls over to tap at the keyboard. Still breathing hard, she grins and lifts the laptop onto her belly to show me the result of this great human-computer concord, this collaboration between a thousand machines, ten times as many humans, and one very smart girl:

It is a washed-out picture of a low stone building, not really more than a big house. Blurry figures are caught crossing the sidewalk in front of it; one of them has a pink fanny pack. The house has iron bars over small windows and a dark shadowed entryway under a black awning. And etched into the stone, gray against gray, there it is: two hands, open like a book.

It's tiny—they aren't any bigger than real hands. You'd probably miss it, just walking by on the sidewalk. The building is on Fifth Avenue, facing Central Park, just down the street from the Guggenheim.

The Unbroken Spine is hiding in plain sight.

# THE LIBRARY

# THE STRANGEST CLERK
# IN FIVE HUNDRED YEARS

I AM LOOKING through a pair of white Storm-trooper binoculars. I am looking at that same tiny gray symbol, two hands spread open like a book, etched into darker gray stone. I'm perched on a bench on Fifth Avenue, my back to Central Park, flanked by a newspaper dispenser and a falafel cart. We're in New York City. I borrowed the binoculars from Mat before we left. He warned me not to lose them.

"What do you see?" Kat asks.

"Nothing yet." There are small windows set high up on the walls, all guarded by heavy bars. It's a boring little fortress.

The Unbroken Spine. It sounds like a band of assassins, not a bunch of book lovers. What's going on in that building? Are there sexual fetishes that involve books? There must be. I try not to imagine how they might work. Do you have to pay money to be a member of the Unbroken Spine? You probably have to pay a lot of money. There are probably expensive cruises. I'm worried about Penumbra. He's in so deep that he can't even see how strange it all is.

It's early in the morning. We came straight from the airport. Neel visits Manhattan all the time for business and I used to take the train down from

Providence, but Kat is a New York neophyte. She gawked at the city's predawn glitter as our plane curled down into JFK, her fingertips on the window's clear plastic, and she breathed, "I didn't realize it was so skinny."

Now we are sitting quietly on a bench in the skinny city. The sky is getting light, but we're cloaked in shadows, breakfasting on perfectly imperfect bagels and black coffee, trying to look normal. The air smells wet, like it's going to rain, and there's a cold wind whipping up the street. Neel is sketching on a little notepad, drawing curvy babes with curvy swords. Kat bought a *New York Times* but couldn't figure out how to operate it, so now she's fiddling with her phone.

"It's official," she says, not looking up. "They're announcing the new Product Management today." She keeps refreshing and refreshing and refreshing; I think her battery is going to die before noon.

I alternate pages of *The Guide to Central Park Birds* (purchased at the JFK bookstore) with furtive glances through Mat's binoculars.

Here's what I see:

As the pitch of the city rises and traffic starts to pick up on Fifth Avenue, a lone figure comes trotting up the opposite sidewalk. It's a man, middle-aged, with a fuzz of brown hair that's blowing in the wind. I fiddle with the focus on the binoculars. He has a round nose and fleshy cheeks that are glowing pink in the cold. He's wearing dark pants and a tweedy jacket that fit him perfectly; they've been tailored to the swell of his belly and the slope of his shoulders. He bounces a little as he walks.

My spider-sense is operational, because sure enough, Round Nose stops at the Unbroken Spine's front door, wiggles a key in the lock, and steps gingerly inside. Twin lamps in small sconces on either side of the door come to life.

I tap Kat's shoulder and point to the glowing lamps. Neel narrows his eyes. Penumbra's train will pull into Penn Station at 12:01 p.m. and until then, we watch and we wait.

Following Round Nose, a thin but steady trickle of incredibly normal-looking New Yorkers passes through the dark doorway. There's a girl in a white blouse and a black pencil skirt; a middle-aged man in a drab green sweater; a guy with a shaved head who looks like he would fit in at Anatomix. Can these all be members of the Unbroken Spine? It doesn't feel right.

Neel whispers, "Maybe they target a different demographic here. Younger. Sneakier."

There are many more New Yorkers who don't pass through the dark doorway, of course. The sidewalks on both sides of Fifth Avenue are full of them, a flux of humanity, tall and short, young and old, cool and uncool. Clots of pedestrians drift past us and block my view. Kat is agog.

"It's so small but there are so many people," she says, watching the human flow. "They're . . . it's like fish. Or birds or ants, I don't know. Some superorganism."

Neel cuts in: "Where did you grow up?"

"Palo Alto," she says. From there to Stanford to Google: for a girl obsessed with the outer limits of human potential, Kat has stayed pretty close to home.

Neel nods knowingly. "The suburban mind cannot comprehend the emergent complexity of a New York sidewalk."

"I don't know about that," Kat says, narrowing her eyes. "I'm pretty good with complexity."

"See, I know what you're thinking," Neel says, shaking his head. "You're thinking it's just an agent-based simulation, and everybody out here follows a pretty simple set of rules"—Kat is nodding—"and if you can figure out those rules, you can model it. You can simulate the street, then the neighborhood, then the whole city. Right?"

"Exactly. I mean, sure, I don't know what the rules are yet, but I could experiment and figure them out, and then it would be trivial—"

"Wrong," Neel says, honking like a game-show buzzer. "You can't do it. Even if you know the rules—and by the way, there are no rules—but

174

even if there were, you can't model it. You know why?"

My best friend and my girlfriend are sparring over simulations. I can only sit back and listen.

Kat frowns. "Why?"

"You don't have enough memory."

"Oh, come on—"

"Nope. You could never hold it all in memory. No computer's big enough. Not even your what's-it-called—"

"The Big Box."

"That's the one. It's not big enough. This box"—Neel stretches out his hands, encompasses the sidewalk, the park, the streets beyond—"is bigger."

The snaking crowd surges forward.

Neel gets bored and walks down the street to the Met, where he intends to snap reference photos of marble breasts from antiquity. Kat composes short urgent messages to Googlers with her thumbs, chasing down rumors of the new PM.

At 11:03 a.m., a stooped figure in a long coat totters up the street. My spider-sense tingles again; I believe I can now detect a certain strain of weirdness with lab-grade precision. The stooped totterer has a face like an old barn owl, with a furry black Cossack's hat pulled down over wiry eyebrows that stick out into space. Sure enough: he ducks into the dark doorway.

At 12:17 p.m., it's finally beginning to rain. We're shielded beneath tall trees, but Fifth Avenue is quickly darkening.

At 12:29 p.m., a taxi stops in front of the Unbroken Spine, and out steps a tall man in a peacoat, pulling it close around his neck as he leans down to pay the driver. It's Penumbra, and it's surreal to see him here, framed by dark trees and pale stone. I've never even imagined him anywhere other than the inside of his bookstore. They're a package deal; you can't have one without the other. But here he is, standing in the middle of the street in Manhattan, fiddling with his wallet.

I hop up and sprint across Fifth Avenue, dodging slow-moving cars. The taxi pulls away like a yellow curtain, and, ta-da! There I am. First Penumbra's face is blank, then his eyes narrow, then he smiles, and then he tips his head back and barks a loud laugh. He keeps laughing, so then I start laughing, too. We stand there for a moment, just laughing at each other. I'm also panting a bit.

"My boy!" Penumbra says. "You might just be the strangest clerk this fellowship has seen in five hundred years. Come, come." He ushers me up onto the sidewalk, still laughing. "What are you doing here?"

"I came to stop you," I say. It sounds strangely serious. "You don't have to—" I'm huffing and puffing. "You don't have to go in there. You don't have to get your book burned. Or whatever."

"Who told you about burning?" Penumbra says quietly, raising an eyebrow.

"Well," I say, "Tyndall heard it from Imbert." Pause. "Who heard it from, uh, Monsef."

"They are wrong," Penumbra says sharply. "I have not come here to talk of punishment." He spits it out: *punishment,* as if it's something far beneath him. "No. I have come to make my case."

"Your case?"

"Computers, my boy," he says. "They hold the key for us. I have suspected it for some time, but never had proof that they could be a boon to our work. You have provided it! If computers can help you solve the Founder's Puzzle, they can do much more for this fellowship." He makes a thin fist and shakes it: "I have come prepared to tell the First Reader that we must make use of them. We must!"

Penumbra's voice has the timbre of an entrepreneur pitching his startup.

"You mean Corvina," I say. "The First Reader is Corvina."

Penumbra nods. "You cannot follow me here"— he waves his hand back toward the dark doorway—"but I would speak to you after I am finished. We will have to consider what equipment to purchase . . . which companies to work with. I will need your help, my boy." He lifts

177

his gaze to look over my shoulder. "And you are not alone, are you?"

I look back across Fifth Avenue, where Kat and Neel are standing, watching us and waiting. Kat waves.

"She works at Google," I say. "She helped."

"Good," Penumbra says, nodding. "That is very good. But tell me: How did you find this place?"

I grin when I tell him: "Computers."

He shakes his head. Then he tucks a hand into his peacoat and pulls out a skinny black Kindle, still activated, showing sharp words against a pale background.

"You got one," I say, smiling.

"Oh, more than one, my boy," Penumbra says, and produces another e-reader—it's a Nook. Then another one, a Sony. Another one, marked KOBO. Really? Who has a Kobo? And did Penumbra just cross the country carrying four e-readers?

"I had a bit of catching up to do," he explains, balancing them in a stack. "But you know, this one"—he produces a final device, this one super-slim and clad in blue—"was my favorite of the bunch."

There's no logo. "What *is* that?"

"This?" He flips the mystery e-reader around in his fingers. "My student Greg—you do not know him, not yet. He lent it to me for the journey." His voice grows conspiratorial. "He said it was a prototype."

The anonymous e-reader is amazing: thin and light, with a skin that's not plastic but cloth, like a hardcover book. How did Penumbra get his hands on a prototype? Who does my boss know in Silicon Valley?

"It is a remarkable device," he says, balancing it with the rest and patting the stack. "This is all quite remarkable." He pauses, then looks up at me. "Thank you, my boy. It is because of you that I am here."

That makes me smile. Go get 'em, Mr. Penumbra. "Where do we meet you?"

"The Dolphin and Anchor," he says. "Bring your friends. You can find it on your own—am I right? Use your computers." He winks, then turns and pushes through the dark doorway into the secret library of the Unbroken Spine.

Kat's phone guides us to our destination. The sky is opening up, so we run most of the way.

When we find it, the Dolphin and Anchor is the perfect refuge, all dark heavy wood and low brassy light. We sit at a round table next to a window flecked with raindrops. Our waiter arrives, and he, too, is perfect: tall and barrel-chested, with a thick red beard and a disposition that warms us all up. We order mugs of beer; he brings those along with a plate of bread and cheese. "Strength in the storm," he says with a wink.

"What if Mr. P doesn't show?" Neel says.

"He'll show," I say. "This isn't what I expected. He's got a plan. I mean—he brought e-readers."

Kat smiles at that but she doesn't look up. She's glued to her phone again. She's like a candidate on election day.

There's a stack of books on the table and a metal cup with pointy pencils that smell fresh and sharp. In the stack, there are copies of *Moby-Dick*, *Ulysses*, *The Invisible Man*—this is a bar for bibliophiles.

There's a pale beer stain on the back cover of *The Invisible Man*, and inside, the margins are mobbed with pencil marks. It's so dense you can barely see the paper behind it—there are dozens of different people's marginalia jostling for space here. I flip through the book; it's jam-packed. Some of the notes are about the text, but more are directed at one another. The margins tend to devolve into arguments, but there are other interactions, too. Some are inscrutable: just numbers back and forth. There's encrypted graffiti:

6HV8SQ was here

I nurse my beer and nibble the cheese and try to follow the conversations through the pages.

Then Kat gives a quiet sigh. I look up across the table, and see her face crumpled into a deep frown. She sets her phone down on the table and covers it with one of the Dolphin and Anchor's thick blue napkins.

"What is it?"

"They emailed out the new PM." She shakes her head. "Not this time." Then she forces a smile and reaches to pick a battered book from the stack. "It's no big deal," she says, flipping pages, making herself busy. "It's like winning the lottery anyway. It was a long shot."

I'm not an entrepreneur, not a business guy, but in that moment I want nothing more than to start a company and grow it to Google size, just so I can put Kat Potente in charge.

There's a gust of wet wind. I look up from *The Invisible Man* to see Penumbra framed in the doorway, the tufts of hair over his ears matted down, turned a shade darker by the rain. His teeth are gritted.

Neel jumps up to usher him toward the table. Kat takes his coat. Penumbra is shivering and saying quietly, "Thank you, dear girl, thank you." He walks stiffly to the table, gripping chair backs for support.

"Mr. P, good to meet you," Neel says, extending a hand. "Love your store." Penumbra gives it a solid shake. Kat waves hello.

"So these are your friends," Penumbra says. "It is good to meet you, both of you." He sits and exhales sharply. "I have not sat across from such young faces in this place since—well, since my own face was so young."

I'm desperate to know what happened in the library.

"Where to begin?" he says. He wipes the dome of his head with one of the napkins. He's frowning, agitated. "I told Corvina what has happened. I told him about the logbook, about your ingenuity."

He's calling it ingenuity; that's a good sign. Our red-bearded waiter arrives bearing another mug of beer and sets it down in front of Penumbra, who waves a hand and says, "Charge this to the Festina Lente Company, Timothy. All of it."

He's in his element. He speaks again: "Corvina's conservatism has deepened, though I barely thought such a thing was possible. He has done so much damage. I had no idea." He shakes his head. "Corvina says California has infected me." He spits it out: *infected*. "Ridiculous. I told him what you did, my boy—I told him what was possible. But he will not budge."

Penumbra lifts his beer to his lips and takes a long sip. Then he looks from Kat to Neel to me, and he speaks again, slowly:

"My friends, I have a proposal for you. But you will need to understand something of this fellowship first. You have followed me to its home, but you do not know anything of its purpose—or have your computers told you that, too?"

Well, I know it involves libraries and novices and people getting bound and books getting burned, but none of it makes any sense. Kat and Neel only know what they've seen on my laptop screen: a sequence of lights making their way through the shelves of a strange bookstore. When you search for "unbroken spine," Google replies: *Did you mean: unicorn sprinkle?* So the correct answer is: "No. Nothing."

"Then we will do two things," Penumbra says, nodding. "First, I will tell you just a little of our history. Then, to understand, you must see the Reading Room. There, my proposal will become clear, and I dearly hope you will accept it."

Of course we'll accept it. That's what you do on a quest. You listen to the old wizard's problem and then you promise to help him.

Penumbra steeples his fingers. "Do you know the name Aldus Manutius?"

Kat and Neel shake their heads, but I nod yes. Maybe art school was good for something after all: "Manutius was one of the first publishers," I say, "right after Gutenberg. His books are still famous. They're beautiful." I've seen slides.

"Yes." Penumbra nods. "It was the end of the fifteenth century. Aldus Manutius gathered scribes and scholars at his printing house in Venice, and there he manufactured the first editions of the classics. Sophocles, Aristotle, and Plato. Virgil, Horace, and Ovid."

I chime in, "Yeah, he printed them using a brand-new typeface, made by a designer named Griffo Gerritszoon. It was awesome. Nobody had ever seen anything like it, and it's still basically the most famous typeface ever. Every Mac comes preinstalled with Gerritszoon." But not Gerritszoon Display. That, you have to steal.

Penumbra nods. "This much is well known to historians and, it appears"—he raises an eyebrow—"to bookstore clerks. It might also be of interest to know that Griffo Gerritszoon's work is the wellspring of our fellowship's wealth. Even today, when publishers buy that typeface, they buy it from us." He goes sotto voce: "And we do not sell it cheap."

I feel the sharp snap of connection: FLC Type Foundry is the Festina Lente Company. Penumbra's cult runs on egregious licensing fees.

"But here is the crux of it," he says. "Aldus Manutius was more than a publisher. He was a philosopher and a teacher. He was the first of us. He was the founder of the Unbroken Spine."

Okay, they definitely did not teach that in my typography course.

"Manutius believed there were deep truths hidden in the writing of the ancients—among them, the answer to our greatest question."

There's a pregnant pause. I clear my throat. "What's . . . our greatest question?"

Kat breathes: "How do you live forever?"

Penumbra turns and levels his gaze on her. His eyes are big and bright and he nods yes. "When Aldus Manutius died," he says quietly, "his friends and students filled his tomb with books—copies of everything he had ever printed."

The wind outside blows hard against the door and makes it rattle.

"They did this because the tomb was empty. When Aldus Manutius died, no body remained."

So Penumbra's cult has a messiah.

"He left behind a book he called CODEX VITAE—book of life. The book was encrypted, and Manutius gave the key to only one person: his great friend and partner, Griffo Gerritszoon."

Amendment: his cult has a messiah and a first disciple. But at least the disciple is a designer. That's cool. And *codex vitae* . . . I've heard that before. But Rosemary Lapin said the books on the Waybacklist were *codex vitae*. I'm confused—

"We, the students of Manutius, have worked for centuries to unlock his *codex vitae*. We believe it contains all the secrets he discovered in his study of the ancients—first among them, the secret to eternal life."

Rain spatters on the window. Penumbra takes a deep breath.

"We believe that when this secret is finally

unlocked, every member of the Unbroken Spine who ever lived . . . will live again."

A messiah, a first disciple, and a rapture. Check, check, and double-check. Penumbra is, right now, teetering right on the boundary between charmingly weird old guy and disturbingly weird old guy. Two things tip the scales toward charm: First, his wry smile, which is not the smile of the disturbed, and micromuscles don't lie. Second, the look in Kat's eyes. She's enthralled. I guess people believe weirder things than this, right? Presidents and popes believe weirder things than this.

"How many members are we talking about here?" Neel asks.

"Not so many," Penumbra says, scooting his chair back and lifting himself up, "that they cannot still fit in a single chamber. Come, my friends. The Reading Room awaits."

# CODEX VITAE

WE WALK THROUGH THE RAIN, all sharing a broad black umbrella borrowed from the Dolphin and Anchor. Neel holds it up above us—the warrior always holds the umbrella—with Penumbra in the middle and Kat and I hugging in close on either side of him. Penumbra doesn't take up much space.

We come to the dark doorway. This place could not possibly be more different from the bookstore in San Francisco: where Penumbra's has a wall of windows and warm light spilling out from inside, this place has blank stone and two dim lamps. Penumbra's invites you inside. This place says: *Nah, you're probably better off out there.*

Kat pulls the door open. I'm the last one through, and I give her wrist a squeeze as I step inside.

I am unprepared for the banality that confronts us. I was expecting gargoyles. Instead, two low couches and a square glass table form a small waiting area. Gossip magazines fan out across the table. Directly ahead, there's a narrow front desk, and behind it sits the young man with the shaved head who I saw on the sidewalk this morning. He's wearing a blue cardigan. Above him, on the wall, square sans-serif capitals announce:

**F L C**

"We are back to see Mr. Deckle," Penumbra says to the receptionist, who barely looks up. There's a door of frosted glass and Penumbra leads us through it. I'm still holding my breath for gargoyles, but no: it's a gray-green still life, a cool savanna of wide monitors and low dividers and curving black desk chairs. It's an office. It looks just like NewBagel.

Fluorescent lights buzz behind ceiling panels. Desks are set up in clusters, and they are manned by the people I saw through the Stormtrooper binoculars this morning. Most of them are wearing headphones; none of them look up from their monitors. Over slumped shoulders, I see a spreadsheet and an inbox and a Facebook page.

I'm confused. This place seems to have plenty of computers.

We weave a path through the pods. All the totems of office ennui have been erected here: the instant coffee machine, the humming half-sized refrigerator, the huge multipurpose laser printer flashing PAPER JAM in red. There's a whiteboard showing faded generations of brainstorms. Right now, in bright blue strokes, it says:

OUTSTANDING LAWSUITS: 7!!

I keep expecting someone to look up and notice our little procession, but they all seem intent on their work. The quiet clatter of keys sounds just like the rain outside. There's a chuckle from the far corner; I look over, and it's the man in the green sweater, smirking into his screen. He's eating yogurt out of a plastic cup. I think he's watching a video.

There are private offices and conference rooms around the perimeter, all with frosted glass doors and tiny nameplates. The one we're vectoring for is at the farthest end of the room and the nameplate reads:

EDGAR DECKLE / SPECIAL PROJECTS

Penumbra clasps a thin hand around the knob, raps once on the glass, and pushes the door open.

The office is tiny, but totally different from the space outside. My eyes stretch to adjust to the new color balance: here, the walls are dark and rich, papered in whirls of gold on green. Here, the floor is made of wood; it springs and whines under my shoes, and Penumbra's heels make light clicks as he moves to close the door behind us. Here, the light is different, because it comes from warm lamps, not overhead fluorescents. And when the door closes, the ambient buzz is banished, replaced by a sweet, heavy silence.

There's a heavy desk here—perfect twin to the one in Penumbra's store—and behind it sits the very first man I spotted on the sidewalk this morning: Round Nose. Here, he's wearing a black robe over his street clothes. It gathers loosely in the front, where it's clasped with a silver pin— two hands, open like a book.

Now we're on to something.

Here, the air smells different. It smells like books. Behind the desk, behind Round Nose, they're packed into shelves set up against the wall, reaching up to the ceiling. But this office isn't that big. The secret library of the Unbroken Spine appears to have approximately the capacity of a regional airport bookstore.

Round Nose is smiling.

"Sir! Welcome back," he says, standing. Penumbra raises his hands, motioning him to sit. Round Nose turns his attention to me and Kat and Neel: "Who are your friends?"

"They are unbound, Edgar," Penumbra says quickly. He turns to us: "My students, this is Edgar Deckle. He has guarded the door to the Reading Room for—what, Edgar? Eleven years now?"

"Eleven exactly," Deckle says, smiling. We're all smiling, too, I realize. He and his chamber are a warm tonic after the cold sidewalk and the colder cubicles.

Penumbra looks at me, his eyes crinkling: "Edgar was a clerk in San Francisco just like you, my boy."

I feel a little whirl of dislocation—the trademark

sensation of the world being more closely knit together than you expected. Have I read Deckle's slanty handwriting in the logbook? Did he work the late shift?

Deckle brightens, too, then goes mock-serious: "Piece of advice. One night, you're going to get curious and wonder if maybe you should check out the club next door." He pauses. "Don't do it."

Yes, he definitely worked the late shift.

There's a chair set up opposite the desk—high-backed, made of polished wood—and Deckle motions for Penumbra to sit.

Neel leans in conspiratorially and jerks a thumb over his shoulder, back toward the office: "So is that all just a front?"

"Oh, no, no," Deckle says. "The Festina Lente Company is a real business. Very real. They license the typeface Gerritszoon"—Kat, Neel, and I all nod sagely, like novices in the know—"and many more. They do other things, too. Like the new e-book project."

"What's that?" I ask. This operation seems a lot more savvy than Penumbra made it out to be.

"I don't understand it completely," Deckle says, "but somehow we identify e-book piracy for publishers." My nostrils flare at that; I've heard the stories of college students sued for millions of dollars. Deckle explains: "It's a new business. Corvina's baby. Apparently it's very lucrative."

191

Penumbra nods. "It is thanks to the labors of those people out there that our store exists."

Well, that's just great. My salary is paid by font licensing fees and copyright infringement cases.

"Edgar, these three have solved the Founder's Puzzle," Penumbra says—Kat and Neel both raise their eyebrows at that—"and the time has come for them to see the Reading Room." The way he says it, I can hear the capital letters.

Deckle grins. "That's terrific. Congratulations and welcome." He nods to a line of hooks on the wall, half of them holding regular jackets and sweaters, the other half hung with dark robes just like his. "So, change into those, for starters."

We shrug out of our wet jackets. As we're pulling on the robes, Deckle explains: "We need to keep things clean down below. I know they look goofy, but they're actually very well designed. They're cut at the sides here so you can move freely"—Deckle swings his arms back and forth—"and they have pockets inside for paper, pencil, ruler, and compass." He pulls his robe wide to show us. "We have writing supplies down below, but you'll have to bring your own tools."

That's almost cute: *Don't forget your ruler on your first day of cult!* But where is "down below"?

"One last thing," Deckle says. "Your phones."

Penumbra holds up empty palms and wiggles his fingers, but the rest of us all surrender our dark trembling companions. Deckle drops them into a shallow wooden bin on the desk. There are three iPhones in there already, along with a black Neo and a battered beige Nokia.

Deckle stands, straightens his robe, braces himself, and gives the shelves behind the desk a sharp shove. They swivel smoothly and silently— it's as if they're weightless, drifting in space—and as they draw apart, they reveal a shadowed space beyond, where wide steps curl down into darkness. Deckle stretches an arm to invite us forward. "*Festina lente*," he says matter-of-factly.

Neel takes a sharp breath and I know exactly what it means. It means: *I have waited my whole life to walk through a secret passage built into a bookshelf.* Penumbra hoists himself up and we follow him forward.

"Sir," Deckle says to Penumbra, standing to one side of the parted shelves, "if you're free later, I'd love to buy you a cup of coffee. There's a lot to talk about."

"So it shall be," Penumbra says with a smile. He claps Deckle on the shoulder as we pass. "Thank you, Edgar."

Penumbra leads us down onto the steps. He goes carefully, clutching the railing, a wide ribbon of wood on heavy metal brackets. Neel hovers close, ready to catch him if he stumbles. The steps are wide and made of pale stone; they curve sharply, a spiral leading us down into the earth, the way barely lit by arc lamps in old wall sconces set at wide intervals.

As we go step-by-step, I begin to hear sounds. Low murmurs; then a louder rumble; then echoing voices. The steps flatten out and there's a frame of light up ahead. We step through. Kat gasps, and her breath comes out in a little cloud.

This is no library. This is the Batcave.

The Reading Room stretches out before us, long and low. The ceiling is crisscrossed with heavy wooden beams. Above and between them, mottled bedrock shows through, all slanted seams and jagged planes, all sparkling with some inner crystal. The beams run the whole length of the chamber, showing sharp perspective like a Cartesian grid. Where they cross, bright lamps hang down and light the space below.

The floor is also bedrock, but polished smooth like glass. Square wooden tables are set up in orderly rows, two of them side by side, all the way back to the end of the chamber. They are simple but sturdy, and each one bears a single massive book. All of the books are black, and all of them are tethered to the tables with thick chains, also black.

There are people around the tables, sitting and standing, men and women in black robes just like Deckle's, talking, jabbering, arguing. There must be a dozen of them down here, and they make it feel like the floor of a very small stock exchange.

The sounds all merge and overlap: the hiss of whispers, the scuffle of feet. The scratch of pen on paper, the squeak of chalk on slate. Coughs and sniffles. It feels more than anything else like a classroom, except the students are all adults, and I have no idea what they're studying.

Shelves line the chamber's long perimeter. They are made from the same wood as the beams and the tables, and they are packed with books. Those books, unlike the tomes on the tables, are colorful: red and blue and gold, cloth and leather, some ragged, some neat. They are a ward against claustrophobia; without them, it would feel like a catacomb down here, but because they line the shelves and lend the chamber color and texture, it actually feels cosseted and comfortable.

Neel makes an appreciative murmur.

"What is this place?" Kat says, rubbing her arms, shivering. The colors might be warm but the air is freezing.

"Follow me," Penumbra says. He makes his way out onto the floor, weaving between squads of black-robes clustered around tables. I hear a snatch of conversation: ". . . Brito is the problem here," a tall man with a blond beard is saying, poking down at the thick black book on the table. "He insisted all operations had to be reversible, when in fact . . ." I lose his voice, but pick up another one: ". . . too preoccupied with the page as a unit of analysis. Think of this book in a different

195

way—it is a string of characters, correct? It has not two dimensions, but one. Therefore . . ."

That's the owl-faced man from the sidewalk this morning, the one with the wiry eyebrows. He's still stooped over, still wearing his furry hat; along with his robe, it makes him look 100 percent like a warlock. He's making sharp strokes with chalk on a small slate.

A loop of chain catches Penumbra's foot and makes a bright clink as he shakes it off. He grimaces and mutters, "Ridiculous."

We follow quietly behind him, a short line of black sheep. The shelves are broken in just a few places: twice by doors on either side of the long chamber, and once at the chamber's terminus, where they give way to smooth bare rock and a wooden dais set up under a bright lamp. It's tall and severe-looking. That must be where they do the ritual sacrifices.

As we pass, a few of the black-robes glance up and stop short; their eyes widen. "Penumbra," they exclaim, smiling, reaching out hands. Penumbra nods and smiles back and takes each hand in turn.

He leads us to an uninhabited table close to the dais, in a soft-shadowed spot between two lamps.

"You have come to a very special place," he says, lowering himself into a chair. We sit, too, negotiating the folds of our new robes. His voice is very quiet, barely audible above the din: "You must never speak of it, or reveal its location, to anyone."

We all nod together. Neel whispers, "This is amazing."

"Oh, it is not the room that is special," Penumbra says. "It is old, certainly. But any vault is the same: a sturdy chamber, built belowground, cold and dry. Unremarkable." He pauses. "It is the room's contents that are remarkable indeed."

We've only been in this book-lined cellar for three minutes and I've already forgotten that the rest of the world exists. I'll bet this place is designed to survive a nuclear war. One of those doors must lead to the stockpile of canned beans.

"There are two treasures here," Penumbra continues. "One is a collection of many books and the other is a single volume." He lifts a bony hand to rest on the black-bound volume chained to our table, identical to all the others. On the cover it says, in tall silver letters: MANVTIVS.

"This is the volume," Penumbra says. "It is the *codex vitae* of Aldus Manutius. It does not exist anywhere outside of this library."

Wait: "Not even in your store?"

Penumbra shakes his head. "No novices read this book. Only the full members of this fellowship—the bound and the unbound. There are not many of us, and we read Manutius only here."

That's what we're seeing all around us—all of

this intense study. Although I've noticed more than a few of the black-robes tipping their noses our way. Maybe not so intense.

Penumbra turns in his chair and waves a hand to indicate the shelves lining the walls. "And this is the other treasure. Following in the Founder's footsteps, every member of this fellowship produces his or her own *codex vitae*, or book of life. It is the task of the unbound. Fedorov, for example, who you know"—he nods to me—"is one of these. When he is finished, he will have poured everything he has learned, all his knowledge, into a book like these."

I think of Fedorov and his snowy-white beard. Yeah, he's probably learned some things.

"We use our logbook," he says to me, "to be sure that Fedorov has earned his knowledge." Penumbra cocks an eyebrow. "We must be sure he understands what he has accomplished."

Right. They have to be sure he didn't just feed a bunch of books into a scanner.

"When Fedorov's *codex vitae* is validated by me, and then accepted by the First Reader, he will become one of the bound. And then, finally, he will make the ultimate sacrifice."

Uh-oh: a dark ritual down at the Dais of True Evil. I knew it. I like Fedorov.

"Fedorov's book will be encrypted, copied, and shelved," Penumbra says flatly. "It will not be read by anyone until after his death."

"That sucks," Neel hisses. I narrow my eyes at him, but Penumbra smiles and raises an open hand.

"We make this sacrifice out of deep faith," he says. "I speak now with utter seriousness. When we unlock Manutius's *codex vitae*, every member of our fellowship who has followed in his footsteps—who has created his own book of life and stored it for safekeeping—will live again."

I struggle to hold back the skepticism that wants so badly to twist across my face.

"What," Neel asks, "like zombies?" He says it a little too loud, and some of the black-robes swivel to look our way.

Penumbra shakes his head. "The nature of immortality is a mystery," he says, speaking so softly that we have to lean closer to hear. "But everything I know of writing and reading tells me that this is true. I have felt it in these shelves and in others."

I don't believe the immortality part, but I do know the feeling that Penumbra is talking about. Walking the stacks in a library, dragging your fingers across the spines—it's hard not to feel the presence of sleeping spirits. That's just a feeling, not a fact, but remember (I repeat): people believe weirder things than this.

"But why can't you decode Manutius's book?" Kat says. This is in her wheelhouse: "What happened to the key?"

"Ah," Penumbra says. "What, indeed." He pauses and takes a breath. Then: "Gerritszoon was as remarkable as Manutius, in his own way. He chose not to pass on the key. For five hundred years . . . we have discussed his decision."

The way he says it makes me think those discussions might have involved the occasional gun or dagger.

"Without it, we have tried every method we can imagine to unlock Manutius's *codex vitae*. We have used geometry. We have searched for hidden shapes. That is the origin of the Founder's Puzzle."

The face in the visualization—of course. I feel another little whirl of dislocation. That was Aldus Manutius staring out of my MacBook.

"We have turned to algebra, logic, linguistics, cryptography . . . we have counted great mathematicians among our number," Penumbra says. "Men and women who won prizes in the world above."

Kat is leaning in so intently she's almost up on top of the table. This is catnip: a code to be cracked *and* the key to immortality, all in one. I feel a little thrill of pride: I'm the one who brought her here. Google is a disappointment today. The real action is down here with the Unbroken Spine.

"What you must understand, my friends," Penumbra says, "is that this fellowship has operated in almost exactly the same way since its formation five hundred years ago." He pokes a finger over to indicate the bustling black-robes: "We use chalk and slate, ink and paper." Here, his tone shifts. "Corvina believes we must adhere to these techniques exactly. He believes that if we change anything at all, we will forfeit our prize."

"And you," I say—you, the man with the Mac Plus—"you disagree."

In reply, Penumbra turns to Kat, and now his voice really is just a breath: "We come now to my proposal. If I am not mistaken, dear girl, your company has shepherded a great number of books"—he pauses, searching for words—"onto digital shelves."

She nods and her reply is a sharp whisper: "Sixty-one percent of everything ever published."

"But you do not have the Founder's *codex vitae*," Penumbra says. "No one does." A pause. "Perhaps you should."

I get it in a flash: Penumbra is proposing bibliographic burglary.

One of the black-robes shuffles past our table carrying a fat green book from the shelves. She's tall and lean, in her forties, with sleepy eyes and black hair chopped short. Beneath her robe, I see a blue floral print. We stay quiet, waiting for her to pass.

"I believe we must break with tradition," Penumbra continues. "I am old, and if it is possible, I would see this work completed before all that is left of me is a book on these shelves."

Another flash: Penumbra is one of the bound, so his own *codex vitae* must be here, in this cave. The thought makes my head spin a little. What's inside? What story does it tell?

Kat's eyes are shining. "We can scan this," she says, patting the book on the table. "And if there's a code, we can break it. We have machines that are so powerful—you have no idea."

There's a murmur in the Reading Room and a ripple of awareness passes through the black-robes. They all sit up straight and make whispers and whistles of attention and warning.

At the far end of the chamber, where the wide steps come down from above, a tall figure has emerged. His robe is different from the rest; it's more elaborate, with extra folds of black fabric around the neck and slashes of red down the sleeves. It's hanging from his shoulders as if he's just thrown it on; underneath, a gleaming gray suit peeks out.

He's heading straight for us.

"Mr. Penumbra," I whisper, "I think maybe—"

"Penumbra," the figure intones. His voice isn't loud, but it comes from down low and it carries through the chamber. "Penumbra," he says again, striding fast. He's old—not as old as Penumbra, but close. He's much more solid, though. He doesn't stoop or totter, and I think he might be hiding pectoral muscles under that suit. His head is shaved starkly bald and he has a dark, neat mustache. He's Nosferatu as a Marine Corps sergeant.

And now I recognize him. This is the man from the photo with young Penumbra, the strong young man giving a thumbs-up in front of the Golden Gate Bridge. This is Penumbra's boss, the one who keeps the lights on at the bookstore, the CEO of the generous Festina Lente Company. This is Corvina.

Penumbra lifts himself up out of his chair. "Please, meet three unbound of San Francisco," he says. To us: "This is the First Reader, and our patron." Suddenly he's playing the solicitous subordinate. He's acting.

Corvina appraises us coldly. His eyes are dark and glinting—there's a fierce, chomping intelligence there. He looks straight at Neel, considering, then says, "Tell me: Which of Aristotle's works did the Founder print first?" The question is soft but implacable, each word a bullet from a silenced pistol.

Neel's face is blank. There's an uncomfortable pause.

Corvina folds his arms and turns to Kat: "Well, what about you? Any idea?"

Kat's fingers twitch like she wants to look it up on her phone.

"Ajax, you have work to do," Corvina says, rounding on Penumbra. Still quiet. "They should be reciting the whole corpus. They should be saying it backwards in the original Greek."

I would frown at that if my head wasn't spinning with the revelation that Penumbra possesses a first name, and that it is—

"They are new to their work," Ajax Penumbra says with a sigh. He's a few inches shorter than Corvina and he's stretching to stand up straight, wobbling slightly. He sweeps his big blue eyes around the room and makes a skeptical face. "I was hoping to inspire them with a visit here, but the chains are a bit much. I am not sure they are in keeping with the spirit—"

"We are not so careless with our books here, Ajax," Corvina cuts in. "Here, we don't lose them."

"Oh, a logbook is hardly the Founder's *codex vitae*, and it was not lost. You grab at any excuse—"

"Because you offer them," Corvina says flatly. His voice is matter-of-fact, but it rings in the chamber. The Reading Room has grown silent now. None of the black-robes are talking, or moving, or possibly even breathing.

Corvina clasps his hands behind his back—a teacher's pose. "Ajax. I'm glad you returned, because I've made my decision, and I wanted to tell you myself." A pause, then a solicitous tilt of the head. "It's time you came back to New York."

Penumbra squints. "I have a store to run."

"No. It cannot continue," Corvina says, shaking his head. "Not filled with books that have nothing to do with our work. Not overflowing with people who know nothing about our responsibility."

Well, I wouldn't say overflowing, exactly.

Penumbra is quiet, eyes downcast, brow deeply wrinkled. His gray hair rises up around his head like a cloud of stray thoughts. If he shaved it off, he might look as sleek and impressive as Corvina. But probably not.

"Yes, I do stock other books," Penumbra says finally. "Just as I have for decades. Just as our teacher did before me. I know you remember that. You know that half my novices come to us because—"

"Because your standards are so low," Corvina interrupts. His gaze strafes across Kat, Neel, and me. "What good are unbound who don't take the work seriously? They make us weaker, not stronger. They put everything at risk."

Kat frowns. Neel's biceps pulse.

"You've spent too long in the wilderness, Ajax. Come back to us. Spend what time remains among your brothers and sisters."

Penumbra's face is a grimace now. "There are novices in San Francisco, and unbound. Many of them." His voice is suddenly husky, and his eyes catch mine. I see a flash of pain, and I know he's thinking of Tyndall and Lapin and the rest, and of me and Oliver Grone, too.

"There are novices everywhere," Corvina says, waving a hand as if to dismiss them. "The unbound will follow you here. Or they will not. But, Ajax, let me be perfectly clear. The Festina Lente Company's support for your store has ended. You will receive nothing more from us."

The Reading Room is utterly silent: no rustle, no clink. The black-robes are all staring down at their books, and they are all listening.

"You have a choice, my friend," the First Reader says gently, "and I am trying to help you see it clearly. We are not so young, Ajax. If you rededicate yourself to our task, there is still time for you to do great work. If not"—his eyes angle up—"well, then you can squander what time remains out there." He gives Penumbra a hard gaze—it's a look of concern, but the really patronizing kind—and repeats, finally: "Come back to us."

Then he spins away and stalks back toward the wide steps, his red-slashed robe fluttering behind him. There's a roar of scratching and scuffling as his subjects all throw themselves into the imitation of study.

When we flee the Reading Room, Deckle asks again about coffee.

"We will need something stronger than that, my boy," Penumbra says, attempting a smile, and almost—but not quite—succeeding. "I would very much like to speak with you tonight . . . Where?" Penumbra turns to me and makes it a question.

"The Northbridge," Neel cuts in. "West Twenty-ninth and Broadway." That's where we're staying, because that's where Neel knows the owner.

We leave our robes and take our phones and wade back out through the gray-green shallows of the Festina Lente Company. As my sneakers scuff the brindled corporate floor-covering material, it occurs to me that we must be directly above the Reading Room—basically walking on its ceiling. I can't decide how far down it is. Twenty feet? Forty?

Penumbra's own *codex vitae* is down there. I didn't see it—it was somewhere on those shelves, one spine among many—but it looms larger in my mind than the black-bound MANVTIVS. We're scurrying away under the shadow of an ultimatum, and it seems to me that Penumbra might be leaving something precious behind.

One of the offices along the wall is larger than the others, its frosted-glass door set apart from the rest. I can see the nameplate clearly now:

MARCUS CORVINA / EXECUTIVE CHAIRMAN

So Corvina has a first name, too.

A shadow moves against the frosted glass, and I realize he's in there. What's he doing? Negotiating with a publisher on the phone, demanding exorbitant sums for the use of grand old Gerritszoon? Offering up the names and addresses of some pesky e-book pirates? Closing down another wonderful bookstore? Talking to his bank, canceling a certain recurring payment?

This isn't just a cult. It's also a corporation, and Corvina is in charge, above and below.

# THE REBEL ALLIANCE

I T'S RAINING HARD in Manhattan now—a dark, noisy deluge. We have taken refuge in the hyper-boutique hotel owned by Neel's friend Andrei, another startup CEO. It is called the Northbridge, and it's the ultimate hacker hideout: power outlets every three feet, air so thick with Wi-Fi you can almost see it, and in the basement, a direct connection to the internet trunk line that runs beneath Wall Street. If the Dolphin and Anchor was Penumbra's place, this is Neel's. The concierge knows him. The valet gives him a high five.

The Northbridge lobby is the hub of the New York startup scene: anywhere two or more people are sitting together, Neel says, it's probably a new company proofreading its articles of incorporation. Huddled together around a low table made from old magnetic-tape canisters, I guess we might qualify—not as a company, but at least as something newly incorporated. We're a little Rebel Alliance, and Penumbra is our Obi-Wan. We all know who Corvina is.

Neel hasn't let up on the First Reader since we emerged:

"And I don't know what's going on with that mustache," he continues.

"He has worn it since the day I met him,"

Penumbra says, mustering a smile. "But he was not so rigid then."

"What was he like?" I ask.

"Like the rest of us—like me. He was curious. Uncertain. Why, I am still uncertain!—about a great many things."

"Well, now he seems pretty . . . self-confident."

Penumbra frowns. "And why not? He is the First Reader, and he likes our fellowship exactly as it is." He bats a thin fist into the soft mass of the couch. "He will not bend. He will not experiment. He will not even let us try."

"But they had computers at the Festina Lente Company," I point out. In fact, they were running a whole digital counterinsurgency.

Kat nods. "Yeah, they actually sound pretty sophisticated."

"Ah, but only above," Penumbra says, wagging a finger. "Computers are fine for the worldly work of the Festina Lente Company—but not for the Unbroken Spine. No, never."

"No phones," Kat says.

"No phones. No computers. Nothing," Penumbra says, shaking his head, "that Aldus Manutius himself would not have used. The electric lights—you would not believe the arguments we had over those lights. It took twenty years." He harrumphs. "I am quite sure Manutius would have been delighted to possess a lightbulb or two."

Everyone is silent.

Finally, Neel speaks: "Mr. P, you don't have to give up. I could fund your store."

"Let us be done with the store," Penumbra says, waving a hand. "I love our customers, but there is a better way to serve them. I will not cling to familiar things as Corvina does. If we can carry Manutius back to California . . . if you, dear girl, can do what you promise . . . none of us will need that place."

We sit and we scheme. In a perfect world, we agree, we would take the *codex vitae* to Google's scanner and let those spider-legs walk all over it. But we can't get the book out of the Reading Room.

"Bolt cutters," Neel says. "We need bolt cutters."

Penumbra shakes his head. "We must do this in secrecy. If Corvina becomes aware of it, he will pursue us, and the Festina Lente Company has tremendous resources."

They know a lot of lawyers, too. Besides, to put Manutius at Google's mercy, we don't need the book in our hands. We need it on a disk. So I ask, "What if we took the scanner to the book instead?"

"It's not portable," Kat says, shaking her head. "I mean, you can move it around, but it's a whole process. It took them a week to get it up and running at the Library of Congress."

So we need something or someone else. We

need a scanner custom-built for stealth. We need James Bond with a library science degree. We need—Wait. I know exactly who we need.

I grab Kat's laptop and click over to Grumble's book-hacking hub. I dig back through the archives—back, back, back—back to his earliest projects, the ones that kicked it all off . . . There it is.

I swivel the screen around for everyone to see. It shows a sharp photo of the GrumbleGear 3000: a book scanner made out of cardboard. Its pieces can be harvested from old boxes; you run them through a laser cutter to carve slots and tabs at all the right angles. You lock the pieces together to make a frame, then break them down flat when you're done. There are two slots for cameras. It all fits into a messenger bag.

The cameras are just crappy tourist point-and-shoots, the kind you can get anywhere. It's the frame that makes the scanner special. With one camera alone, you'd be stretching to hold the book at the right angle, fumbling with every page-turn. It would take days. But with two cameras mounted side by side on the GrumbleGear 3000, controlled by Grumble's software, you get a two-page spread in one snap, perfectly focused, perfectly aligned. It's high-speed but low-profile.

"It's made from paper," I explain, "so you can get it through a metal detector."

"What, so you can sneak it onto a plane?" Kat asks.

"No, so you can sneak it into a library," I say. Penumbra's eyes widen. "Anyway, he posted the schematics. We can download them. We just need to round up the materials and find a laser cutter."

Neel nods and waves a finger in a circle, circumscribing the lobby. "This is the nerdiest place in New York. I think we can get our hands on a laser cutter."

Assuming we can get a GrumbleGear 3000 assembled and working, we'll need time undisturbed in the Reading Room. Manutius's *codex vitae* is huge, and scanning it will take hours.

Who will do the deed? Penumbra is too wobbly for stealth. Kat and Neel are credible accomplices, but I have other plans. As soon as the possibility of a book-scanning mission arose, I made a decision: I would do it alone.

"I want to come with you," Neel insists. "This is the exciting part!"

"Don't make me use your Rockets & Warlocks name," I say, holding up a finger, "not with a girl in the room." I make my face serious. "Neel, you have a company, with employees and customers. You have responsibilities. If you get caught, or jeez, I don't know, *arrested,* that's a problem."

"And you don't think getting arrested is a problem for you, Claymore Red—"

"Ah!" I cut him off. "First: I have no actual responsibilities. Second: I'm basically already a novice of the Unbroken Spine."

"You did solve the Founder's Puzzle." Penumbra nods. "Edgar would vouch for you."

"Besides," I say, "I'm the rogue in this scenario."

Kat raises an eyebrow and I explain quietly, "He's the warrior, you're the wizard, I'm the rogue. This conversation never happened."

Neel nods once, slowly. His face is scrunched up but he's no longer protesting. Good. I'll go in alone, and I'll leave not with one book, but two.

There's a whip of cold wind from the Northbridge's front doors and Edgar Deckle comes bounding in out of the rain, his round face framed by the hood of a plasticky purple jacket pulled tight. Penumbra waves him over. Kat's gaze meets mine; she looks nervous. This will be a crucial meeting. If we want access to the Reading Room and to MANVTIVS, Deckle is the key, because Deckle has the key.

"Sir, I heard about the store," he says, panting and setting himself down on the couch next to Kat. He gingerly peels back his hood. "I don't know what to say. It's terrible. I'll talk to Corvina. I can convince him—"

Penumbra holds up a hand, and then he tells

Deckle everything. He tells him about my logbook, about Google and the Founder's Puzzle. He tells him about his pitch to Corvina, about the First Reader's rejection.

"We'll work on him," Deckle says. "I'll mention it from time to time, to see if—"

"No," Penumbra cuts in. "He is beyond reason, Edgar, and I do not have the patience. I am quite a bit older than you, my boy. I believe the *codex vitae* can be decoded today—not in a decade, not in a hundred years, but today!"

It occurs to me that Corvina isn't the only one with outsized confidence. Penumbra really does believe that computers can deliver the goods. Is it strange that I, the person who rekindled this project, don't feel so sure?

Deckle's eyes go wide. He glances around as if there might be a black-robe lurking here in the Northbridge. Not likely; I doubt anyone in this lobby has touched a physical book in years.

"You're not serious, sir," he whispers. "I mean, I remember, when you made me type all the titles into the Mac, you were so excited—but I never thought . . ." He takes a breath. "Sir, this is not how the fellowship works."

So it was Edgar Deckle who built the bookstore's database. I feel a surge of clerkly affection. We've both laid our fingers on the same short, clackety keyboard.

Penumbra shakes his head. "It only seems

strange because we are stuck, my boy," he says. "Corvina has held us frozen. The First Reader has not been true to the spirit of Manutius." His eyes are like blue laser beams and he jabs a long finger down into the magnetic-tape table. "He was an entrepreneur, Edgar!"

Deckle is nodding, but he still looks nervous. His cheeks are pink and he's running his knuckles through his hair. Is this how all schisms start? Huddled circles, whispered sales pitches?

"Edgar," Penumbra says evenly, "of all my students, you are the dearest to me. We spent many years together in San Francisco, working side by side. You possess the true spirit of the Unbroken Spine, my boy." He pauses. "Lend us the key to the Reading Room for one night. That is all I ask. Clay will not leave a trace. I promise you."

Deckle's expression is blank. His hair is damp and disheveled. He searches for words: "Sir. I didn't think you—I never imagined—sir." He is quiet. The Northbridge lobby doesn't exist. The whole universe is Edgar Deckle's face, and the thoughtful turn of his lips, and the signs that he might say no, or—

"Yes." He draws himself taller. He takes a deep breath, and he says again, "Yes. Of course I'll help you, sir." He nods sharply, and smiles. "Of course."

Penumbra grins. "I do know how to pick the

right clerks," he says, reaching across to slap Deckle's shoulder. He barks a laugh. "I do know how to pick them!"

The scheme is set.

Tomorrow, Deckle will bring a spare key sealed in an envelope addressed to me and deliver it to the Northbridge concierge. Neel and I will find a way to manufacture the GrumbleGear, Kat will make her appearance at Google's New York office, and Penumbra will meet with a handful of black-robes who are sympathetic to his cause. When night falls, I will take scanner and key and make my way to the secret library of the Unbroken Spine, where I will liberate MANVTIVS—along with one other.

But that's all tomorrow. Right now Kat has retired to our room. Neel has docked with a group of New York startup dudes. Penumbra is sitting at the hotel bar alone, nursing a heavy tumbler of something golden, lost in thought. He cuts a strange figure in this place: older than everyone else in the lobby by several decades, the top of his head a pale beacon in the calibrated gloom.

I'm sitting alone on one of the low couches, staring at my laptop, wondering how we can get ourselves in front of a laser cutter. Neel's friend Andrei gave us leads on two different Manhattan hacker spaces, but only one had a laser cutter, and it's booked solid for weeks. Everybody's making something.

It occurs to me that Mat Mittelbrand might know someone, somewhere. There's got to be a special-effects shop in this city that possesses the tool we need. I tap out a distress signal on my phone:

**Need a laser cutter ASAP in new york. Any ideas?**

Thirty-seven seconds elapse, and Mat texts back:

**Ask grumble.**

Of course. I've spent months browsing the pirate library, but never posted anything. Grumble's site features a bustling forum where people request particular e-books and then complain about the quality of what they receive. There's also a technical subforum where people talk about the nuts and bolts of book digitization; this is where Grumble himself appears, answering questions with brevity, precision, and all-lowercase letters. This subforum is where I'll ask for help:

**Hi everybody. I'm a silent member of the Grumblematrix, speaking up for the first**

**time. Tonight I find myself in New York City, in need of an Epilog laser cutter (or similar) as required by the instructions for the GrumbleGear 3000. I intend to carry out a clandestine scan ASAP, and the target is one of the most important books in the history of printing. In other words: this might be bigger than Potter. Any help?**

I take a breath, check three times for typos, then submit the post. I hope the Festina Lente Company's pirate patrol isn't reading this.

Rooms at the Northbridge are a lot like the white shipping containers on Google's campus: long and boxy, with hookups for water, power, and internet. There are narrow beds, too, but those are clearly a reluctant concession to the frailties of wetware.

Kat is sitting cross-legged on the floor in her underwear and red T-shirt, leaning in to her laptop. I'm on the lip of the bed above her with my Kindle drawing power from her USB port—um, not a euphemism—reading *The Dragon-Song Chronicles* for the fourth time. She's finally perking up again after the disappointment of the PM, and, twisted around to look at me, she says, "This is really exciting. I can't believe I've never heard of Aldus Manutius." His Wikipedia entry is open on her screen. I recognize the look on her face—it's the same one that shows up when she talks about the Singularity. "I always thought the key to immortality would be, like, tiny robots fixing things in your brain," she says. "Not books."

I have to be honest: "I'm not sure books are the key to anything. I mean, come on. This is a cult. It really is." She frowns at that. "But a lost book written by Aldus Manutius himself is still pretty important, no matter what. After this, we can get Mr. Penumbra back to California. We'll run the store on our own. I've got a marketing plan."

None of that registers with Kat. She says, "There's a team in Mountain View—we should tell them about this. It's called Google Forever. They work on life extension. Cancer treatment, organ regeneration, DNA repair."

This is getting silly. "Maybe a little cryogenics on the side?"

She glances up at me defensively. "They're taking a portfolio approach." I run my fingers through her hair, which is still damp from the shower. She smells like citrus.

"I just don't get it," she says, twisting back around to look up at me. "How can you stand it that our lives are so short? They're *so short,* Clay."

To be honest, my life has exhibited many strange and sometimes troubling characteristics, but shortness is not one of them. It feels like an eternity since I started school and a techno-social epoch since I moved to San Francisco. My phone couldn't even connect to the internet back then.

"Every day you learn something amazing," Kat says, "like, there's a secret underground library in New York City"—she pauses and gapes for effect, and it makes me laugh—"and you realize there's so much more that's waiting. Eighty years isn't enough. Or a hundred. Whatever. It's just *not*." Her voice goes a little ragged, and I realize how deep this current runs within Kat Potente.

I lean down, kiss her above the ear, and whisper: "Would you really freeze your head?"

"I would absolutely, positively freeze my head." She looks up at me and her face is serious. "I'd freeze yours, too. And in a thousand years, you'd thank me."

# POP-UP

**W**HEN I WAKE UP in the morning, Kat is gone, already headed for Google's New York office. On my laptop, there's an email waiting—a message relayed from Grumble's forum. The timestamp says 3:05 a.m., and it's from—holy shit. It's from Grumble himself. The message says simply:

**bigger than potter huh? tell me what you need.**

My pulse pounds in my ears. This is awesome. Grumble lives in Berlin, but he seems to spend most of his time traveling, doing special scanning ops in London or Paris or Cairo. Maybe sometimes New York. Nobody knows his real name; nobody knows what he looks like. He might be a she, or even a collective. In my imagination, though, Grumble is a he, not much older than me. In my imagination, he works solo—shuffling into the British Library in a puffy gray parka, wearing the cardboard components of his book scanner like a bulletproof vest under his clothes—but he has allies every-where.

Maybe we'll meet up. Maybe we'll become friends. Maybe I'll become his hacker apprentice.

But I have to play it cool, or he'll probably think I'm from the FBI or, worse, the Festina Lente Company. So I write:

**Hey Grumble! Thanks for replying, man. Big fan of your**

Okay, no. I lean on the delete key and start again:

**Hey. We can get the cameras and the cardboard, but we can't find a laser. Can you help? P.S. Okay admittedly J. K. Rowling is a pretty big deal . . . but so was Aldus Manutius.**

I hit send, smack my MacBook shut, and retreat into the bathroom. I think about hacker heroes and frozen heads while I scrub shampoo into my hair under the hot industrial blast of the Northbridge's shower, obviously designed for robots, not for men.

Neel is waiting for me in the lobby, finishing a bowl of plain oatmeal and slurping a shake made from blended kale.

"Hey," he says, "does your room have a biometric lock?"

"No, just a card key."

"Mine's supposed to recognize my face, but it

wouldn't let me in." He frowns. "I think it only works for white people."

"You should sell your friend some better software," I say. "Expand into the hospitality business."

Neel rolls his eyes. "Right. I don't think I want to expand into any more markets. Did I tell you I got an email from Homeland Security?"

I freeze. Does this have anything to do with Grumble? No, that's ridiculous. "You mean, like, recently?"

He nods. "They want an app to help them visualize different body types under heavy clothing. Like, burkas and stuff."

Okay, whew. "Are you going to do it?"

He grimaces. "No way. Even if it wasn't a gross idea—which it is—I'm doing too much already." He slurps his shake and makes a bright cylinder of green zoom up the straw.

"You like it," I say lightly. "You love having a finger in eleven different pots."

"Sure, fingers in pots," he says. "Not, like, whole bodies in pots. Dude, I don't have partners. I don't have business development people. And I don't even do the fun stuff anymore!" He's talking about code—or maybe boobs, I'm not sure. "Honestly, what I really want to do is, like, be a VC."

Neel Shah, venture capitalist. We'd never have dreamed that in sixth grade.

"So why don't you?"

"Um, I think you might overestimate how much money Anatomix throws off," he says, raising his eyebrows. "This isn't exactly Google over here. To be a VC, you need a lot of C. All I've got is a bunch of five-figure contracts with video game companies."

"And movie studios, right?"

"Shh," Neel hisses, casting his eyes around the lobby. "Nobody can know about those. There are some very serious documents, dude." He pauses. "There are documents with Scarlett Johansson's signature on them."

We take the subway. Grumble's next message came through after breakfast, and it said:

**theres a grumblegear3k waiting for you at 11 jay street in dumbo. ask for the hogwarts special. hold the shrooms.**

It is probably the coolest message that has ever appeared in my inbox. It's a dead-drop, and Neel and I are headed there now. We are going to supply a secret passphrase and get a special-ops book scanner in return.

The train rumbles and sways through its tunnel below the East River. The windows are all dark. Neel is lightly gripping the bar overhead and he says:

"You sure you don't want to get into business development? You could head up the burka project." He grins and lifts his eyebrows, and I realize he's serious, at least about the BD part.

"I am the absolute worst person you could get to do BD for your company," I say. "I guarantee it. You'd have to fire me. It would be awful." I'm not kidding. Working for Neel would violate the terms of our friendship. He'd be Neel Shah, boss, or Neel Shah, business mentor—no longer Neel Shah, dungeon master.

"I wouldn't fire you," he says. "I'd just demote you."

"To what, Igor's apprentice?"

"Igor already has an apprentice. Dmitriy. He's supersmart. You could be Dmitriy's apprentice."

I'm sure Dmitriy is sixteen. I don't like the sound of this. I change course:

"Hey, what about making your own movies?" I say. "Really show off Igor's chops. Start another Pixar."

Neel nods at that, then he's quiet a moment, chewing it over. Finally: "I would totally do that. If I knew a filmmaker, I would fund him in a second." He pauses. "Or her. But if it was a her, I'd probably fund her through my foundation."

Right: the Neel Shah Foundation for Women in the Arts. It's a tax shelter created at the behest of Neel's slick Silicon Valley accountant. Neel asked me to build a placeholder website to make it look more legit and it is, to date, the second-most-depressing thing I have ever designed. (The NewBagel to Old Jerusalem rebranding still holds the top slot.)

"So go find a filmmaker," I say.

"*You* go find a filmmaker," Neel shoots back. Very sixth-grade. Then something lights up in his eyes: "Actually . . . that's perfect. Yes. In exchange for funding this adventure, Claymore Redhands, I ask this boon of you." His voice goes low and dungeon master-y: "You will find me a filmmaker."

My phone guides us to the address in Dumbo. It's on a quiet street along the water, next to a fenced-in lot bristling with ConEdison transformers. The building is dark and narrow, even skinnier than Penumbra's and much more run-down. It looks like there's been a fire here recently; long black streaks rise up around the doorframe. The space would look derelict if not for two things: One, a wide vinyl sign stuck crookedly to the front that says POP-UP PIE. Two, the warm rising smell of pizza.

Inside, it's a wreck—yes, there was definitely a fire here—but the air is dense and fragrant, full of carbohydrates. Up front, there's a card table with a dented money box. Behind it, a gang of ruddy-cheeked teenagers is milling around a makeshift kitchen. One is spinning dough in wobbly circles above his head; another is chopping tomatoes, onions, and peppers. Three more are just standing around, talking and laughing. There's a tall pizza oven behind them, bare banged-up metal with a wide blue racing stripe down the middle. It has wheels.

There's music blaring from a set of plastic speakers, a crunchy warbling tune that I suspect no more than thirteen people in the world have ever heard.

"What can I get you guys?" one of the teenagers calls out above the music. Well, he might not actually be a teenager. The staff here inhabits a whiskerless in-between space; they probably go to art school. Our host is wearing a white T-shirt that shows Mickey Mouse grimacing and brandishing an AK-47.

Okay, I'd better get this right: "One Hogwarts Special," I call back to him. Insurgent Mickey nods once. I add, "But hold the shrooms." Pause. "The mushrooms, I mean." Pause. "I think." But Insurgent Mickey has already turned away from us, consulting with his colleagues.

"Did he hear you?" Neel whispers. "I can't eat pizza. If we actually end up with a pizza, it's going to be your responsibility to consume it. Do not let me have any. Even if I ask for some." He pauses. "I'll probably ask for some."

"Tie you to the mast," I say. "Like Odysseus."

"Like Captain Bloodboots," Neel says.

In *The Dragon-Song Chronicles*, Fernwen the scholarly dwarf convinces the crew of the *Starlily* to tie Captain Bloodboots to the mast after he tries to cut the singing dragon's throat. So, yes. Like Captain Bloodboots.

Insurgent Mickey is back with a pizza box. That was fast. "That'll be sixteen-fifty," he says. Wait, did I do something wrong? Is this a joke? Did Grumble send us on a wild-goose chase? Neel raises his eyebrows but produces a crisp twenty-dollar bill and hands it over. In return, we receive an extra-large pizza box, with POP-UP PIE stamped across the top in runny blue ink.

The box isn't hot.

Outside on the sidewalk, I crack it open. Inside, there are tidy stacks of heavy cardboard, all long flat shapes with slots and tabs where they fit together. It's a GrumbleGear, all in pieces. The edges are burned black. These shapes have been made with a laser cutter.

Written in thick marker strokes on the underside of the box's lid is a message from Grumble, whether by his own hand or his Brooklyn minion's, I will never know:

SPECIALIS REVELIO

On the way back, we stop at a gray-market electronics shop and pick out two cheap digital cameras. Then we make our way to the

Northbridge through the streets of lower Manhattan, Neel carrying the pizza box, me with the cameras in a plastic bag bouncing against my knee. We have everything we need. MANVTIVS will be ours.

The city is all bright squalls of traffic and commerce. Taxis honk underneath lights turning gold; long lines of shoppers clank up and down Fifth Avenue. There are loose crowds on every street corner, laughing and smoking and selling kebabs. San Francisco is a good city, and beautiful, but it's never this alive. I take a deep breath—the air is cool and sharp, scented with tobacco and mystery meat—and I think of Corvina's warning to Penumbra: *You can squander what time remains out there.* Jeez. Immortality in a book-lined catacomb down beneath the surface of the earth, or death up here, with all this? I'll take death and a kebab. And what about Penumbra? Somehow he seems more like a man of the world, too. I think of his bookstore, with those wide front windows. I think of his first words to me—"What do you seek in these shelves?"—delivered with a big, welcoming smile.

Corvina and Penumbra were fast friends once; I've seen photographic proof. Corvina must have been so different then . . . really literally a different person. At what point do you make that call? At what point should you just give someone a new name? *Sorry, no, you don't get to be Corvina anymore. Now you're Corvina 2.0*—a dubious upgrade. I think of the young man in the old photo giving a thumbs-up. Is he gone forever?

"It really would be better if the filmmaker was female," Neel is saying. "Seriously. I need to put more money into that foundation. I've only given one grant, and it was to my cousin Sabrina." He pauses. "I think that might have been illegal."

I try to imagine Neel forty years from now: bald, suit-wearing, a different person. I try to imagine Neel 2.0 or Neel Shah, business mentor—a Neel with whom I can no longer be friends—but I just can't do it.

Back at the Northbridge, I'm surprised to find Kat and Penumbra sitting together on the low couches, deep in conversation. Kat is gesturing enthusiastically and Penumbra is smiling, nodding, his blue eyes shining.

When Kat looks up, she's smiling. "There was another email," she blurts. Then she pauses, but her face is alive, jumping, like she can't contain whatever comes next: "They're expanding the PM to a hundred and twenty-eight, and—I'm one of them." Her micromuscles are on fire, and she almost shrieks it: "I got picked!"

My mouth hangs open a little bit. She jumps up and hugs me, and I hug her back, and we dance around in a little circle in the ultracool Northbridge lobby.

"What does that even mean?" Neel says, setting down the pizza box.

"I think it means this side project just got some executive support," I say, and Kat throws her arms up in the air.

To celebrate Kat's success, all four of us sidle up to the Northbridge lobby bar, which is tiled with tiny matte-black integrated circuits. We sit on tall stools and Neel buys a round of drinks. I sip something called the Blue Screen of Death, which is in fact neon-blue, with a bright LED winking inside one of the ice cubes.

"So let me get this straight—you're one–one-twenty-eighth of Google's CEO?" Neel says.

"Not exactly," Kat says. "We have a CEO, but Google is way too complicated for one person to run alone, so the Product Management helps out. You know . . . should we enter this market, should we make that acquisition."

"Dude!" Neel says, leaping up off his stool. "Acquire me!"

Kat laughs. "I'm not sure 3-D boobs—"

"It's not just boobs!" Neel says. "We do the whole body. Arms, legs, deltoids, you name it."

Kat just smiles and sips her drink. Penumbra is nursing an inch of golden scotch in a thick-bottomed tumbler. He turns to Kat.

233

"Dear girl," he says. "Do you think Google will still exist in a hundred years?"

She's quiet a moment, then nods sharply. "Yes, I do."

"You know," he says, "a rather famous member of the Unbroken Spine was fast friends with a young man who founded a company of similar ambition. And he said exactly the same thing."

"Which company?" I ask. "Microsoft? Apple?" What if Steve Jobs dabbled in the fellowship? Maybe that's why Gerritszoon comes preinstalled on every Mac . . .

"No, no," Penumbra says, shaking his head. "It was Standard Oil." He grins; he's caught us. He swirls his glass and says, "You have found your way into a story that has been unfolding for a very long time. Some of my brothers and sisters would say that your company, dear girl, is no different from all the others that have come before. Some of them would say no one outside the Unbroken Spine has ever had anything to offer us."

"Some of them, like Corvina," I say flatly.

"Yes, Corvina." Penumbra nods. "Others, too." He looks at the three of us together—Kat and Neel and me—and he says quietly, "But I am glad to have you as my allies. I do not know if you understand how historic this work is going to be. The techniques we have developed over centuries, aided by new tools . . . I believe we will succeed. I believe it in my bones."

• • •

Together, with Neel reading the instructions from my laptop and Penumbra handing me the pieces, we assemble the GrumbleGear 3000 for the first time. The components are cut from corrugated cardboard and they make a satisfying *thwack* when you thump them with your finger. Slotted together, they achieve a preternatural structural integrity. There's an angled bed for a book and two long arms above it, each with a cunning socket for a camera—one for each page in a two-page spread. The cameras connect to my laptop, which is now running a program called Grumble-Scan. The program, in turn, hands the images off to a hard drive, a matte-black terabyte tucked into a slender box of Bicycle playing cards. The box is a nice roguish touch from Neel.

"Who designed this thing again?" he asks, scrolling through the instructions.

"A guy named Grumble. He's a genius."

"I should hire him," Neel says. "Good programmer. Great sense of spatial relationships."

I open my *Guide to Central Park Birds* and set it up on the scanner. Grumble's design isn't much like Google's—it has no spidery page-turning appendages, so you have to do that part yourself, and trigger the cameras, too—but it works. Flip, flash, snap. The migratory pattern of the American robin spools onto the disguised hard drive. Then I break the scanner back down into flat pieces with Kat keeping time. It takes forty-one seconds.

With this contraption in tow, I'll return to the Reading Room just a little past midnight tonight. I'll have the place entirely to myself. With maximum speed and stealth, I will scan not one but two books, then flee the scene. Deckle has warned me to be done and departed, leaving no trace, by first light.

# THE BLACK HOLE

I T'S JUST PAST MIDNIGHT. I walk quickly up Fifth Avenue, eyeing the dark mass of Central Park across the street. The trees are black silhouettes against a blotchy gray-purple sky. Yellow taxis are the only cars on the street, despondently circling for fares. One of them flashes its brights at me; I shake my head no.

Deckle's key goes *click* in the dark doorway of the Festina Lente Company, and just like that, I am inside.

There's a dot of light blinking red in the darkness, and thanks to Deckle's intel, I know it's a silent alarm that signals a very private security firm. My heart beats faster. Now I have thirty-one seconds to enter the code, which I do: 1-5-1-5. That's the year Aldus Manutius died—or, if you subscribe to the stories of the Unbroken Spine: the year he didn't.

The front room is dark. I pull a headlamp out of my bag and wind the strap around my forehead. It was Kat who suggested a headlamp instead of a flashlight. "So you can focus on flipping the pages," she said. The light flashes across the FLC on the wall, casting sharp shadows behind the capitals. I briefly consider some extracurricular espionage here—could I delete their database of e-book pirates?—but decide my real mission is risky enough.

I stalk through the silent expanse of the outer office, sweeping the headlamp through cubicles on either side. The refrigerator rattles and hums; the multipurpose printer blinks forlornly; screen savers twist across monitors, casting weak blue light into the room. Otherwise, nothing moves or makes a sound.

In Deckle's office, I skip the costume change and keep my phone securely in my pocket. I give the shelves a gentle push, and I'm surprised at how easily they split and swivel back, silent and weightless. This secret way is well oiled indeed.

Beyond, it is all blackness.

Suddenly this seems like a very different undertaking. Up until this moment, I'd still been imagining the Reading Room as it was yesterday afternoon: bright, bustling, and if not welcoming then at least well lit. Now I am basically looking into a black hole. This is a cosmic entity from which no matter or energy have ever escaped, and I am about to step straight into it.

I tilt my headlamp down. This is going to take a while.

I should have asked Deckle about the light switch. Why didn't I ask Deckle about the light switch?

My footfalls make long echoes. I've stepped through the passageway into the Reading Room, and it is pure pitch-black, the blackest void I have ever encountered. It's also freezing.

I take a step forward and decide to keep my head down, not up, because when I look down, the headlamp's light reflects on smooth rock, and when I look up, it disappears into nothing.

I want to scan these books and get out of this place. First I need to find one of the tables. There are dozens. This isn't going to be a problem.

I start by tracing the chamber's perimeter, trailing my fingers along the shelves, feeling the bumps of the spines as I go. My other arm is outstretched and sensing, like a mouse's whisker.

I hope there aren't mice in here.

There. My headlamp catches a table edge, and then I see a heavy black chain and the book that it binds. The cover bears tall silver letters that reflect brightly back at me: MANVTIVS.

From my messenger bag, I produce first my laptop and then the dismantled skeleton of the GrumbleGear. The assembly process is more difficult in the darkness, and I fumble with the slots and tabs for too long, afraid I'll break the cardboard. The cameras come out of my bag next, and I give one of them a test snap. The flash explodes and lights up the whole chamber for a bright microsecond and immediately I regret it, because my vision is ruined, swimming with wide purple spots. I blink and wait and wonder about the mice and/or bats and/or minotaur.

MANVTIVS is truly gigantic. Even if it wasn't chained to the table, I don't know how somebody would get one of these books out of here. I have to wrap both arms around it in an awkward embrace to haul it up onto the scanner. I'm afraid the cardboard won't bear the load, but physics is on my side tonight. Grumble's design holds strong.

So I start scanning. Flip, flash, snap. The book is just like all the rest I've seen in the Waybacklist: a dense matrix of coded characters. Flip, flash, snap. The second page is the same as the first, and so is the third, and the seventh. I fall into a trance, turning the wide monotonous pages and taking their measure. Flip, flash, snap. The grim letters of MANVTIVS are all that exist in the universe; in between camera flashes, I see only flat buzzing darkness. I feel with my fingers to find the next page.

There's a shake. Is someone down here? Something just made the table shake.

It shakes again. I try to say *Who's there?* but it catches in my throat, which is parched, and I make a little croak instead.

Another shake. Then, before I have time to formulate a terrifying theory about the Horned Guardian of the Reading Room—obviously Edgar Deckle's werebeast form—there's more shaking, and the cave rumbles and roars and I have to clutch the scanner to keep it upright. In a flood of relief, I realize it's the subway, just the subway, cruising through bedrock next door. The noise echoes back into itself and becomes a low bellow in the darkness of the cave. Finally, it passes, and I start scanning again.

Flip, flash, snap.

Many minutes pass, or maybe more than minutes, and bleakness washes over me. Maybe it's the fact that I didn't have any dinner, so my blood sugar is bottoming out, or maybe it's the fact that I'm standing alone in a freezing pitch-black subterranean vault. But whatever the cause, the effect is real: I feel keenly the stupidity of this entire enterprise, this absurd cult. Book of life? This is barely a book at all. *The Dragon-Song Chronicles: Volume III* is a better book than this.

Flip, flash, snap.

But of course: I can't read it. Would I say the same thing about a book in Chinese or Korean or Hebrew? The big Torahs in Jewish temples look like this, right? Flip, flash, snap—heavy grids of inscrutable symbols. Maybe it's my own limitation that's getting to me. Maybe it's the fact that I can't understand what I'm scanning. Flip, flash, snap. What if I could read this? What if I could glance across the page and, you know, get the joke? Or gasp at the cliff-hanger?

Flip, flash, snap.

No. Turning the pages of this encoded codex, I realize that the books I love most are like open cities, with all sorts of ways to wander in. This thing is a fortress with no front gate. You're meant to scale the walls, stone by stone.

I'm cold and tired and hungry. I have no idea how much time has passed. It feels like maybe my entire life has been spent in this chamber, with the occasional dream of a sunny street. Flip flash snap, flip flash snap, flip flash snap. My hands are cold claws, curled and cramped as if I've been playing video games all day.

Flip, flash, snap. This is a terrible video game.

At last, I'm done.

I lace my fingers together and bend them backward, pressing them out into space. I jump up and down, trying to restore my bones and muscles to some semblance of normal hominid configuration. It doesn't work. My knees hurt. My back is cramped. There are jets of pain shooting out of my thumbs, up into my wrists. I hope it isn't permanent.

I shake my head. I'm feeling really dismal. I should have brought a granola bar. Suddenly I am sure that starving to death in a pitch-black cave is the very worst way to die. That makes me think of the *codex vitae* lining the walls, and suddenly I get the creeps. How many dead souls are sitting—waiting—on the shelves all around me?

One soul matters more than the rest. It's time to accomplish this mission's second objective.

Penumbra's *codex vitae* is here. I'm cold, shivering, and I want to leave this place, but I came here to liberate not only Aldus Manutius, but Ajax Penumbra, too.

To be clear: I don't believe in this. I don't believe any of these books can confer immortality. I just clawed my way through one of them; it's moldy paper bound in moldier leather. It's a hunk of dead tree and dead flesh. But if Penumbra's *codex vitae* is the great work of his life—if he really did pour everything he learned, all his knowledge, into one book—then, you know, I think somebody ought to make a backup.

It might be a long shot, but I'll never have this chance again. So I start along the perimeter, doubled over, trying to read the spines sideways. One look confirms that they are not shelved alphabetically. No, of course they're not. They're probably grouped according to some supersecret intra-cult rank, or favorite prime number, or inseam, or something. So I just go shelf by shelf, deeper and deeper into the darkness.

The variation between books is incredible. Some are fat, some are skinny; some are tall like atlases, some squat like paperbacks. I wonder if there's a logic to that, too; is some sort of status encoded into each book's format? Some are bound in cloth, others in leather, and many in materials that I don't recognize. One shines bright in the light of my headlamp; it's clad in thin aluminum.

Thirteen shelves in, there's still no sign of

PENVMBRA, and I'm afraid I might have missed him. The headlamp casts a narrow cone of light, and I'm not seeing every spine, especially the ones down by the floor—

There's a blank space in the shelves. No: upon closer inspection, it's not blank, but black. It's a blackened husk of a book, with the name still faintly visible on the spine:

MOFFAT

It can't be . . . Clark Moffat, author of *The Dragon-Song Chronicles*? No, it can't.

I paw at the spine and pull it out, and as I do, the book disintegrates. The covers hold together, but a sheaf of blackened pages comes loose inside and falls onto the floor. I hiss, "Shit!" and shove what remains of the book back onto the shelf. This must be what they mean by burning. The book is ruined, just a blackened placeholder. Maybe it's a warning.

My hands are blackened now, too, slick with soot. I clap them together and bits of MOFFAT float to the floor. Maybe it's an ancestor or a second cousin. There's more than one Moffat in the world.

I reach down to scoop up the charred remains and my headlamp catches a book, tall and skinny, with golden letters spaced out along the spine:

PENVMBRA

It's him. I almost can't bring myself to touch it. It's right there—I found it—but suddenly it feels too intimate, like I'm about to look through Penumbra's tax returns or his underwear drawer. What's inside? What story does it tell?

I hook a finger into the top of the binding and angle it slowly away from the shelf. This book is beautiful. It's taller and skinnier than its neighbors, with super-stiff binding boards. Its dimensions remind me more of an oversized children's book than an occult diary. The cover is pale blue, exactly the color of Penumbra's eyes, and with some of the same luminescence, too: the color shifts and glimmers in the glare of the headlamp. It's soft under my fingers.

The remains of MOFFAT are a dark smear at my feet, and I won't let the same thing happen to this book, no matter what. I will scan PENVMBRA.

I carry my erstwhile employer's *codex vitae* back over to the GrumbleGear and—why am I so nervous?—I open to the first page. It's the same jumble of characters as all the rest, of course. Penumbra's *codex vitae* is no more readable than any of the others.

Because it's so slender—a mere fraction of MANVTIVS—it shouldn't take long, but I find myself flipping more slowly, trying to glean something, anything, from the pages. I relax my eyes, defocus them, so the letters become a dappling of shadows. I want so badly to see something in this mess—honestly, I want something magical to happen. But no: if I really want to read my weird old friend's opus, I'll need to join his cult. There are no free stories in the secret library of the Unbroken Spine.

It takes longer than it should, but at last I'm finished and the pages of PENVMBRA are safe on the hard drive. More so than with MANVTIVS, I feel like I just accomplished something important. I snap my laptop shut, shuffle over to the place where I found the book—marked by MOFFAT's remains on the floor—and slot the glimmering blue *codex vitae* back into place.

I give it a pat on the spine and say, "Sleep well, Mr. Penumbra."

Then the lights come on.

I'm blinded and stricken, blinking and panicking. What just happened? Did I set off an alarm? Did I trigger some trap laid for over-reaching rogues?

I claw my phone out of my pocket and swipe madly at the screen, bringing it back to life. It's almost eight in the morning. How did this happen? How long was I circumnavigating the shelves here? How long was I scanning PENVMBRA?

The lights are on, and now I hear a voice.

When I was a kid, I had a pet hamster. He always seemed to be afraid of absolutely everything—permanently trapped and trembling.

This made hamster ownership pretty much totally unpleasant for the whole eighteen months that it lasted.

Now, for the first time in my life, I empathize 100 percent with Fluff McFly. My heart is beating at hamster-speed and I am throwing my eyes around the room, looking for some way out. The bright lamps are like prison-yard spotlights. I can see my own hands, and I can see the pile of charred paper at my feet, and I can see the table with my laptop and the skeletal scanner set up on top of it.

I can also see the dark shape of a door directly across the chamber.

I sprint to my laptop, scoop it up, then grab the scanner, too—crushing the cardboard under my arms—and make for the door. I have no idea what it is or where it leads—to the canned beans?—but now I hear voices, plural.

My fingers are on the door handle. I hold my breath—please, please be unlocked—and I push it down. Poor tormented Fluff McFly never felt anything like the relief of that door giving way. I slide through and close it behind me.

On the other side, it's all darkness again. I stand frozen for a moment, cradling my awkward cargo in my arms, my back pressed up against the door. I force myself to take shallow breaths; I ask my hamster-heart to please, please slow down.

There is the sound of motion and conversation behind me. The door is not set tightly into its frame of rock; it's like one of those bathroom stalls that feels way too see-through. But it does give me the chance to set the scanner aside and flatten myself down on the cold, smooth floor and peek through the half inch of empty space beneath it:

Black-robes are flooding into the Reading Room. There are a dozen here already, and more coming down the steps. What's going on? Did Deckle forget to check the calendar? Did he betray us? Is today the annual convention?

I sit up straight and do the first thing a person is supposed to do in an emergency, which is send a text message. No such luck. My phone flashes NO SERVICE, even if I stand on tiptoe and wave it up near the ceiling.

I need to hide. I'll find a little spot, curl up in a ball, and wait until tomorrow night to slink out. There will be the issue of hunger and thirst, and maybe going to the bathroom . . . but one thing at a time. My eyes are adjusting to the darkness again, and if I beam my headlamp around in a wide circle, I can make out the shape of the space around me. It's a small, low-ceilinged chamber packed with dark shapes, all interconnected and overlapping. In the gloom, it looks like something from a science fiction movie: there are sharp-edged metal ribs and long tubes that reach up into the ceiling.

I am still feeling my way forward when there's a soft click from the door, which sends me back into hamster mode. I scuttle forward and crouch down behind one of the dark shapes. Something pokes me in the back and wobbles there, so I reach around to steady it—it's an iron rod, painfully cold and slippery with dust. Can I whack the black-robe with this rod? Where will I whack him? In the face? I'm not sure I can whack somebody in the face. I'm a rogue, not a warrior.

Warm light falls into the chamber, and I see a figure framed in the doorway. It is a round figure. It's Edgar Deckle.

He shuffles through, and there's a sloshing sound. He's carrying a mop and bucket, which he holds awkwardly with one hand while he feels along the wall. There's a low buzz, and the room is bathed in orange light. I grimace and squint.

Deckle makes a sharp gasp when he sees me crouched in the corner, iron rod raised like some Gothic baseball bat. His eyes go wide. "You were supposed to be gone by now!" he hisses.

I decide not to reveal that I got distracted by MOFFAT and PENVMBRA. "It was really dark," I say.

Deckle sets aside his mop and bucket with a clack and a plop. He sighs and wipes a black sleeve across his forehead. I lower the rod. I can see now that I'm crouched next to a huge furnace; the rod is an iron poker.

I survey the scene, and it's not science fiction anymore. I'm surrounded by printing machines. There are refugees from many eras: an old Monotype bristling with knobs and levers; a wide, heavy cylinder set on a long track; and something straight out of Gutenberg's garage—a heavy whorled block of wood with an enormous corkscrew poking out at the top.

There are cases and cabinets. There are tools of the printing trade laid out on a wide, weathered table: fat book blocks and tall spools of heavy thread. Under the table, there are lengths of chain piled up in wide loops. The stove next to me has a wide, smiling grille, and at the top, it sprouts a fat pipe that disappears into the chamber's ceiling.

Here, deep beneath the streets of Manhattan, I have discovered the world's weirdest print shop.

"But you got it?" Deckle whispers.

I show him the hard drive in its Bicycle box.

"You got it," he breathes. The shock doesn't last long; Edgar Deckle is quickly recomposing himself. "Okay. I think we can make this work. I think—yes." He nods to himself. "Let me just take these"—he lifts three heavy books, all identical, up off the table—"and I'll be right back. Stay quiet."

He balances the books against his chest and goes back the way he came, leaving the light on behind him.

I wait and inspect the print shop. The floor is beautiful: a mosaic of characters, each in its own tile, each deeply etched. The alphabet at my feet.

There's one metal case much larger than the rest. The top has a familiar symbol: two hands, open like a book. Why do organizations need to mark everything with their insignia? It's like a dog peeing on every tree. Google is the same way. So was NewBagel.

Using both hands, I grunt and lift the case's lid. Inside, it's divided into compartments—some long, some wide, some perfectly square. They all hold shallow piles of metal type: stubby little 3-D letters, the kind you line up on a printing press to make words and paragraphs and pages and books. And suddenly I know what this is.

This is Gerritszoon.

The door clicks again and I whirl to look: Deckle stands there with his hand tucked into his cloak. I am briefly gripped with the certainty that he's been playing dumb, that he's betrayed us after all, that he's been sent back to kill me now. He will do Corvina's handiwork—maybe flatten my skull with the Gutenberg press. But if he's bent on clerkicide, he's putting on a good show: his face is open, friendly, conspiring.

"That's the inheritance," Deckle says, nodding to the Gerritszoon case. "Pretty great, huh?"

He strolls over as if we're just hanging out here,

deep beneath the surface of the earth, and reaches down to run round pink fingers through the type. He picks up a tiny *e* and holds it up to his eye. "The most-used letter in the alphabet," he says, turning it around, inspecting it. He frowns. "It's really worn down."

The subway rumbles through bedrock nearby and it makes the whole room clatter. The Gerritszoon type clinks and shifts; there's a tiny avalanche of *a*'s.

"There's not very much of it," I say.

"It wears out," Deckle says, tossing the *e* back into its compartment. "We break letters but we can't make new ones. We lost the originals. One of the great tragedies of the fellowship." He looks up at me. "Some people think if we change typefaces, new *codex vitae* won't be valid. They think we're stuck with Gerritszoon forever."

"Could be worse," I say. "It's probably the best—"

There's a noise from the Reading Room; a bright bell clangs and makes a long, lingering echo. Deckle's eyes flash. "That's him. Time to go." He gently closes the case, reaches around to the back of his waistband, and pulls out a folded square of black fabric. It's another robe.

"Put this on," he says. "Stay quiet. Stay in the shadows."

# BINDING

THERE'S A CROWD of black-robes at the end of the chamber, down by the wooden dais—dozens of them. Is this everybody? They're talking and whispering, pushing the tables and chairs back. They're setting things up for a show.

"Guys, guys!" Deckle calls out. The black-robes part and make way for him. "Who's got mud on their shoes? I see those prints. I just mopped yesterday."

It's true: the floor shines like glass, reflecting the colors on the shelves, beaming them back as pale pastels. It's beautiful. The bell clangs again, echoing in the cave and making a harsh chorus with itself. The black-robes are forming up in front of the dais, facing a single figure, who is of course Corvina. I position myself directly behind a tall blond-haired scholar. My laptop and the crumpled carcass of the GrumbleGear are stuffed back into my bag, which is slung over my shoulder and concealed under my brand-new black robe. I pull my head down toward my shoulders. These robes should really have hoods.

The First Reader has a stack of books in front of him on the dais, and he taps them with sturdy fingers. They're the books Deckle retrieved from the print shop moments ago.

"Brothers and sisters of the Unbroken Spine,"

Corvina calls out. "Good morning. *Festina lente.*"

"*Festina lente*," the black-robes all murmur in return.

"I have gathered you here to speak of two things," Corvina says, "and this is the first." He lifts one of the blue-bound books and holds it up for everyone to see. "After many years of work, your brother Zaid has presented his *codex vitae.*"

Corvina nods, and one of the black-robes steps forward and turns to face the crowd. The man is in his fifties, thickset under his robe. He has a face like a boxer, with a smooshed-down nose and splotchy cheeks. This must be Zaid. He's standing straight, his hands clasped behind his back. His face is pinched; he's trying hard for fortitude.

"Deckle has validated Zaid's work and I have read his book," Corvina says. "I have read it as closely as I know how." He really is a charismatic dude—his voice has a quiet but irresistible confidence. There's a pause, and the Reading Room is silent. Everyone is waiting for the First Reader's judgment.

Finally, Corvina says simply, "It is masterful."

The black-robes whoop and rush forward to embrace Zaid and shake his hands two at a time. Three scholars near me start belting out a song, which sounds like a for-he's-a-jolly-good-fellow sort of tune, but I'm not sure because it's in Latin. I clap my hands to fit in. Corvina raises a hand to quiet the crowd. They move back and settle down.

Zaid is still standing up in front, and now he raises a hand to cover his eyes. He's crying.

"Today, Zaid is bound," Corvina says. "His *codex vitae* has been encrypted. Now it will be shelved, and the key will remain secret until his death. Just as Manutius chose Gerritszoon, Zaid has chosen a trusted brother to carry his key." Corvina pauses. "It is Eric."

Scattered cheers again. I know Eric. There he is in the front row, a pale face under a splotchy black beard: Corvina's courier to the store in San Francisco. Black-robes are clapping him on the shoulders, too, and I can see him smiling, a bloom of color on his cheeks. Maybe he's not so bad. That's quite a responsibility, keeping Zaid's key. Is he allowed to write it down somewhere?

"Eric will also be one of Zaid's couriers, along with Darius," Corvina says. "Brothers, come forward."

Eric takes three sure steps forward. So does another black-robe, this one with golden skin like Kat's and a tight cap of brown curls. They both unbutton their robes. Underneath, Eric is wearing his slate-gray slacks below a crisp white shirt. Darius is in jeans and a sweater.

Edgar Deckle also steps out of the crowd, carrying two wide sheets of thick brown paper. One at a time, he hoists a book from the dais, wraps it crisply, and hands the package off to a courier: first Eric, then Darius.

"Three copies," Corvina says. "One for the library"—he lifts the blue-bound book again—"and two for safekeeping. Buenos Aires and Rome. We entrust Zaid to you, brothers. Take his *codex vitae* and do not sleep until you have seen it shelved."

So I understand Eric's visit better now. He came from here. He was carrying a fresh *codex vitae*, delivering it for safekeeping. And, of course, being a jerk about it.

"Zaid adds to our burden," Corvina says gravely, "just as all the bound before him have added to it. Year by year, book by book, our responsibility grows heavier." He swivels his gaze to take in all of the black-robes. I suck in my breath and scrunch in my shoulders and try to disappear behind the tall blond-haired scholar. "We must not falter. We must unlock the Founder's secret, so that Zaid and all who came before him can live on."

There's a deep murmur from the crowd. Up in front, Zaid is no longer crying. He's composed himself, and now his face looks proud and severe.

Corvina is silent for a moment. Then he says, "There is something else we must speak of."

He gives a little wave with his hand and Zaid returns to the crowd. Eric and Darius head for the steps. I think for a moment about following them, but quickly reconsider. Right now my only hope is to blend in completely—to crouch in this shadow, not of normalcy, but of deep strangeness.

"I have spoken recently with Penumbra," Corvina says. "He has friends in this fellowship. I count myself among them. So, I feel compelled to tell you about our conversation."

There are whispers all around.

"Penumbra is responsible for a great transgression—one of the greatest imaginable. Thanks to his negligence, one of our volumes was stolen."

Murmurs and groans.

"A logbook containing details of the Unbroken Spine, its work in San Francisco for years, unencrypted, laid out for anyone to read."

My back is sweating under the robe and my eyes feel itchy. The hard drive in its Bicycle box is a lump of lead in my pocket. I try to appear as unconcerned and uninvolved as possible. Mostly this involves looking at my shoes.

"It was a grave mistake, and not the first that Penumbra has made."

More groans from the black-robes. Corvina's disappointment, his disdain, is feeding into them, circling back, amplifying. The tall dark shapes have all drawn together into one big sulking shadow. It's a massacre of crows. I've already picked out a path toward the steps. I'm ready to run for it.

"Note this well," Corvina says, his voice rising

just a little. "Penumbra is one of the bound. His *codex vitae* sits on these shelves, just as Zaid's will. Yet his destiny is not assured." His voice is swift and sure, and it carries through the chamber: "Brothers and sisters, let me be clear: when a burden is this heavy and a purpose this serious, friendship is no shield. Another mistake, and Penumbra will be burned."

There are gasps at this, followed by quick whispered exchanges. Glancing around, I see expressions of shock and surprise. The First Reader might have gone too far just then.

"Do not take your work for granted," he says more gently, "whether you are bound or unbound. We must be disciplined. We must be determined. We cannot allow ourselves to be"—he pauses here—"distracted." He takes a breath. He could be a presidential candidate—a good one—stumping with total conviction and sincerity. "It is the text that matters, brothers and sisters. Remember this. Everything we need is already here in the text. As long as we have that, and as long as we have our minds"—he raises a finger and taps his sleek forehead—"we don't need anything else."

After that, the crows take flight. Black-robes swirl around Zaid, congratulating him, asking him questions. Above his rough red cheeks, his eyes are still wet.

The Unbroken Spine is returning to its labors.

Black-robes are bending down over black books and pulling the chains tight. Near the dais, Corvina confers with a middle-aged woman. She's making broad gestures, explaining something as he gazes down and nods. Deckle is hovering just behind them. His eyes meet mine. He makes a sharp motion with his chin, and the message is clear: *Go.*

I keep my head down and my bag tucked in tight and I march the length of the chamber, keeping close to the shelves. But halfway to the steps, I trip on a chain and stumble down onto one knee. My palm smacks the floor and a black-robe cocks an eye at me. He's tall, with a beard that juts out from his jaw like a bullet.

I say softly: *"Festina lente."*

Then I look straight down and shuffle fast toward the steps. I take them two at a time all the way back up to the surface of planet earth.

I meet Kat, Neel, and Penumbra in the North-bridge lobby. They are sitting, waiting, on massive gray couches with coffee and breakfast set up in front of them; the scene is an oasis of sanity and modernity. Penumbra is frowning.

"My boy!" he says, rising to his feet. He looks me up and down and raises an eyebrow. I realize I'm still wearing the black robe. I shrug my bag onto the floor and peel it off. It's smooth in my hands, shiny in the lobby's half-light.

"You had us worried," Penumbra says. "What took you so long?"

I explain what happened. I tell them Grumble's scanner worked, and then I dump the contraption's crumpled remains out onto the low table. I tell them about Zaid's ceremony.

"A binding," Penumbra says. "They are few and far between. Unlucky that it would happen today." He tilts his chin. "Or lucky, perhaps. Now you know more of the patience that the Unbroken Spine demands."

I wave down a Northbridge waiter and desperately order a bowl of oatmeal and a Blue Screen of Death. It's still early in the morning but I need a drink.

Then I tell them what Corvina said about Penumbra.

My erstwhile employer waves a bony hand: "His words do not matter. Not anymore. What matters is what is on those pages. I cannot believe it worked. I cannot believe we have in our possession the *codex vitae* of Aldus Manutius!"

Kat nods, grinning. "Let's get started," she says. "We can OCR the book and make sure everything works."

She hauls out her MacBook and brings it to life. I plug in the tiny hard drive and copy its contents—most of them. I drag MANVTIVS over to Kat's laptop, but I keep PENVMBRA for myself. I'm not going to tell Penumbra, or anyone, that I scanned his book. That can wait—with luck, maybe forever. Manutius's *codex vitae* is a project. Penumbra's is just an insurance policy.

I eat my oatmeal and watch the progress bar grow. It finishes copying with a quiet *plink* and then Kat's fingers fly across the keyboard. "All right," she says. "It's on its way. We're going to need help back in Mountain View to actually crack the code . . . but we can at least kick off the Hadoop job to turn the pages into plain text. Ready?"

I smile. This is exciting. Kat's cheeks are glowing; she's in digital empress mode. Also, I think the Blue Screen of Death is going to my head. I hoist my blinking glass: "Long live Aldus Manutius!"

Kat thunks a finger down on her keyboard. Pictures of pages start flying to far-off computers, where they will become strings of symbols that can be copied and, soon, decoded. No chains can hold them now.

While Kat's computer goes to work, I ask Penumbra about the burned book marked MOFFAT. Neel is listening, too.

"Was it him?" I ask.

"Yes, of course," Penumbra says. "Clark Moffat. He did his work here, in New York. But before that, my boy—he was our customer." He grins and winks. He thinks this will impress me, and he's right. I'm retroactively starstruck.

261

"But that was not a *codex vitae* you held," Penumbra says, shaking his head. "Not anymore."

Obviously. It was a book of ashes. "What happened?"

"He published it, of course."

Wait, I'm confused: "The only books Moffat ever published were *The Dragon-Song Chronicles*."

"Yes." Penumbra nods. "His *codex vitae* was the third and final volume of the saga he started before he joined us. It was a tremendous profession of faith to finish this work, then surrender it to the fellowship's shelves. He presented it to the First Reader—this was Nivean, before Corvina—and it was accepted."

"But he took it back."

Penumbra nods. "He could not make the sacrifice. He could not leave his final volume unpublished."

So Moffat couldn't remain part of the Unbroken Spine because Neel and I and countless other nerdy sixth-graders all had our minds blown by the third and final volume of *The Dragon-Song Chronicles*.

"Man," Neel says, "this explains a lot."

He's right. The third volume blows middle-school minds because it's a total curveball. The tone shifts. The characters change. The plot goes off the rails and begins to obey some hidden logic. People always assumed it was because Clark

Moffat started doing psychedelic drugs, but the truth is even stranger.

Penumbra frowns. "I believe Clark made a tragic mistake."

Mistake or not, what a world-bending decision. If *The Dragon-Song Chronicles* were never completed, I'd never have been friends with Neel. He wouldn't be sitting here. Maybe I wouldn't be sitting here. Maybe I'd be surfing in Costa Rica with some bizarro-universe best friend. Maybe I'd be sitting in a gray-green office.

Thank you, Clark Moffat. Thank you for your mistake.

# THE DRAGON-SONG CHRONICLES, VOLUME II

**B**ACK IN SAN FRANCISCO, I find Mat and Ashley together in the kitchen, both scarfing complicated salads, both wearing stretchy bright-colored athletic gear. Mat has a carabiner clipped at his waist.

"Jannon!" he exclaims. "Have you ever been rock-climbing?"

I concede that I have not. As a rogue, I prefer athletic activities that require agility, not strength.

"See, that's what I thought, too," Mat says, nodding, "but it's not strength. It's strategy." Ashley eyes him proudly. He continues, waving a forkful of greens, "You have to learn each course as you go—come up with a plan, try it out, adjust. Seriously, my brain is more tired than my arms right now."

"How was New York?" Ashley asks politely.

I'm not sure how to respond. Something like: *Well, the mustachioed master of the secret library is going to be pissed that I copied the entirety of his ancient codebook and delivered it to Google, but at least I got to stay at a nice hotel?*

Instead, I say, "New York was good."

"They've got some great climbing gyms." She shakes her head. "Nothing out here even compares."

"Yeah, the interior design at Frisco Rock City definitely . . . leaves something to be desired," Mat says.

"That purple wall . . ." Ashley shudders. "I think they just bought whatever paint was on sale."

"And a climbing wall is such an opportunity," Mat says. He's getting excited. "What a canvas! Three stories to cover with anything you want. Like a matte painting. There's a guy at ILM . . ."

I leave them chattering happily together about all the details.

At this point, the best option is sleep, but I dozed on the plane and now I'm restless, like something in my brain is still circling the runway, refusing to come in for a landing.

I find Clark Moffat (unburned and intact) on my own short shelves. I'm still making my way through the series again slowly, and now I'm on *Volume II*, near the end. I flop down on my bed and try to see it with new eyes. I mean: this book was written by a man who walked the same streets as me, who looked up at the same shadowed shelves. He joined the Unbroken Spine and he left the Unbroken Spine. What did he learn along the way?

I flip to where I left off.

The heroes, a scholarly dwarf and a dethroned prince, are making their way through a deadly swamp to the Citadel of the First Wizard. I know

266

what's going to happen next, of course, because I've read this book three times before: the First Wizard is going to betray them and hand them over to the Wyrm Queen.

I always know it's coming, and I know it needs to happen (because how else are they going to get into the Wyrm Queen's tower and ultimately defeat her?) but it always kills me to read this part. Why can't things just work out? Why can't the First Wizard just give them a mug of coffee and a safe place to stay for a while?

Even with all my new knowledge, the story seems about the same as before. Moffat's prose is fine: clear and steady, with just enough sweeping statements about destiny and dragons to keep things well inflated. The characters are appealing archetypes: Fernwen the scholarly dwarf is the everynerd, doing his best to live through the adventure. Telemach Half-Blood is the hero you wish you could be. He always has a plan, always has a solution, always has secret allies that he can call upon—pirates and sorcerers whose allegiance he earned with long-ago sacrifices. In fact, I'm just getting to the part where Telemach is going to blow the Golden Horn of Griffo to raise the dead elves of the Pinake Forest, who are all bound to him because he liberated their—

The Golden Horn of Griffo.

Huh.

Griffo, like Griffo Gerritszoon.

I open my laptop and start taking notes. The passage continues:

"The Golden Horn of Griffo is finely wrought," Zenodotus said, tracing his finger along the curve of Telemach's treasure. "And the magic is in its making alone. Do you understand? There is no sorcery here—none that I can detect."

Fernwen's eyes widened at that. Hadn't they just braved a swamp of horrors to reclaim this enchanted trumpet? And now the First Wizard claimed it carried no real power at all?

"Magic is not the only power in this world," the old mage said gently, handing the horn back to its royal owner. "Griffo made an instrument so perfect that even the dead must rise to hear its call. He made it with his hands, without spells or dragon-songs. I wish that I could do the same."

I don't know what that means—but I think it means something.

From there, the plot is familiar: while Fernwen and Telemach slumber (at last) in richly furnished chambers, the First Wizard steals the horn. Then he lights a red lantern and sends it dancing aloft, a signal to the Wyrm Queen's dark marauders in the Pinake Forest. They are busy there among the trees—hunting down old elf graves, digging up bones, grinding them to dust—but they know what that signal means. They descend on the citadel, and when Telemach Half-Blood startles awake in his chamber, he is surrounded by tall shadows. They howl and strike.

And that's where the second book ends.

"It was amazing," Kat says. We're sharing a gluten-free waffle in the Gourmet Grotto and she's telling me about the inaugural gathering of the new Product Management. She's wearing a cream-colored blouse with a daggerlike collar; underneath, her T-shirt winks red at her throat.

"Totally amazing," she continues. "Best meeting ever. Completely . . . structured. You know exactly what's happening all the time. Everybody brings a laptop—"

"Do people even look at one another?"

"Not really. Everything that matters is on your screen. There's an agenda that rearranges itself. There's a back-channel chat. And there's fact-checking! If you get up to speak, there are people cross-referencing your claims, supporting and refuting you—"

It sounds like an engineer's Athens.

"—and the meeting is really long, like six hours, but it feels like no time, because you're thinking so hard. You get totally wrung out. There's so much information to absorb and it comes so fast. And they—we—make decisions really fast, too.

After somebody calls for a vote, it happens live, and you have to cast yours right away, or delegate it to someone else . . ."

Now it sounds more like a reality show. This waffle is terrible.

"There's an engineer named Alex, he's a big deal, he built most of Google Maps, and I think he likes me—he delegated his vote to me once already, which is pretty crazy, I'm brand-new—"

I think I'd like to delegate my fist to Alex's face.

"—and there are tons of designers, more designers than usual. Somebody said they tweaked the selection algorithm. I think maybe that's why I got in, because I'm a designer and a programmer. It's an optimal combination. Anyway." She finally takes a breath. "I made a presentation. Which, I guess, you're not really supposed to do at your first PM. But I asked Raj and he said it might be okay. Maybe even a good idea. Make an impression. Whatever." Another breath. "I told them about Manutius."

She did it.

"How it's this amazing ancient book, totally a historical treasure, totally old knowledge, OK—"

She actually did it.

"—and then I explained how there's this nonprofit that's trying to break the code—"

"Nonprofit?"

"It sounds better than, like, secret society. Anyway, I said they're trying to break the code, and of course people perked up at that, because everybody at Google likes codes—"

Books: boring. Codes: awesome. These are the people who are running the internet.

"—and I said, maybe we should spend some time on this, because it could be the start of a whole new thing, like some sort of public service code-breaking thing—"

This is a girl who knows her audience.

"—and everybody thought that sounded like a great idea. We voted on it."

Amazing. No more sneaking around. Thanks to Kat, we now have Google's official backing. It's surreal. I wonder when the code-breaking will commence.

"Well, I'm supposed to organize it." She ticks through the tasks on her fingers: "I'll round up some volunteers. Then we'll get the systems configured, and make sure the text all looks okay—Jad can help with that. We need to talk to Mr. Penumbra, for sure. Maybe he can come to Mountain View? Anyway. I think we can be ready in, like . . . two weeks. Say, two weeks from today." She nods sharply.

A fellowship of secret scholars spent five hundred years on this task. Now we're penciling it in for a Friday morning.

# THE ULTIMATE OK

PENUMBRA AGREES to keep the bookstore open until the bank account runs dry, so I go back to work, and I go back with a mission. I order a book distributor's catalog. I run another Google ad campaign, a bigger one. I email the organizer of San Francisco's big literary festival, which runs for a whole week and draws free-spending readers from as far away as Fresno. It's a long shot, but I think we can do it. I think we can get some real customers. Maybe we don't need the Festina Lente Company. Maybe we can turn this place into a real business.

Twenty-four hours after the start of the ad campaign, eleven lonely souls have wandered in, which is pretty exciting, because before, there was only one lonely soul—me. These new customers nod when I ask about the ads, and then four of them actually buy something. Three of those four pick up a copy of the new Murakami, which I've set up in a neat little stack next to a card that explains how awesome it is. The card is signed *Mr. Penumbra* in a simulation of his spidery script because I think that's probably what people want to see.

Past midnight, I spot North Face from Booty's out on the sidewalk, walking with her head down, headed for the bus stop. I run to the front door.

"Albert Einstein!" I shout, leaning out into the sidewalk.

"What?" she says. "My name is Daphne—"

"We've got the Einstein biography," I say, "by Isaacson. The guy who did Steve Jobs. Still want it?"

She smiles and turns on her heels—which are very high—and that makes five books for the night, a new record.

There are new books coming in every day. When I arrive to start my shift, Oliver shows me the boxes in a pile, his eyes wide and slightly suspicious. He's been a bit unsettled ever since I returned and told him everything I'd learned in New York.

"I thought there was something strange going on," he said quietly, "but I always figured it was drugs."

"Holy shit, Oliver! What?"

"Well, yeah," he said. "I thought maybe some of those books were full of cocaine."

"And you never bothered to mention this?"

"It was just a theory."

Oliver thinks I am being too liberal with our dwindling funds: "Don't you think we should try to make the money last as long as we can?"

"Spoken like a true preservationist," I cluck. "Money isn't like terra-cotta. We can make more of it if we try. We have to try."

So now we've got teenage wizards. We've got vampire police. We've got a journalist's memoir, a designer's manifesto, a celebrity chef's graphic novel. In a nostalgic gesture—maybe a slightly defiant one, too—we've got the new edition of *The Dragon-Song Chronicles*, all three volumes. I also ordered the old audiobook edition for Neel. He doesn't really read books anymore, but maybe he can listen while he lifts weights.

I try to get Penumbra excited about all of this—our nightly receipts are still just double digits, but that's a whole digit more than we used to have—but he's preoccupied with the Great Decoding. One cold Tuesday morning, he strolls into the store with a cup of coffee in one hand and his mystery e-reader in the other, and I show him what I've added to the shelves:

"Stephenson, Murakami, the latest Gibson, *The Information*, *House of Leaves*, fresh editions of Moffat"—I point them out as I go. Each one has a little shelf talker, and they're all signed *Mr. Penumbra*. I was worried he might feel protective of his imprimatur, but he doesn't even notice.

"Very good, my boy," he says with a nod, still looking down at the e-reader. He doesn't have any idea what I just said. His shelves are getting away from him. He nods and makes a quick swipe across the e-reader's screen, then looks up. "There will be a meeting later today," he says. "The Googlers are visiting the store"—he makes it three syllables, *Goo-gull-urz*—"to meet us and discuss our techniques." He pauses. "I believe you should attend as well."

So that afternoon, just after lunchtime, there is a great convening of the old guard and the new at Mr. Penumbra's 24-Hour Bookstore. The most senior of Penumbra's students are present: white-bearded Fedorov and a woman named Muriel with short-cropped silver hair. I've never seen her before; she must visit during the day. Fedorov and Muriel are following their teacher. They're going rogue.

There's a contingent from Google, selected and sent over by Kat. They are Prakesh and Amy, both even younger than me, and Jad from the book scanner. He looks up and down the short shelves admiringly. Maybe I can sell him something later.

Neel is at a Google developer conference downtown—he wants to meet more of Kat's colleagues and sow the seeds of an Anatomix acquisition—but he sent Igor, who is brand-new to these proceedings but seems to grasp everything instantly. Actually, he might be the smartest person in the store.

All together, young and old, we stand around the front desk with volumes from the Waybacklist opened wide for inspection. It's a crash course on the centuries-old work of the Unbroken Spine.

"Dese are books," Fedorov says, "not simply strings of letters." He traces his fingers across the page. "So ve must celculate not only letter-vise, but also page-vise. Some of de most cemplicated encryption schemes rely on dis page-vise cemposition."

The Googlers nod and take notes on their laptops. Amy has her iPad set up with a little keyboard.

The bell above the door tinkles, and a rangy man with black-rimmed glasses and a long ponytail comes hustling into the store. "Sorry I'm late," he heaves, out of breath.

"Hello, Greg," says Penumbra.

"Hey, Greg," says Prakesh at the same time.

They look at each other, then across to Greg.

"Yep," Greg says. "This is weird."

It turns out that Greg—the source of Penumbra's mystery e-reader!—is both a hardware engineer at Google and a novice in the San Francisco chapter of the Unbroken Spine. It also turns out that he is invaluable. He translates between Penumbra's bookstore crew and the Googlers, explaining parallel processing to one group and folio sizes to the other.

Jad from the book scanner is also crucial, because he's actually done this before. "There will be OCR errors," he explains. "For instance, a lowercase *f* will come through as an *s*." He types them on his laptop so we can see them side by side. "Lowercase *rn* looks like *m*. Sometimes *A* becomes *4*, and there's so much stuff like that. We'll have to compensate for all those possible errors."

Fedorov nods and interjects, "End for de optical eigenvectors of de text, as vell."

The Googlers stare blankly at him.

"Ve must also cempensate for de optical eigenvectors," he repeats, as if stating the obvious.

The Googlers look across to Greg. He's staring blankly, too.

Igor raises a skinny hand and says neatly, "I tink ve could make a tree-dimensional metrix of ink-saturation values?"

Fedorov's white beard splits into a grin.

I'm not sure what will happen when Google cracks MANVTIVS. Of course, there are things that I know will *not* happen: Penumbra's passed-away brothers and sisters will not rise. They will not reappear. They will not even make spectral blue cameos, Jedi-style. Real life is not like *The Dragon-Song Chronicles*.

But it might still be big news. I mean, a secret book from the first great publisher, digitized, decoded, and made public? *The New York Times* might blog about that.

We decide we ought to invite the whole San

Francisco fellowship down to Mountain View to watch it happen. Penumbra gives me the task of telling the members I know best.

I begin with Rosemary Lapin. I take the steep hike up to her hillside hobbit-hole and knock three times on her door. It opens just a crack, and a single wide Lapin-eye blinks out at me.

"Oh!" she squeaks, and opens the door the rest of the way. "It's you! Did you—that is, have you—that is—what happened?"

She brings me in, opening windows and waving her hands in the air to clear away the smell of pot, and I tell her the tale over tea. Her eyes are wide, devouring; I can sense she wants to go immediately to the Reading Room and don one of those black robes. I tell her she might not have to. I tell her the Unbroken Spine's great secret might be unlocked in just a few days.

Her face is blank. "Well, that's something," she says finally.

Honestly, I expected a little more excitement.

I tell Tyndall, and his reaction is better than Lapin's, but I'm not sure if he's excited about the pending revelation or if this is just how he responds to everything. Maybe if I told him that Starbucks was introducing a new latte that smelled like books he'd say the same thing:

"Fabulous! Euphoric! Essential!" His hands are up on his head, working their way into tangles of curly gray. He's walking around his apartment—a tiny one-room studio out near the ocean, where you can hear the foghorns murmuring to one another—going in quick circles, his elbows brushing the walls and knocking framed photos into odd angles. One of them clatters to the floor, and I reach down to pick it up.

It shows a cable car at a crazy angle, completely packed with passengers, and up at the front, in a neat blue uniform, it's Tyndall himself: younger and skinnier, with hair that's black instead of gray. He's wearing a broad grin, hanging half-out of the car, waving at the camera with his free arm. Tyndall the cable car conductor; yes, I can see it. He must have been—

"Magnificent!" He's still orbiting. "Unspeakable! When? Where?"

"Friday morning, Mr. Tyndall," I tell him. Friday morning, at the bright glowing center of the internet.

I don't see Kat for almost two weeks. She's busy organizing everything for the Great Decoding, and busy with other Google projects, too. The Product Management is an all-you-can-eat buffet, and she's hungry. She hasn't replied to any of my flirty emails, and when she texts me, her messages are two words long.

Finally, we meet on Thursday night for a desultory date over sushi. It's cold, and she's wearing a heavy houndstooth blazer over a thin gray sweater and a shiny blouse. There's no sign of her red T-shirt anymore.

Kat gushes about Google's projects, all revealed to her now. They are making a 3-D web browser. They are making a car that drives itself. They are making a sushi search engine—here she pokes a chopstick down at our dinner—to help people find fish that is sustainable and mercury-free. They are building a time machine. They are developing a form of renewable energy that runs on hubris.

With each new mega-project she describes, I feel myself shrink smaller and smaller. How can you stay interested in anything—or anyone—for long when the whole world is your canvas?

"But what I'm really interested in," Kat says, "is Google Forever." Right: life extension. She nods. "They need more resources. I'm going to be their ally on the PM—really try to make their case. It might be the most important work we can do, in the long run."

"I don't know, the car sounds pretty awesome—"

"Maybe we'll give them something to work with tomorrow," Kat continues. "What if we find something crazy in this book? Like, a DNA sequence? Or the formula for some new drug?" Her eyes are shining. I have to hand it to her: she has a real imagination for immortality.

"You're giving a medieval publisher a lot of credit," I say.

"They figured out the circumference of the earth

a thousand years before they invented printing," she sniffs. Then she pokes a chopstick at me: "Could *you* figure out the circumference of the earth?"

"Well—no." I pause for a moment. "Wait, could you?"

She nods. "Yeah, it's actually pretty easy. The point is, they knew their stuff back then. And there's stuff they knew that we still haven't rediscovered. OK and TK, remember? Old knowledge. This might be the ultimate OK."

After dinner, Kat won't come back to the apartment with me. She says she has email to read, prototypes to review, wiki pages to edit. Did I really just lose out to a wiki on a Thursday night?

I walk alone in the darkness and wonder how a person would begin to determine the circumference of the earth. I have no idea. I'd probably just google it.

# THE CALL

I T IS THE NIGHT before the morning on which Kat Potente has scheduled an all-out assault on the centuries-old *codex vitae* of Aldus Manutius. Her Googler platoon is assembled. Penumbra's posse is invited. It's exciting—I have to admit, it's really exciting—but it's also unnerving, because I have no idea what's next for Mr. Penumbra's 24-Hour Bookstore. The man himself hasn't said a word, but I feel like Penumbra might be winding this place down. Because, I mean, sure: Who needs the burden of an old bookstore when eternal life is imminent?

We'll see what tomorrow holds. It's going to be a good show, whatever happens. Maybe afterward he'll be ready to talk about the future. I still want to buy a billboard on that bus shelter.

It's a quiet night, with only two customers so far. I browse the shelves, straightening my new acquisitions. I promote *The Dragon-Song Chronicles* to a higher shelf, then idly flip the first volume over in my hands. The back cover bears a small black-and-white portrait of Clark Moffat in his thirties. He has shaggy blond hair and a bushy beard, and he's wearing a plain white T-shirt, grinning a toothy grin. Below the portrait, it says:

Clark Moffat (1952–1999) was a writer who lived in Bolinas, California. He is best known for the bestselling *The Dragon-Song Chronicles*, as well as *Further Tales of Fernwen*, a book for children. He graduated from the United States Naval Academy and served as a communications specialist aboard the nuclear submarine U.S.S. *West Virginia.*

Something occurs to me. It's something I've never done before—something I've never thought to do, not in all the time I've worked here. I'm going to search for someone in the logbooks.

It's logbook VII I want, the one I smuggled down to Google, because it runs through the mid-eighties and early nineties. I find the raw text on my laptop and command-F a particular description: someone with shaggy blond hair and a beard.

It takes a while, trying different keywords, skimming through false positives. (There are a lot of beards in here, it turns out.) I'm looking at OCR'd text, not handwriting, so I can't tell who wrote what here, but I know some of these must be Edgar Deckle's notes. It would be nice if he was the one who—There.

Member number 6HV8SQ:

The novice takes possession of KINGSLAKE with thanks and good cheer. Wears a white T-shirt celebrating the bicentennial. Levi 501 jeans and heavy work boots. Voice rough with smoke; package of cigarettes, approximately half-empty, visible in pocket. Pale blond hair is longer than has ever been recorded by this clerk. Upon remark, the novice explains: "I want it wizard-length." Monday the 23rd of September, 1:19 in the morning. Clear skies and the smell of the ocean.

That's Clark Moffat. It's got to be. The note is after midnight, which means the late shift, which means "this clerk" is indeed Edgar Deckle. There's another one:

The novice is moving quickly through the Founder's Puzzle. But even more than his speed, it is his confidence that is striking. There is none of the hesitation or frustration that has characterized other novices (this clerk included). It is as if he is playing a familiar song or dancing a familiar dance. Blue T-shirt, Levi 501s, work boots. Hair is longer still. Receives BRITO. Friday the 11th of October, 2:31 in the morning. A foghorn sounds.

It goes on. The notes are concise but the message is clear: Clark Moffat was a savant of the Unbroken Spine. Is it possible . . . was he the dark moss constellation in the visualization? Was he the one who raced around the Founder's whole face in the time it took other novices to trace out an eyelash or an earlobe? There's probably some way to link specific notes to the visualization and—

The bell tinkles and I jerk my head up out of the endless scrolling text. It's late, and I expect to see a member of the fellowship, but instead it's Mat Mittelbrand, hauling a black plastic case. It's huge, bigger than he is, and it's stuck in the doorway.

"What are you doing here?" I ask, helping to pry it loose. The case's surface is tough and knobby and it has heavy metal buckles.

"I'm here on a mission," Mat says, breathing hard. "This is your last night, right?"

I've been complaining to him about Penumbra's neglect. "Maybe," I say. "Probably. What's all this?"

He tips his case over on the floor, flips the buckles (they make a serious-sounding *snap snap*), and opens it wide. Inside, cushioned in a bed of gray foam, there's photography gear: crystalline lights with sturdy wire shields, thick collapsible aluminum stalks, and wide coils of bright orange cable.

"We're going to document this place," Mat says. He sets his hands on his hips and peers appreciatively around. "It must be recorded."

"So, what, like—a photo shoot?"

Mat shakes his head. "No, that would be selective recording. I hate selective recording.

We're going to take a picture of every surface, from every angle, under bright, even light." He pauses. "So we can re-create it."

My mouth hangs open.

He continues, "I've done photo recon on castles and mansions. This store is tiny. It'll only take three or four thousand shots."

Mat's intention is completely over-the-top, obsessive, and maybe impossible. In other words: it's perfect for this place.

"So, where's the camera?" I ask.

On cue, the bell over the front door tinkles again, and Neel Shah comes barreling through with a monstrous Nikon hanging from his neck and a bottle of bright green kale juice in either hand. "Got some refreshments," he says, holding them aloft.

"You two are going to be my assistants," Mat says. He taps the black plastic case with his toe. "Start setting up."

The bookstore is bursting with heat and light. Mat's lamps are daisy-chained together, all plugged into the one power outlet behind the front desk. I'm pretty sure it's going to blow a fuse, or maybe a whole street-level transformer. Booty's neon sign might be at risk tonight.

Mat is up on one of Penumbra's ladders. He's using it as a makeshift dolly, with Neel pushing him slowly across the span of the store. Mat holds the Nikon steady in front of his face and fires off a shot for each of Neel's long, even strides. The camera triggers the lights, which are set up in all the corners and behind the front desk, and they all go *pop pop* with every shot.

"You know," Neel says, "we could use these shots to make a 3-D model." He looks over at me. "I mean, another one. Yours was good."

"No, I get it," I say. I'm at the front desk, making a checklist of all the details we need to capture: the tall letters on the windows and their rough, crenelated edges, worn away by time. The bell and its clapper and the curling iron bracket that holds it in place. "Mine looked like Galaga."

"We can make it interactive," Neel says. "First-person view, totally photorealistic and explorable. You could choose the time of day. We can make the shelves cast shadows."

"No," Mat groans from the ladder. "Those 3-D models suck. I want to make a miniature store with miniature books."

"And a miniature Clay?" Neel asks.

"Sure, maybe a little LEGO dude," Mat says. He hauls himself up higher on the ladder and Neel starts pushing him back across the store. The lights go *pop pop,* leaving red spots in my eyes. Neel is ticking off the advantages of 3-D models as he pushes the ladder: they're more detailed, more immersive, you can make infinite copies. Mat is groaning. *Pop pop.*

In all the bright noise, I almost miss the ring.

It's just a tickle in my ear, but yes: somewhere in the bookstore, a phone is ringing. I cut through the shelves parallel to the photo shoot, with the lights still going *pop pop,* and emerge into the tiny break room. The sound is coming from Penumbra's study. I push through the door marked PRIVATE and hop up the steps.

The *pop pop* of the lights is softer up here, and the *ring ring* from the phone (next to the old modem) is loud and insistent, produced by some powerful old-fashioned mechanical noisemaker. It keeps ringing, and it occurs to me that my usual strategy for strange phone calls—wait them out—might not work here.

*Ring ring.*

These days, the phone only carries bad news. It's all "your student loan is past due" and "your uncle Chris is in the hospital." If it's anything fun or exciting, like an invitation to a party or a secret project in the works, it will come through the internet.

*Ring ring.*

Okay, well, maybe it's an inquisitive neighbor calling to ask what the commotion is all about—all the flashing lights. Maybe it's North Face over at Booty's checking to make sure everything's okay. That's sweet. I pick up the phone and announce, with relish: "Mr. Penumbra's 24-Hour Bookstore."

"You must stop him," a voice says, without introduction or preamble.

"Um, I think you have the wrong number." It's not North Face.

"I definitely do not have the wrong number. I know you. You're the boy—you're the clerk."

I recognize the voice now. The quiet power. The crisp syllables. It's Corvina.

"What's your name?" he says.

"I'm Clay." But then: "You probably want to talk to Penumbra directly. You should call back in the morning . . ."

"No," Corvina says matter-of-factly. "Penumbra's not the one who stole our most precious treasure." He knows. Of course he knows. How? Another one of his crows, I suppose. Word must have gotten out here in San Francisco.

"Well, it's really not technically stealing, I don't think," I say, looking down at my shoes as if he's here in the room with me, "because, I mean, it's probably in the public domain . . ." I trail off. This is not going to get me anywhere.

"Clay," Corvina says, smooth and dark, "you must stop him."

"I'm sorry, but I just don't believe in your . . . religion," I say. I would probably not be able to say this to his face. I'm clutching the black curve of the phone tight to my cheek. "So I don't think it matters if we scan an old book. Or if we don't. I don't think it's, like, of any cosmic importance whatsoever. I'm just helping my boss—my friend."

"You're doing exactly the opposite," Corvina says quietly.

I don't have any response to that.

"I know you don't believe what we believe," he says. "Of course you don't. But you don't need faith to realize that Ajax Penumbra is on the razor's edge." He pauses to let that sink in. "I've known him longer than you have, Clay—far longer. So let me tell you about him. He's always been a dreamer, a great optimist. I understand why you're drawn to him. All of you in California—I used to live there. I know what it's like."

Right. The young man in front of the Golden Gate Bridge. He's smiling at me across the room, giving me a big thumbs-up.

"You probably think I'm just the cold New York CEO. You probably think I'm too severe. But, Clay—sometimes discipline is the truest form of kindness."

He's using my first name a lot. Mostly it's salesmen who do that.

"My friend Ajax Penumbra has tried many things in his life—many schemes—and they have always been so elaborate. He has always been just on the cusp of a breakthrough—in his own mind, at least. I've known him for fifty years, Clay— fifty years! And in that time, do you know how many of his schemes have succeeded?"

I don't like where—

"None. Zero. He has maintained that store where you're standing—barely—and accomplished absolutely nothing else of note. And this, the last and greatest of his schemes—it will not succeed, either. You just said so yourself. It is foolishness, and it will fail, and what then? I worry about him, Clay, truly—as his oldest friend."

I know he's using a Jedi mind trick on me right now. But it's a really good Jedi mind trick.

"Okay," I say, "I get it. I know Penumbra's a little weird. Obviously. What am I supposed to do?"

"You must do what I can't. I would delete the copy you stole. I would delete every copy. But I'm too far away, so you must help me, and you must help our friend."

Now it sounds like he's standing right beside me:

"You must stop Penumbra, or this final failure will destroy him."

The phone is back in its cradle, even though I am not totally conscious of having hung up. The store is quiet; there's no more *pop pop* from the front. I cast my eyes slowly around Penumbra's study, at the wreckage of decades of digital dreams, and Corvina's warning starts to make sense. I think of the look on Penumbra's face as he was explaining his scheme to us in New York, and it makes even more sense. I look across at the photo again. Suddenly it's not Corvina who's the wayward friend—it's Penumbra.

Neel appears at the top of the stairs.

"Mat needs your help," he says. "You have to hold a light or something."

"Okay, sure." I take a sharp breath, push Corvina's voice out of my head, and follow Neel back down into the store. We've raised a lot of dust, and now the lamps are making bright shapes in the air, punching through spaces in the shelves, catching feathery motes—microscopic scraps of paper, bits of Penumbra's skin, of mine—and making them shine.

"Mat's pretty good at this, huh?" I say, peering around at the otherworldly effect.

Neel nods. "He's amazing."

Mat hands me a giant sheet of glossy white poster board and tells me to hold it steady. He's capturing the front desk up close, getting deep into the grain. The poster board is reflecting so subtly that I cannot detect its effect on the wood, but I assume it is making a crucial contribution to the brightness and evenness of the light.

Mat starts shooting again, and the big lights are just calmly beaming now, so I can hear the camera go *click click*. Neel is standing behind Mat, holding a light with one hand, slurping his second kale juice with the other.

As I stand holding the poster board, I think:

Corvina doesn't really care about Penumbra. This is about control, and he's trying to turn me into his instrument. I'm grateful for the geographical distance between us; I'd hate to experience that voice in person. Or maybe he wouldn't bother with persuasion in person. Maybe he'd show up with a gang of black-robes. But he can't, because we're in California; the continent is our shield. Corvina caught on too late, so his voice is all he's got.

Mat pushes in even closer, apparently going for molecular detail on the front desk, the place where I've spent so much of my life recently. I'm presented, for a moment, with a nicely framed portrait: compact curled-up Mat, sweating, holding his camera up to his eye, and big broad Neel, smiling, holding the light steady, slurping his kale juice. My friends, making something together. This requires faith, too. I can't tell what this poster board is doing, but I trust Mat. I know it's going to be beautiful.

Corvina's got it wrong. Penumbra's schemes didn't fail because he's a hopeless crackpot. If Corvina's right, it means nobody should ever try anything new and risky. Maybe Penumbra's schemes failed because he didn't have enough help. Maybe he didn't have a Mat or a Neel, an Ashley or a Kat—until now.

Corvina said: *You must stop Penumbra.*

No, just the opposite. We're going to help him.

Dawn comes, and when it does, I know not to expect Penumbra. He is headed not to the store that bears his name, but to Google. In just about two hours, the project that Penumbra and his brothers and sisters have toiled over for decades, for centuries, is coming to fruition. He's probably eating a celebratory bagel somewhere.

Here in the store, Mat packs the lights back into their gray foam sarcophagus. Neel takes the bent-up white poster board out to the trash can. I coil up the orange cables and straighten the front desk. Everything looks the same; nothing has moved. And yet, something is different. We took photos of every surface: the shelves, the desk, the door, the floor. We took photos of the books, all of them, the ones in the front and the Waybacklist, too. We didn't capture the pages inside, of course—that would be a project of a different scale. If you're ever playing Super Bookstore Brothers, navigating a 3-D simulacrum of Penumbra's bookstore with pink-yellow light coming in the front windows and a foggy particle effect rising in the back, and you decide you want to actually read one of the beautifully textured books: too bad. Neel's model might match the store's volume but never its density.

"Breakfast?" Neel asks.

"Breakfast!" Mat agrees.

So we leave. That's it. I turn off the lights and

pull the door tight behind me. The bell makes its bright tinkle. I never did get a key.

"Let me see the photos," Neel says, grabbing at Mat's camera.

"Not yet, not yet," Mat says, tucking it under his arm. "I need to grade them. This is just raw material."

"Grade them? Like A-B-C?"

"Color grading—color correction. Translation: I need to make them look awesome." He raises an eyebrow. "I thought you worked with movie studios, Shah."

"He told you?" Neel spins to look at me with wide eyes: "You told him? There are *documents!*"

"You should stop by ILM next week," Mat says calmly. "I'll show you some stuff."

They're both far up the sidewalk now, halfway to Neel's car, but I'm still standing at the wide front windows with their big gold type: MR. PENUMBRA'S in beautiful Gerritszoon. It's dark inside. I press my hand onto the fellowship's symbol—two hands, open like a book—and when I take it away, there's an oily, five-fingered print left behind.

# A REALLY BIG GUN

I T'S FINALLY TIME to break a code that has waited five hundred years.

Kat has requisitioned Google's data visualization amphitheater with its massive screens. She's moved tables from the lunch tent into position down in front; it looks like mission control, picnic-style.

The day is beautiful; a sharp blue sky is dotted with wispy white clouds, all commas and curlicues. Hummingbirds hover down to investigate the screens, then zip back out across the bright open lawns. There's music in the distance; the Google brass band is practicing an algorithmically generated waltz.

Down below, Kat's handpicked code-breaking squad is setting up. Laptops are coming out, each one encrusted with a different collection of colorful stickers and holograms, and the Googlers are plugging into power and fiber optics, flexing their fingers.

Igor is among them. His brilliance at the bookstore earned him a special invitation: today, he's allowed to play in the Big Box. He's leaning in to his laptop, his skinny hands a bluish blur, and two Googlers are watching wide-eyed over his shoulder.

Kat is making the rounds, conferring with

Googlers one by one. She smiles and nods and pats them on the back. Today, she's a general, and these are her troops.

Tyndall, Lapin, Imbert, and Fedorov are all here, along with the rest of the local novices. They're sitting up on the lip of the amphitheater, all in a row along the highest stone step. More are arriving. Silver-haired Muriel is here, and so is Greg the ponytailed Googler. He's standing with the fellowship today.

Most of the fellowship's members are in late middle age. Some, like Lapin, look pretty old, and a few are older still. There's an ancient man in a wheelchair, eyes lost in shadowed sockets, his cheeks pale and wrinkled like tissue paper, pushed by a young attendant in a neat suit. The man croaks a faint greeting to Fedorov, who clasps him by the hand.

Finally, there's Penumbra. He's holding court at the amphitheater's edge, explaining what's about to happen. He's smiling and waving his arms, pointing down at the Googlers at their tables, pointing over to Kat, over to me.

I haven't told him about the call from Corvina, and I don't plan to. The First Reader doesn't matter anymore. What matters are the people here in this amphitheater and the puzzle up on those screens.

"Come over here, my boy, come over here," he

says. "Meet Muriel properly." I smile and shake her hand. She's beautiful. Her hair is silver, almost white, but her skin is smooth, with just the lightest lace of microwrinkles around her eyes.

"Muriel runs a goat farm," Penumbra says. "You should take your, ah, friend, you know"—he tilts his head down toward Kat—"you should take her down. The tour is wonderful."

Muriel smiles lightly. "The spring is the best time," she says. "That's when we have baby goats." To Penumbra she says, mock-scoldingly, "You're a good ambassador, Ajax, but I wish I could get you down there more often." She winks at him.

"Oh, the store has kept me busy," he says, "but now, after this?" He waves his hands and opens his face wide with a little who-knows-what-could-happen frown. "After this, anything is possible."

Wait a second—is there something going on there? There couldn't be anything going on there.

There might be something going on there.

"Okay, quiet down, everybody. Quiet down!" Kat shouts from the front of the amphitheater. She looks up to address the crowd of scholars gathered on the stone steps: "So, I'm Kat Potente, the PM for this project. I'm glad you're all here, but there are a few things you should know. First, you can use the Wi-Fi, but the fiber optics are for Google employees only."

I glance across the assembled mass of the fellowship. Tyndall has a pocket watch connected to his pants with a long chain, and he's checking the time. I don't think this is going to be a problem.

Kat glances down at a printed-out checklist. "Second, don't blog, tweet, or live-stream anything you see here."

Imbert is adjusting an astrolabe. Seriously: not a problem.

"And third"—she grins—"this isn't going to take long, so don't get too comfortable."

Now she shifts to address her troops: "We don't know what kind of code we're dealing with yet," she says. "We need to figure that out first. So we'll be working in parallel. We've got two hundred virtual machines ready and waiting in the Big Box, and your code will run in the right place automatically if you just tag it CODEX. Everybody ready?"

The Googlers all nod. One girl straps on a pair of dark goggles.

"Hit it."

The screens leap to life, a blitzkrieg of data visualization and exploration. The text of MANVTIVS blinks bright and jagged, set in the squared-off letters favored by code and console. This isn't a book anymore; it's a data dump. Scatter plots and bar charts unfurl across the screens. At Kat's command, Google's machines crunch and recrunch the data nine hundred different ways. Nine thousand. Nothing yet.

The Googlers are looking for a message—any message—in the text. It might be a whole book, it might be a few sentences, it might be a single word. Nobody, not even the Unbroken Spine, knows what's waiting there, or how Manutius encrypted it, and that makes this a very hard problem. Luckily, the Googlers love very hard problems.

Now they get more creative. They make crosses and spirals and galaxies of color dance across the screens. The graphs grow new dimensions—first they become cubes and pyramids and blobs, then they sprout long tentacles. My eyes swim as I try to follow along. A Latin lexicon flashes across one screen—an entire language examined in milliseconds. There are n-gram graphs and Vonnegut diagrams. Maps appear, with letter sequences somehow translated into longitudes and latitudes and plotted across the world, a dusting of dots through Siberia and the South Pacific.

Nothing.

The screens flicker and flash as Googlers try every angle. The fellowship is murmuring. Some are still smiling; others are starting to frown. When a giant chessboard appears on one screen with a pile of letters on every square, Fedorov sniffs and mutters, "Ve tried det in 1627."

Is that why Corvina believes this project won't

succeed—because the Unbroken Spine has literally tried it all? Or is it simply because this is cheating—because old Manutius never had any bright screens or virtual machines? If you follow them, those two lines of reasoning close together like a trap, and they lead you straight down to the Reading Room, with its chalk and its chains, and nowhere else. I still don't believe the secret to immortality is going to pop up on one of those screens, but jeez, I want Corvina to be wrong. I want Google to crack this code.

"Okay," Kat announces, "we just got another eight hundred machines." Her voice rises and carries across the lawn: "Go deeper. More iterations. Don't hold back." She walks from table to table, consulting and encouraging. She's a good leader—I can see it in the Googlers' faces. I think Kat Potente has found her calling.

I watch Igor bang his head against the text. First he translates each line of letters into a molecule and simulates a chemical reaction; on-screen, the solution dissolves into a gray sludge. Then he makes letters into tiny 3-D people and sets them up in a simulated city. They wander around bumping into buildings and forming crowded clumps in the street until Igor destroys it all with an earthquake. Nothing. No message.

Kat hikes up the steps, squinting into the sun, shading her eyes with her hand. "This code is tough," she admits. "Like, crazy tough."

Tyndall sprints around the amphitheater's edge and leaps over Lapin, who squeaks and shields herself. He grabs Kat's arm. "You must compensate for the phase of the moon at the time of writing! The lunar offset is essential!"

I reach over and detach his shivering claw from her sleeve. "Mr. Tyndall, don't worry," I say. I've already watched a line of half-eaten moons parade across the screens. "They know your techniques." And Google is nothing if not thorough.

While the screens flash and blur down below, a team of Googlers wanders through the fellowship—young people with clipboards and friendly faces, asking questions like: When were you born? Where do you live? What's your cholesterol?

I wonder who they are.

"They're from Google Forever," Kat says, a bit sheepishly. "Interns. I mean, it's a good opportunity. Some of these people are so old and still so healthy."

Lapin is describing her work at Pacific Bell to a Googler holding a skinny video camera. Tyndall is spitting into a plastic vial.

One of the interns approaches Penumbra, but he waves her away without a word. His gaze is fixed on the screens below. He's utterly absorbed, his blue eyes wide and shining like the sky above. Unbidden, Corvina's warning echoes in my head: *And this, the last and greatest of his schemes—it will not succeed, either.*

But it's not just Penumbra's scheme anymore. This has gotten much bigger than that. Look at all these people—look at Kat. She's back up at the front of the amphitheater, typing furiously into her phone. She pushes it back into her pocket and squares to face her team.

"Hold up a second," she shouts, waving her arms in the air. "Hold it!" The code-breaking roulette slowly spins to a halt. On one screen, the letters of MANVTIVS are twisting in space, all rotating at different speeds. On another, some sort of super-complicated knot is trying to untie itself.

"The PM is doing us a big favor," Kat announces. "Whatever you've got running, tag it CRITICAL. We're going to farm that code out to the whole system in about ten seconds."

Wait—the whole system? As in, the *whole* system? The Big Box?

Kat is grinning. She's an artillery officer who's just gotten her hands on a really big gun. Now she looks up at her audience—the fellowship. She cups her hands around her mouth: "That was just the warm-up!"

There's a countdown splashed across the screens. Giant rainbow numbers go 5 (red), 4 (green), 3 (blue), 2 (yellow) . . .

And then, on a sunny Friday morning, for three seconds, you can't search for anything. You can't check your email. You can't watch any videos. You can't get directions. For just three seconds, nothing works, because every single one of Google's computers around the world is dedicated to this task.

Make that a really, *really* big gun.

The screens go blank, pure white. There's nothing to show because too much is happening now, more than you could ever display on a bank of four screens, or forty, or four thousand. Every transformation that can be applied to this text is being applied. Every possible error is being accounted for, every optical eigenvalue is being inveigled. Every question you can ask a sequence of letters is being asked.

Three seconds later, the interrogation is complete. The amphitheater is quiet. The fellowship is holding its breath—except for the oldest, the man in the wheelchair, who's drawing a long, rattling wheeze in through his mouth. Penumbra's eyes are shining and expectant.

"Well? What have we got?" Kat says.

The screens are bright, and they hold the answer.

"Guys? What have we got?"

Silence from the Googlers. The screens are blank. The Big Box is empty. After all that: nothing. The amphitheater is silent. Across the lawn, one of the brass band's snare drums goes *rat-a-tat*.

I find Penumbra's face in the crowd. He looks utterly stricken, still staring down at the screens, waiting for something, anything, to appear. You can see the questions piling up on his face: *What does this mean? What did they do wrong? What did I do wrong?*

Down below, the Googlers are wearing sour expressions, whispering to one another. Igor is still bent over his keyboard, still trying things. Sparks of color flash and fizzle on his screen.

Kat comes slowly up the steps. She looks dejected and disheartened—worse than when she thought she'd been passed over for the PM. "Well, I guess they're wrong," she says, waving weakly at the fellowship. "There's no message here. It's just noise. We tried everything."

"Well, not *everything,* right—"

She looks up hotly. "Yes, everything. Clay: we just dialed in the equivalent of, like, a million years' worth of human effort. It came up empty." Her face is flushed—angry, or embarrassed, or both. "There's nothing here."

Nothing.

What are the possibilities here? Either this code is so subtle, so complex, that the most powerful computational force in the history of the world can't crack it—or there's nothing here at all, and the fellowship has been wasting its time, all five hundred years of it.

I try to find Penumbra's face again. I search the amphitheater, casting my eyes up and down the mass of the fellowship. There's Tyndall, whispering to himself; Fedorov, sitting in a pensive lump;

Rosemary Lapin, smiling faintly. And then I spot him: a tall stick figure wobbling across Google's green lawns, almost to the stand of trees on the other side, moving fast, not looking back.

*And this, the last and greatest of his schemes—it will not succeed, either.*

I start to jog after him, but I'm out of shape, and how is he so fast, anyway? I huff and puff across the lawn, toward the spot where I saw him last. When I get there, he's gone. Google's chaotic campus rises up all around me, rainbow arrows pointing every way at once, and here the walkways curve off in five different directions. He's gone.

*It is foolishness, and it will fail, and what then?*
Penumbra is gone.

# THE TOWER

# LITTLE BITS OF METAL

**M**ATROPOLIS HAS TAKEN OVER the living room. Mat and Ashley have hauled the couch away, and to navigate around the room you follow a narrow channel between the card tables: the winding Mittelriver, complete with two bridges. The commercial district has matured, and new towers push past the old airship dock, nearly touching the ceiling. I suspect Mat might build something up there, too. Soon Matropolis will annex the sky.

It's past midnight, and I can't sleep. I still haven't been able to reclaim my circadian rhythm, even though it's been a week since our late-night photo shoot. So now I am lying on the floor, drowning deep in the Mittelriver, dubbing *The Dragon-Song Chronicles*.

The audiobook edition I bought for Neel was produced in 1987 and the distributor's catalog did not specify that it still comes on cassette tapes. Cassette tapes! Or maybe it did specify that, and I just missed it in the excitement of the bulk order. In any case, I still want Neel to have the audiobooks, so I bought a black Sony Walkman for seven dollars on eBay and I am now playing the tapes into my laptop, rerecording them, shepherding them one by one into the great digital jukebox in the sky.

The only way to do this is in real time, so basically I have to sit and listen to the first two volumes in their entirety again. But that's not so bad, because the audiobooks are read by Clark Moffat himself. I've never heard him speak, and it's spooky, knowing what I know about him now. He has a good voice, gravelly but clear, and I can imagine it echoing in the bookstore. I can imagine the first time Moffat came through the door—the tinkle of the bell, the creak of the floorboards.

Penumbra would have asked: *What do you seek in these shelves?*

Moffat would have looked around, taken the measure of the place—noticed the shadowy reaches of the Waybacklist, certainly—and then he might have said: *Well, what would a wizard read?*

Penumbra would have smiled at that.

Penumbra.

He has vanished, and his bookstore stands derelict. I have no idea where to find him.

In a flash of genius, I checked the domain registration for penumbra.com, and sure enough: he owns it. It was purchased in the primordial era of the web by Ajax Penumbra and renewed in 2007 with an optimistic ten-year term . . . but the registration only lists the store's address on Broadway. Further googling yielded nothing. Penumbra casts only the faintest digital shadow.

In another, somewhat dimmer flash of genius, I tracked down silver-haired Muriel and her goat farm, just south of San Francisco in a foggy cluster of fields called Pescadero. She hadn't heard from him, either. "He's done this before," she said. "Gone away. But—he does usually call." Her smooth face made a little frown and the microwrinkles around her eyes darkened. When I left, she gave me a little palm-sized wheel of fresh goat cheese.

And so, in a final desperate flash, I opened the scanned pages of PENVMBRA. Google couldn't crack MANVTIVS, but these latter-day *codex vitae* were not so cunningly encrypted, and besides (I was fairly sure), there was actually something in this book to be decoded. I sent Kat an inquiring text message, and her response was short and definitive: *No.* Thirteen seconds later: *Absolutely not.* Seven more: *That project is done.*

Kat had been deeply disappointed when the Great Decoding failed. She had really believed there would be something profound waiting for us in that text; she had *wanted* there to be something profound. Now she was throwing herself into the PM and mostly ignoring me. Except, of course, to say *Absolutely not.*

But that was probably for the best. The two-page spreads on my laptop screen—heavy Gerritszoon glyphs lit harshly by the GrumbleGear camera flashes—still made me feel strange. Penumbra's expectation was that his *codex vitae* wouldn't be read until after he was gone. I decided I wouldn't crack open a man's book of life just to find his home address.

Finally, genius depleted, I checked with Tyndall and Lapin and Fedorov. None of them had heard from Penumbra, either. They were all preparing to move east, to take refuge with the Unbroken Spine in New York and join Corvina's chain gang there. If you ask me, it's futile: we took Manutius's *codex vitae* and bent it until it broke. At best, the fellowship is founded on a false hope, and at worst, it's founded on a lie. Tyndall and the rest haven't faced up to this, but at some point they'll have to.

If all of this seems grim: it is. And I feel terrible because, if you trace it back step-by-step, you cannot avoid the fact that all of it is my fault.

My mind is wandering. It's taken me many nights to get this far again, but Moffat is finally wrapping up *Volume II*. I've never listened to an audiobook before, and I have to say, it's a totally different experience. When you read a book, the story definitely happens inside your head. When you listen, it seems to happen in a little cloud all around it, like a fuzzy knit cap pulled down over your eyes:

*"The Golden Horn of Griffo is finely wrought,"* Zenodotus said, *tracing his finger along the curve of Telemach's treasure. "And the magic is in its*

*making alone. Do you understand? There is no sorcery here—none that I can detect."*

Moffat's Zenodotus voice is not what I expected. Instead of a rich, dramatic wizard's rumble, it's clipped and clinical. It's the voice of a corporate magic consultant.

*Fernwen's eyes widened at that. Hadn't they just braved a swamp of horrors to reclaim this enchanted trumpet? And now the First Wizard claimed it carried no real power at all?*

*"Magic is not the only power in this world," the old mage said gently, handing the horn back to its royal owner. "Griffo made an instrument so perfect that even the dead must rise to hear its call. He made it with his hands, without spells or dragon-songs. I wish that I could do the same."*

With Moffat reading, I can hear the sinister intent in the First Wizard's voice. It's so obvious what's coming:

*"Even Aldrag the Wyrm-Father would envy such a thing."*

Wait, what?

So far, every line out of Moffat's mouth has been pleasant repetition. His voice has been a needle bobbing comfortably through a deep groove in my brain. But that line—I have never read that line.

That line is new.

My finger twitches over the Walkman's pause button, but I don't want to mess up Neel's

315

recording. Instead, I pad quickly to my room and pull *Volume II* from the shelf. I flip to the end, and yes, I'm right: there's no mention of Aldrag the Wyrm-Father here. He was the first dragon to sing, and he used the power of his dragon-song to forge the first dwarves out of molten rock, but that's not the point—the point is, that line is *not* in the book.

So what else isn't in the book? What else is different? Why is Moffat freestyling?

These audiobooks were produced in 1987, just after *Volume III* had been published. Therefore, it was also just after Clark Moffat's entanglement with the Unbroken Spine. My spider-sense is tingling: this is connected.

But I can think of only three people in the world who might possess clues to Moffat's intent. The first is the dark lord of the Unbroken Spine, but I have absolutely no desire to communicate with Corvina or any of his henchmen at the Festina Lente Company, above- or belowground. Besides, I'm still afraid my IP address might be listed on one of their pirate rosters.

The second is my erstwhile employer, and I have a deep desire to communicate with Penumbra, but I don't know how. Lying here on the floor, listening to the hiss of empty tape, I realize something very sad: this skinny, blue-eyed man bent my life into a crazy curlicue . . . and all I know about him is what it says on the front of his store.

There is a third possibility. Edgar Deckle is technically part of Corvina's crew, but he has a few things going for him:

1. He's an established coconspirator.
2. He guards the door to the Reading Room, so he must be pretty high up in the fellowship, and therefore have access to many secrets.
3. He knew Moffat. And, most important of all:
4. He's in the phone book. Brooklyn.

It feels appropriately weighty and Unbroken Spine-ish to send him a letter. This is something I haven't done in more than a decade. The last letter I wrote in ink on paper was a mushy missive to my long-distance pseudo-girlfriend in the gold-tinted week after science camp. I was thirteen. Leslie Murdoch never wrote back.

For this new epistle, I select heavy archival-grade paper. I purchase a sharp-tipped rollerball pen. I carefully compose my message, first explaining all that transpired up on Google's bright screens and then asking Edgar Deckle what he knows, if anything, about Clark Moffat's audiobook editions. I crumple six sheets of the archival-grade paper in the process because I keep misspelling words or smashing them together. My handwriting is still terrible.

Finally, I drop the letter into a bright blue mailbox and hope for the best.

Three days later, an email appears. It's from Edgar Deckle. He proposes that we video chat.

Well, fine.

It's just past noon on a Sunday when I click the green camera icon. The feed comes to life and there is Deckle, peering down into his computer, his round nose slightly foreshortened. He's sitting in a narrow, light-filled room with yellow walls; I think there's a skylight somewhere up above him. Behind his fuzzy crown of hair, I can see copper cooking pots hanging from hooks, and the front of a gleaming black refrigerator festooned with bright magnets and faint drawings.

"I liked your letter," Deckle says, smiling, holding up the archival-grade paper folded into neat thirds.

"Right, well. I figured. Anyway."

"I already knew what happened in California," he says. "Word travels fast in the Unbroken Spine. You shook things up."

I expected him to be angry about all that, but he's smiling. "Corvina took some heat. People were angry."

"Don't worry, he did his best to stop it."

"Oh, no—no. They were angry we hadn't tried it

already ourselves. 'This upstart Google shouldn't have all the fun,' they said."

That makes me smile. Maybe Corvina's rule isn't as absolute as it seems.

"But you're still at it?" I ask.

"Even though Google's mighty computers didn't find anything?" Deckle says. "Sure. I mean, come on. I have a computer." He flicks a finger against the lid of his laptop and it makes the camera wobble. "They're not magic. They're only as capable as their programmers, right?"

Yeah, but those were some pretty capable programmers.

"To tell you the truth," Deckle says, "we did lose some people. A few of the younger folks, unbound, still just starting out. But that's fine. It's nothing compared to—"

There's a blur of motion behind Deckle, and a tiny face appears up over his shoulder, stretching to see the screen. It's a little girl, and I am astonished to see that she is a miniature Deckle. She has sunny blond hair, long and tangled, and she has his nose. She looks about six years old.

"Who's that?" she says, pointing at the screen. So, Edgar Deckle is hedging his bets: immortality by book and immortality by blood. Do any of the others have kids?

"That's my friend Clay," Deckle says, curling his arm around her waist. "He knows Uncle Ajax. He lives in San Francisco, too."

"I like San Francisco!" she says. "I like whales!"

Deckle leans in close to his daughter and stage-whispers, "What sound does a whale make, sweetie?"

The girl wriggles out of his grasp, stands up straight on tiptoe, and makes a sort of moo-meow sound while doing a slow pirouette. It's her whale impression. I laugh, and she looks at the screen with bright eyes, enjoying the attention. She makes the whale-song again, this time spinning away, her feet slipping on the kitchen floor. The moo-meow fades into the next room.

Deckle smiles and watches her go. "So, to get to the point," he says, turning back to me, "no: I can't help you. I saw Clark Moffat at the store, but after he solved the Founder's Puzzle—in about three months—he headed straight for the Reading Room. I never saw him after that, and I definitely don't know anything about his audiobook. To tell you the truth, I hate audiobooks."

But an audiobook is like a fuzzy knit cap pulled down over your—

"You know who you should talk to, right?"

Of course I do: "Penumbra."

Deckle nods. "He held the key to Moffat's *codex vitae*—did you know that? They were close, at least for a while there."

"But I can't find him," I say dejectedly. "He's like a ghost." Then I realize I'm talking to the man's favorite novice. "Wait—do you know where he lives?"

"I do," Deckle says. He looks straight into the camera. "But I'm not going to tell you."

My dismay must be all over my face, because Deckle immediately holds up his hands and says: "Nope, I'm going to trade you. I broke every rule in the book—and it's a very old book—and I gave you the key to the Reading Room when you needed it, right? Now I want you to do something for me. In exchange, I will happily tell you where to find our friend Mr. Ajax Penumbra."

This kind of calculation is not what I expected from friendly, smiling Edgar Deckle.

"Do you remember the Gerritszoon type I showed you down in the print shop?"

"Yeah, of course." Down in the subterranean copy shop. "Not much left."

"Right. I think I told you this: the originals were stolen. It was a hundred years ago, just after we arrived in America. The Unbroken Spine went berserk. Hired a crew of detectives, paid off the police, caught the thief."

"Who was it?"

"One of us—one of the bound. His name was Glencoe, and his book had been burned."

"Why?"

"They caught him having sex in the library," Deckle says matter-of-factly. Then he raises a finger and says, sotto voce, "Which, by the way, is still frowned upon, but would not get you burned today."

So the Unbroken Spine does make progress— slowly.

"Anyway, he swiped a stack of *codex vitae* and some silver forks and spoons—we had a fancy dining room back then. And he scooped up the Gerritszoon punches. Some say it was revenge, but I think it was more like desperation. Latin fluency doesn't get you far in New York City."

"You said they caught him."

"Yep. He couldn't find anyone to buy the books, so we got those back. The spoons were long gone. And the Gerritszoon punches—they were gone, too. They've been lost ever since."

"Weird story. So?"

"I want you to find them."

Um: "Seriously?"

Deckle smiles. "Yes, seriously. I know they might be at the bottom of a dump somewhere. But it's also possible"—his eyes glint—"that they're hiding in plain sight."

Little bits of metal, lost a hundred years ago. It would probably be easier to go looking for Penumbra door-to-door.

"I think you can do this," Deckle says. "You seem very resourceful."

One more time: "Seriously?"

"Drop me a line when you find them. *Festina lente.*" He smiles and the feed cuts to black.

Okay, now I'm angry. I'd expected Deckle to help me. Instead, he's giving me homework. Impossible homework.

But: *You seem very resourceful.* That's something I haven't heard before. I think about the word. Resourceful: full of resources. When I think of resources, I think of Neel. But maybe Deckle is right. Everything I've done so far, I've done by calling in favors. I do know people with special skills, and I know how to put their skills together.

And come to think of it, I have just the resource for this.

To find something old and obscure, something strange and significant, I turn to Oliver Grone.

When Penumbra disappeared and the store shut down, Oliver leapt so nimbly to a new job that I suspected he'd had it in his back pocket for a while. The job is at Pygmalion, one of the true-believer indies, a no-bullshit bookstore set up by Free Speech Movement alumni on Engels Street over in Berkeley. So now Oliver and I are sitting together in Pygmalion's cramped café, tucked behind the sprawling FOOD POLITICS section. Oliver's legs are too big for the tiny table, so he's stretching them out to one side. I'm nibbling a scone made with raspberries and bean sprouts.

Oliver seems happy working here. Pygmalion is huge, almost a whole city block stacked with books, and it is supremely well organized. Bright blocks of color on the ceiling mark out the sections and matching stripes run in tight patterns across the floor like a rainbow circuit board. When I arrived, Oliver was carrying an armload of heavy tomes toward the ANTHROPOLOGY shelves. Maybe his big build isn't a linebacker's after all; maybe it's a librarian's.

"So what's a punch?" Oliver says. His knowledge of obscure objects doesn't run quite so deep after you get past the twelfth century, but I am undeterred.

I explain that the system of movable type relies on tiny metal characters that can be slotted into rows that stack up to make pages. For hundreds of years, the characters were made individually, each one cast by hand. To cast the characters, you needed an original model, carved from hard metal. That model was called a punch, and there was a punch for each letter.

Oliver is quiet for a moment, and his eyes have a distant look. Then he says, "So. I should tell you. There are really two kinds of objects in the world. This is going to sound sort of spacey, but . . . some things have an aura. Others don't."

Well, I'm banking on aura. "We're talking about one of the key assets of a centuries-old cult here."

He nods. "That's good. Everyday objects . . . household objects? They're gone." He snaps his fingers: *poof.* "We're really lucky when we find, like, an awesome salad bowl. But religious objects? You would not believe how many ceremonial urns are still hanging around. Nobody wants to be the guy to throw away the urn."

"So if I'm lucky, nobody wanted to be the guy to throw away Gerritszoon, either."

"Yep, and if somebody stole it, that's a good sign. Getting stolen is one of the best things that can happen to an object. Stolen stuff recirculates. Stays out of the ground." Then he presses his lips tight. "But don't get your hopes up."

Too late, Oliver. I swallow the last of my scone and ask, "So if you've got an aura, where does that get you?"

"If these punches exist anywhere in my world," Oliver says, "there's one place you're going to find them. You need a seat at the Accession Table."

# FIRST GRADE

TABITHA TRUDEAU IS OLIVER'S BEST friend from Berkeley. She is short and solid, with curly brown hair and big intimidating eyebrows behind thick black glasses. She is now the deputy director of the most obscure museum in the whole Bay Area, a tiny place in Emeryville called the California Museum of Knitting Arts and Embroidery Sciences.

Oliver introduced us with an email and explained to Tabitha that I am on a special mission that he looks kindly upon. He also relayed to me the tactical advice that a donation wouldn't hurt. Unfortunately, any reasonable donation would constitute at least 20 percent of my worldly wealth, but I still have a patron, so I replied to Tabitha and told her I might have a thousand dollars to pass along (courtesy of the Neel Shah Foundation for Women in the Arts)—if she can help me out.

When I meet her at the museum—it's just Cal Knit to those in the know—I feel an immediate kinship, because Cal Knit is almost as weird as Penumbra's. It's just one big room, a converted schoolhouse now lined with bright displays and kid-sized activity stations. In a wide bucket next to the door, knitting needles are lined up like an armory: fat ones, skinny ones, some made of bright plastic, some made of wood carved into anthropomorphic shapes. The room smells overwhelmingly of wool.

"How many visitors do you get here?" I ask, inspecting one of the wooden needles. It's like a very slender totem pole.

"Oh, a lot," she says, hitching up her glasses. "Mostly students. There's a bus on its way right now, so we'd better get you set up."

She's sitting at the museum's front desk, where a small sign says FREE ADMISSION WITH YARN DONATION. I find Neel's check in my pocket and smooth it out on the desk. Tabitha takes it with a grin.

"Have you ever used one of these before?" she says, clicking a key on a blue computer terminal. It beeps brightly.

"Never," I say. "I didn't even know it was a thing until two days ago."

Tabitha looks up, and I follow her gaze: a school bus is rounding the corner into the museum's tiny parking lot. "Well," she says, "it's a thing. You'll figure it out. Just don't, like, give our stuff away to some other museum."

I nod and scooch in behind the desk, trading places with her. Tabitha buzzes around the museum, straightening chairs and swabbing plastic tables with antiseptic wipes. As for me: the Accession Table is set.

The Accession Table, I learned from Oliver, is

an enormous database that tracks all artifacts in all museums, everywhere. It's been around since the middle of the twentieth century. Back then it ran on punch cards passed around, copied, kept in catalogs. In a world where artifacts are always on the move—from a museum's third subbasement, up to the exhibition hall, over to another museum (which is in Boston or Belgium)—it is a necessity.

Every museum in the world uses the Accession Table, from the humblest community history co-op to the most opulent national collection, and every museum has an identical monitor. It's the Bloomberg terminal of antiquity. When any artifact is found or purchased, it gets a new record in this museological matrix. If it's ever sold or burned to a crisp, the record is dropped. But as long as any scrap of canvas or sliver of stone remains in any collection anywhere, it's still on the books.

The Accession Table helps catch forgeries: each museum sets up its terminal to watch for new records bearing suspicious similarities to artifacts already in its collection. When the Accession Table sounds its alarm, it means that somewhere, someone has just been duped.

If the Gerritszoon punches exist in any museum in the world, they'll be listed in the Accession Table. All I need is a minute on the terminal. But, to be clear, a curator at any legitimate museum would be appalled at this request. These terminals constitute the secret knowledge of this particular cult. So Oliver proposed that we find a back door: a small museum with a guardian friendly to our cause.

The chair behind the front desk creaks under my weight. I expected the Accession Table to be a little more high-tech, but in fact it looks like an artifact itself. It's a bright blue monitor, not of recent vintage; the pixels peek out through thick glass. New acquisitions all over the world scroll up the side of the screen. There are Mediterranean ceramic plates and Japanese samurai swords and Mughal fertility statues—pretty hot Mughal statues, all hips, totally yakshini—and more, lots more, there are old stopwatches and crumbling muskets and even books, nice old books bound in blue with fat golden crosses on their covers.

How do curators not just stare at this terminal all day long?

First-graders are streaming into Cal Knit, yelping and shrieking. Two boys grab knitting needles out of the bucket by the front door and start dueling, making buzzing light-saber noises accompanied by sprays of saliva. Tabitha shepherds them to the activity stations and starts her spiel. There's a poster on the wall behind her that says KNITTING IS NEAT.

Back to the Accession Table. On the other side of the terminal, there are graphs, obviously configured by Tabitha. They track accession activity in different areas of interest, areas such as TEXTILES and CALIFORNIA and NO ENDOWMENT. TEXTILES is a spiky little mountain range of activity; CALIFORNIA has a clear upward slope; NO ENDOWMENT is flatlined.

Okay. Where's the search box?

Over by Tabitha, the yarn has come out. First-graders are digging through wide plastic containers, looking for their favorite colors. One of them falls in and shrieks, and her two friends start poking her with needles.

There is no search box.

I jab random keys until the word DIRECTORY lights up at the top of the screen. (It was F5 that did it.) Now a rich, detailed taxonomy unfurls before me. Someone somewhere has categorized everything everywhere:

METAL, WOOD, CERAMIC.
15TH CENTURY, 16TH CENTURY, 17TH
  CENTURY.
POLITICAL, RELIGIOUS, CEREMONIAL.

But wait—what's the difference between RELIGIOUS and CEREMONIAL? There's a sinking feeling in my stomach. I start exploring METAL but there are only coins and bracelets and fishing hooks. No swords—I think those are filed under WEAPONS. Maybe WAR. Maybe POINTY THINGS.

Tabitha is leaning in close with one of the first-graders, helping him cross two knitting needles together to make his first loop. His brow is furrowed with utter concentration—I saw that look in the Reading Room—and then he gets it, the loop forms, and he breaks into a wide giggling grin.

Tabitha looks back my way. "Found it yet?"

I shake my head. No, I have not found it yet. It's not in 15TH CENTURY. Well, maybe it is in 15TH CENTURY, but everything else is in 15TH CENTURY, too—that's the problem. I'm still stuck looking for a needle in a haystack. Probably an ancient Song Dynasty haystack that the Mongols burned along with everything else.

I slump forward with my face in my hands, staring into the blue terminal, which is showing me a picture of some lumpy green coins salvaged from an old Spanish galleon. Did I just waste a thousand of Neel's dollars? What am I supposed to do with this thing? Why hasn't Google indexed museums yet?

A first-grader with bright red hair runs up to the front desk, giggling and choking herself with a tangle of green yarn. Um—nice scarf? She grins and jumps up and down.

"Hi there," I say. "Let me ask you a question." She giggles and nods. "How would you find a needle in a haystack?"

The first-grader pauses, pensive, tugging on

the green yarn around her neck. She's really thinking this over. Tiny gears are turning; she's twisting her fingers together, pondering. It's cute. Finally, she looks up and says gravely, "I would ask the hays to find it." Then she makes a quiet banshee whine and bounces away on one foot.

An ancient Song Dynasty gong thunders in my head. Yes, of course. She's a genius! Giggling to myself, I pound the escape key until I'm free of the terminal's awful taxonomy. Instead, I choose the command that says, simply, ACCESSION.

It's so simple. Of course, of course. The first-grader is right. It's easy to find a needle in a haystack! *Ask the hays to find it!*

The accession form is long and complicated, but I race through it:

CREATOR: Griffo Gerritszoon
YEAR: 1500 (approx.)
DESCRIPTION: Metal type. Gerritszoon
   punches. Full font.
PROVENANCE: Lost ca. 1900. Recovered
   via anonymous gift.

I leave the rest of the fields empty and thwack the return key to submit this new artifact, entirely made-up, to the Accession Table. If I understand this right, it's now scrolling across all the other terminals, just like this one, in every museum in the world. Curators are checking it out, cross-referencing it—thousands of them.

A minute ticks past. Another. A slouchy first-grader with a dark mop of hair slinks up to the desk, stands on tiptoe, and leans in conspiratorially. "Do you have any games?" he whispers, pointing to the terminal. I shake my head sadly. Sorry, kid, but maybe—

The Accession Table goes *whoop whoop*. It's a high, rising sound, like a fire alarm: *whoop whoop*. The slouchy kid jumps, and the first-graders all turn my way. Tabitha does, too, with one of her big eyebrows arched up.

"Everything okay over there?"

I nod, too excited to speak. A message in fat red letters blinks angrily at the bottom of the screen:

ACCESSION DENIED

Yes!

ARTIFACT EXISTS

Yes yes yes!

PLEASE CONTACT: CONSOLIDATED UNIVERSAL LONG-TERM STORAGE LLC

The Accession Table rings—wait, it can ring? I peer around the side of the terminal and see a bright blue telephone handset clipped into place there. Is this the museum emergency hotline? *Help, King Tut's tomb is empty!* It rings again.

"Hey, dude, what are you doing over there?" Tabitha calls across the room.

I wave brightly—everything is just fine—then snatch up the handset, clutch it close, and whisper, "Hello. Cal Knit."

"This is Consolidated Universal Long-Term Storage calling," says the voice on the other end of the line. It's a woman, and she speaks with just the tiniest twang. "Put me through to accessions, could you please?"

I look across the room: Tabitha is pulling two first-graders out of a cocoon of green and yellow yarn. One of them is a little red in the face, like she's been suffocating. On the phone I say, "Accessions? That's me, ma'am."

"Oh, you are so polite! Well, listen darlin', somebody's taking you for a ride," she says. "The—let's see—ceremonial artifact you just submitted is already on file over here. Had it for years. You *always* need to check first, hon."

It's all I can do not to jump up and start dancing behind the desk. I compose myself and say into the phone, "Gosh, thanks for the heads-up. I'll get this guy out of here. He's totally sketchy, says he's part of a secret society, they've had it for hundreds of years—you know, the usual."

The woman sighs sympathetically. "Story of my *life,* hon."

"Listen," I say lightly, "what's your name?"

"Cheryl, hon. I'm real sorry about this. Nobody likes a call from Con-U."

"That's not true! I appreciate your diligence, Cheryl." I'm playing the part: "But we're pretty small. I've actually never heard of Con-U . . ."

"Darlin', are you serious? We are *only* the largest and most advanced off-site storage facility serving the historical entertainment sector anywhere west of the Mississippi," she says in one breath. "Over here in Nevada. You ever been to Vegas?"

"Well, no—"

"Driest place in the whole United States, hon."

Perfect for stone tablets. Okay, this is it. I make the pitch: "Listen, Cheryl, maybe you can help me out. Here at Cal Knit, we just got a big grant from, uh, the Neel Shah Foundation—"

"That sounds nice."

"Well, it's big by our standards, which isn't that big at all. But we're putting together a new exhibition, and . . . you've got the real Gerritszoon punches, right?"

"I don't know what those are, hon, but it says here we've got 'em."

"Then we'd like to borrow them."

I get the details from Cheryl, say thanks and goodbye, and fit the blue handset back into place.

A ball of green yarn comes arcing through the air and lands on the front desk, then rolls into my lap, unraveling as it goes. I look up, and it's the redheaded first-grader again, standing on one foot, sticking her tongue out at me.

The first-graders jostle and fidget on their way back out into the parking lot. Tabitha closes the front door, locks it, and limps back to the front desk. She has a faint red scratch across her cheek.

I start spooling up the green yarn. "Rough class?"

"They're quick with those needles," she says, sighing. "What about you?"

I've written the name of the storage facility and its Nevada address on a Cal Knit memo pad. I spin it around to show her.

"Yeah, that's not surprising," she says. "Probably ninety percent of everything on that screen is in storage. Did you know the Library of Congress keeps most of its books outside of D.C.? They have, like, seven hundred miles of shelves. All warehouses."

"Ugh." I hate the sound of that. "What's the point, if nobody ever gets to see it?"

"It's a museum's job to keep things for posterity," Tabitha sniffs. "We have a temperature-controlled storage unit full of Christmas sweaters."

Of course. You know, I'm really starting to think the whole world is just a patchwork quilt of crazy little cults, all with their own secret spaces, their own records, their own rules.

• • •

On the train back to San Francisco, I type three short messages into my phone.

One is to Deckle, and it says: *I'm on to something.*

Another is to Neel, and it says: *Can I borrow your car?*

The last is to Kat, and it says simply: *Hello.*

# THE STORM

CONSOLIDATED UNIVERSAL Long-Term Storage is a long, low span of gray that squats on the side of the highway just outside of Enterprise, Nevada. As I pull into the long parking lot, I can feel its blank mass pressing down on my spirit. It is industrial-park desolation given shape and form, but at least it holds the promise of treasures within. The Applebee's three miles up the highway is also depressing, but there you know exactly what's waiting inside.

To get into Con-U, I pass through two metal detectors and an X-ray machine and then I am patted down by a security guard named Barry. My bag, jacket, wallet, and pocket change are all confiscated. Barry checks for knives, scalpels, picks, awls, scissors, brushes, and cotton swabs. He checks the length of my nails, then makes me pull on pink latex gloves. Finally, he puts me in a white Tyvek jumpsuit with elastic at the wrists and built-in booties for my shoes. When I emerge into the dry, immaculate air of the storage facility, I am a man made perfectly inert: I cannot chip, scratch, fade, corrode, or react with any physical substance in the known universe. I guess I could still lick something. I'm surprised Barry didn't tape my mouth shut.

Cheryl meets me in a narrow hallway, harshly lit

by overhead fluorescents, in front of a door with the words ACCESSION/DEACCESSION stenciled on it in tall black letters. They look like they want to say REACTOR CORE.

"Welcome to Nevada, hon!" She waves and smiles a wide smile that makes her cheeks bunch up. "Awful nice to see a new face out here." Cheryl is a middle-aged woman with frizzy black hair. She's wearing a green cardigan with a neat zigzag pattern and dusty blue mom-jeans—no Tyvek suit for her. Her Con-U badge hangs on a lanyard around her neck, and the photo on the badge looks ten years younger.

"Okay, hon. The intermuseum loan form is here." She hands me a crinkly sheet of pale green paper. "And this is the checkout manifest." Another paper, this one yellow. "And you'll have to sign this one." It's pink. Cheryl takes a long breath. Her brow furrows, and she says, "Now, listen, hon. Your institution isn't nationally accredited, so we can't do the pick and pack for you. Against the rules."

"Pick and pack?"

"Sorry about that." She hands me a previous-generation iPad wrapped in a tire-tread rubber casing. "But here's a map. We have these neat pads now." She smiles.

The iPad shows a tiny hallway (she pokes at it with her finger—"See, we're right here") that runs out into a gigantic rectangle, which is blank. "And that's the facility, through there." She lifts her arm, which jangles with bracelets, and points down the hallway toward wide double doors.

One of the forms—the yellow one—tells me the Gerritszoon punches are on shelf ZULU-2591. "So where do I find that?"

"Honestly, hon, it's hard to say," Cheryl says. "You'll see."

The Con-U storage facility is the most amazing space I have ever seen. Keep in mind that I recently worked at a vertical bookstore and have even more recently visited a secret subterranean library. Keep in mind, also, that I saw the Sistine Chapel when I was a kid, and, as part of science camp, I got to visit a particle accelerator. This warehouse has them all beat.

The ceiling hangs high above, ribbed like an airplane hangar. The floor is a maze of tall metal shelves loaded with boxes, canisters, containers, and bins. Simple enough. But the shelves—the shelves are all moving.

For a moment I feel sick, because my vision is swimming. The whole facility is writhing like a bucket of worms; it's that same overlapping, hard-to-follow motion. The shelves are all mounted on fat rubber tires, and they know how to use them. They move in tight, controlled bursts, then break into smooth sprints through channels of open floor. They pause and politely wait for one another; they team up and form long caravans. It's uncanny. It's totally "Sorcerer's Apprentice."

So the iPad's map is blank because the facility is rearranging itself in real-time.

The space is dark, with no lights overhead, but each shelf has a small orange lamp mounted on top, flashing and rotating. The lamps cast strange spinning shadows as the shelves make their complex migrations. The air is dry—really dry. I lick my lips.

A shelf carrying a rack of tall spears and lances comes whizzing past me. Then it takes a sharp turn—the lances rattle—and I see that it's bound for wide doors on the far wall. There, cool blue light spills into the darkness, and a team in Tyvek lifts boxes off the shelves, checks them against clipboards, then carries them out of sight. Shelves line up like schoolchildren, fidgeting and jostling; then, when the white-suits are done, they scoot away and merge back into the maze.

Here, in the most advanced off-site storage facility serving the historical entertainment sector anywhere west of the Mississippi, you don't find the artifacts. The artifacts find you.

The iPad blinks at me, now showing a blue dot labeled ZULU-2591 near the center of the floor. Okay, that's helpful. It must be a transponder tag. Or a magic spell.

There's a thick yellow line painted on the floor in front of me. I edge one toe across, and the shelves nearby all swerve and recoil. That's good. They know I'm here.

So then I push slowly into the maelstrom. Some shelves don't slow down, but bend their trajectories to coast just behind or just ahead of me. I walk evenly, taking slow, deliberate steps. As they migrate around me, the shelves make a parade of wonders. There are huge urns glazed in blue and gold, strapped down and packed with foam; wide glass cylinders full of brown formaldehyde, tentacles inside dimly visible and undulating; slabs of crystal poking out of rough black rock glowing green in the darkness. One shelf holds a single oil painting, six feet tall: a portrait of a scowling merchant prince with a skinny mustache. His eyes seem to follow me as the painting curves out of sight.

I wonder if Mat's miniature city—well, now Mat and Ashley's—will end up on shelves like these one day. Will they strap it in sideways? Or will they carefully dismantle it and store all the buildings separately, each one wrapped in gauze? Will the shelves drift apart and go their separate ways? Will Matropolis spread out through the facility like so much stardust? So many people dream of getting something into a museum . . . is this what they have in mind?

The outer perimeter of the facility is like a highway; this must be where all the popular artifacts hang out. But as I follow the iPad and make my way toward the center of the floor, things slow down. Here, there are racks of wicker masks, tea sets packed in foam peanuts, thick metal panels crusted with dry barnacles. Here, there's an airplane propeller and a three-piece suit. Here, things are weirder.

It's not all shelves, either. There are rolling vaults—huge metal boxes set up on tank treads. Some of them crawl slowly forward; some sit in place. All of them have complicated locks and glinting black cameras perched on top. One has a bright biohazard warning splashed across the front; I make a wide path around it.

Suddenly there's a hydraulic snap and one of the vaults heaves to life. It jerks forward, orange lamps flashing. I jump out of the way, and it trundles through the spot where I just stood. The shelves all move and make room as the vault begins its journey, slowly, toward the wide doors.

It occurs to me that if I'm flattened here, no one will find me for a while.

There's a flicker of motion. The part of my brain that is devoted to the detection of other human beings (and especially muggers, murderers, and enemy ninjas) lights up like one of the orange lamps. There's a person coming through the darkness. Hamster-mode: engage. Somebody's running right at me, coming fast, and he looks like Corvina. I whirl to face him, put my hands up in front of me, and yell: "Ah!"

It's that painting again—the mustachioed merchant prince. It's come back around for another look. Is it following me? No—of course not. My heart is racing. Calm down, Fluff McFly.

In the very center of the facility, nothing moves. It's hard to see in here; the shelves have shut off their lamps, maybe to save battery power or maybe just out of despair. It's quiet—the eye of the storm. Bars of light from the busy perimeter poke through and briefly illuminate dented brown boxes, stacks of newsprint, slabs of stone. I check the iPad and find the blinking blue dot. I think it's close, so I start checking the shelves.

They all have a thick layer of dust. Shelf by shelf, I wipe them off and check the labels. In tall black digits on shiny yellow, they read: BRAVO-3877. GAMMA-6173. I keep checking, using my phone as a flashlight. TANGO-5179. ULTRA-4549. Then: ZULU-2591.

I'm expecting a heavy case, some finely wrought ark for Gerritszoon's great creation. Instead, it's a cardboard box with the flaps folded in. Inside, each punch is wrapped in its own plastic bag with a rubber band to hold it tight. They look like old car parts.

But then I lift one out—it's the *X,* and it's heavy—and a bright wash of triumph floods through me. I can't believe I'm holding this in my hand. I can't believe I found them. I feel like

Telemach Half-Blood with the Golden Horn of Griffo. I feel like the hero.

Nobody's looking. I hoist the $X$ high in the air like a mythic sword. I imagine lightning streaking down through the ceiling. I imagine the Wyrm Queen's dark legion falling silent. I make a quiet energy-overload noise: *pshowww!*

Then I wrap both arms around the box, heave it up off the shelf, and wobble back out into the storm.

# THE DRAGON-SONG
# CHRONICLES, VOLUME III

**B**ACK IN CHERYL'S OFFICE, I fill out my paperwork and wait patiently while she updates the Accession Table. The terminal on her desk is just like the one at Cal Knit: blue plastic, thick glass, built-in handset. Next to it, she has a page-a-day calendar with pictures of cats dressed up as famous figures. Today's is a fuzzy white Julius Caesar.

I wonder if Cheryl realizes how historically significant the contents of this cardboard box are.

"Oh, honey," she says, waving her hand, "everything in there is a treasure to somebody." She leans in close to the terminal, double-checking her work.

Huh. Right. What else is slumbering in the eye of the storm, waiting for the right person to come along and pick it up?

"You want to set that down, hon?" Cheryl asks, tipping her chin at the box between my arms. "Looks heavy."

I shake my head. No, I do not want to set it down. I'm afraid it might vanish. It still seems impossible that I'm holding the punches. Five hundred years ago, a man named Griffo Gerritszoon carved these shapes—these ones exactly. Centuries passed, and millions, maybe billions, of people saw the impressions they made, although most didn't realize it. Now I'm cradling them like a newborn. A really heavy newborn.

Cheryl taps a key and the printer next to her terminal starts to purr. "Almost done, hon."

For objects of deep aesthetic value, the punches don't look like much. They're just skinny sticks of dark alloy, raw and scratched, and only at the very ends do they become beautiful, the glyphs emerging from the metal like mountaintops in the fog.

I suddenly think to ask, "Who owns these?"

"Oh, nobody does," Cheryl says. "Not anymore. If somebody owned 'em you'd be talkin' to them, not me!"

"So . . . what are they doing here?"

"Gosh, we're like an orphanage for a lot of things," she says. "Let's see here." She tilts her glasses and scratches at her mouse's scroll wheel. "The Flint Museum of Modern Industry sent 'em over, but of course they went under in '88. Real cute place. Real nice curator, Dick Saunders."

"And he just left everything here?"

"Well, he came and picked up some old cars and took 'em away on a flatbed truck, but the rest, he just signed it over to the Con-U collection."

Maybe Con-U should put on an exhibit of its own: Anonymous Artifacts of the Ages.

"We try to auction things off," Cheryl says, "but some of it . . ." She shrugs. "Like I said, everything's a treasure to somebody. But a lot of times, you can't find that somebody."

That's depressing. If these little objects, so significant to the history of printing and typography and human communication, were lost in a giant storage unit . . . what chance do any of us have?

"Okay, Mis-ter Jannon," Cheryl says with mock formality, "you're all set." She tucks the printout into the box and pats me on the arm. "That's a three-month loan, and you can extend it to a year. Ready to change out of that long underwear?"

I drive back to San Francisco with the punches in the passenger seat of Neel's hybrid. They fill the interior with a dense annealed odor that makes my nose itch. I wonder if I should wash them in boiling water or something. I wonder if the smell is going to stick to the seats.

It's a long drive home. For a while I watch the Toyota's energy-management control panel and try to beat my fuel efficiency from before. But that gets boring fast, so I plug in the Walkman and start up the audiobook version of *The Dragon-Song Chronicles: Volume III*, read by Clark Moffat himself.

I roll my shoulders back, grip the wheel at ten and two, and settle into the strangeness. I'm flanked by brothers of the Unbroken Spine, separated by centuries: Moffat on the stereo,

Gerritszoon in the passenger seat. The Nevada desert is blank for miles, and high in the Wyrm Queen's tower, things are getting super-weird.

Keep in mind that this series starts with a singing dragon lost at sea, calling out to dolphins and whales for help. It gets rescued by a passing ship that also happens to be carrying a scholarly dwarf. The dwarf befriends the dragon and nurses it back to health, then saves its life when the ship's captain comes in the night to cut the dragon's throat and get the gold in its gullet, and that's just the first five pages—so, you know, for this story to get even weirder is a not-insignificant development.

But, of course, now I know the reason: the third and final volume of *The Dragon-Song Chronicles* served double duty as Moffat's *codex vitae*.

All of the action in this installment takes place in the Wyrm Queen's tower, which turns out to be almost a world unto itself. The tower reaches up to the stars, and each floor has its own set of rules, its own puzzles to solve. The first two volumes have adventures and battles and, of course, betrayals. This one is all puzzles, puzzles, puzzles.

It begins with the friendly ghost who appears to release Fernwen the dwarf and Telemach Half-Blood from the Wyrm Queen's dungeon and start them on their ascent. Moffat describes the ghost through the Toyota's speakers:

*It was tall, made of pale blue light, a creature*

*with long arms and long legs and the shadow of a smile, and above it all, eyes that shone bluer still than its body.*

Wait a second.

*"What do you seek in this place?" the shade asked plainly.*

I fumble to rewind the tape. First I overshoot the mark, so I have to fast-forward, then I miss it again, so I have to rewind, and then the Toyota shakes as it crosses the rumble strips. I pull the steering wheel and point the car straight down the highway and finally press play:

*. . . eyes that shone bluer still than its body. "What do you seek in this place?" the shade asked plainly.*

Again:

*. . . bluer still than its body. "What do you seek in this place?"*

It is unmistakable: Moffat is doing Penumbra's voice there. This part of the book isn't new; I remember the friendly blue ghost in the dungeon from my first reading. But, of course, back then I had no way of knowing Moffat might encode an eccentric San Francisco bookseller into his fantasy epic. And likewise, when I walked through the front door of the 24-Hour Bookstore, I had no way of knowing I'd met Mr. Penumbra a few times already.

Ajax Penumbra is the blue-eyed shade in the dungeon of the Wyrm Queen's tower. I am absolutely sure of it. And to hear Moffat's voice, the rough affection in it, as he finishes the scene . . .

*Fernwen's small hands burned on the ladder. The iron was ice-cold, and it seemed each rung bit him, tried its evil best to send him plummeting back into the dark depths of the dungeon. Telemach was high above, already pulling himself through the portal. Fernwen glanced down below. The shade was there, standing just inside the secret door. It grinned, a pulse of light through spectral blue, and waved its long arms and called out:*

*"Climb, my boy! Climb!"*

*And so he did.*

. . . incredible. Penumbra has already earned a touch of immortality. Does he know?

I accelerate back up to cruising speed, shaking my head and smiling to myself. The story is accelerating, too. Now Moffat's gravelly voice carries the heroes from floor to floor, solving riddles and recruiting allies along the way—a thief, a wolf, a talking chair. Now, for the first time, I get it: the floors are a metaphor for the code-breaking techniques of the Unbroken Spine. Moffat is using the tower to tell the story of his own path through the fellowship.

This is all so obvious when you know what to listen for.

At the very end, after a long weird slog of a story, the heroes arrive at the tower's summit, the spot from which the Wyrm Queen looks out across the world and plots domination. She is there, waiting for them, and she has her dark legion with her. Their black robes seem more significant now.

While Telemach Half-Blood leads his band of allies into the final battle, Fernwen the scholarly dwarf makes an important discovery. In the cataclysmic commotion, he sneaks over to the Wyrm Queen's magic telescope and peeks through. From this vantage point, impossibly high up, he can see something amazing. The mountains that divide the Western Continent form letters. They are, Fernwen realizes, a message, and not just any message, but the message promised long ago by Aldrag the Wyrm-Father himself, and when Fernwen speaks the words aloud, he—

Holy shit.

When I finally cross the bridge back into San Francisco, Clark Moffat's voice in the closing chapters has a new warble; I think the cassette might be stretched out from my rewinding and replaying, rewinding and replaying, again and again. My brain feels a little stretched out, too. It's carrying a new theory that started as a seed but is now growing fast, all based on what I've just heard.

Moffat: You were brilliant. You saw something

that no one else in the whole history of the Unbroken Spine ever saw. You raced through the ranks, you became one of the bound, maybe just to get access to the Reading Room—and then you bound up their secrets in a book of your own. You hid them in plain sight.

It took me hearing them to get it.

It's late, past midnight. I double-park Neel's car in front of the apartment and bang the wide button that sets the hazard lights blinking. I jump out, heave the cardboard box from the passenger seat, and dash up the steps. My key scratches the lock—I can't find it in the darkness, and my hands are full, and I'm vibrating.

"Mat!" I run to the stairs and call up to his room: "Mat! Do you have a microscope?"

There's a murmuring, a faint voice—Ashley's—and Mat appears at the top of the stairs, wearing just his boxer shorts, which are printed with a full-color reproduction of a Salvador Dalí painting. He's waving a giant magnifying glass. It's huge and he looks like a cartoon detective. "Here, here," he says softly, scampering down to hand it off. "Best I can do. Welcome back, Jannon. Don't drop it." Then he hops back up the stairs and shuts his door with a quiet click.

I take the Gerritszoon originals into the kitchen and turn all the lights on. I feel crazy, but in a good way. Carefully, I lift one of the punches out of the box—the *X* again. I pull it out of its plastic bag, wipe it down with a towel, and hold it under the glare of the stove's fluorescent light. Then I steady Mat's magnifying glass and peer through.

The mountains are a message from Aldrag the Wyrm-Father.

# THE PILGRIM

I T IS ONE WEEK LATER, and I have got the goods, in more ways than one. I emailed Edgar Deckle and told him he had better come out to California if he wants his punches. I told him he had better come out to Pygmalion on Thursday night.

I invited everyone: my friends, the fellowship, all the people who helped along the way. Oliver Grone convinced his manager to let me use the back of the store, where they have A/V gear set up for book readings and poetry slams. Ashley baked vegan oat cookies, four plates of them. Mat set up the chairs.

Now Tabitha Trudeau sits in the front row. I introduce her to Neel Shah (her new benefactor) and he immediately proposes a Cal Knit exhibit that will have, as its focus, the way boobs look in sweaters.

"It's very distinct," he says. "The sexiest of all apparel. It's true. We ran a focus group." Tabitha frowns and knits her brows together. Neel goes on: "The exhibit could have classic movie scenes looping, and we could track down the actual sweaters they wore and hang them up . . ."

Rosemary Lapin sits in the second row, and next to her are Tyndall, Fedorov, Imbert, Muriel, and more—most of the same crowd that came out to

Google on a bright morning not so long ago. Fedorov has his arms crossed and his face set in a skeptical mask, as if to say, *I've been through this once before,* but that's okay. I'm not going to disappoint him.

There are two unbound brothers from Japan, too—a pair of young mop-haired men in skinny indigo jeans. They heard a rumor through the grapevine of the Unbroken Spine and decided it would be worth their while to find a last-minute flight to San Francisco. (They were correct.) Igor is sitting with them, chatting comfortably in Japanese.

There's a laptop set up in the front row so Cheryl from Con-U can watch. She's beaming in via video chat, her frizzy black hair taking up the whole screen. I invited Grumble to join in, too, but he's on a plane tonight—headed for Hong Kong, he says.

Darkness blooms through the bookstore's front door: Edgar Deckle has arrived, and he's brought an entourage of New York black-robes with him. They aren't actually wearing their robes, not here, but their attire still marks them as strange outsiders: suits, ties, a charcoal skirt. They come streaming through the door, a dozen of them— and then, there's Corvina. His suit is gray and gleaming. He's still an imposing dude, but here he seems diminished. Without all the pageantry and the backdrop of bedrock, he's just an old—

His dark eyes flash up and find me. Okay, maybe not that diminished.

Pygmalion's customers turn to watch, eyebrows raised, as the black-robes march through the store. Deckle is wearing a light smile. Corvina is all sharp gravity.

"If you truly have the Gerritszoon punches," he says flatly, "we will take them."

I steel my spine and tilt my chin up a little. We're not in the Reading Room anymore. "I do have them," I say, "but that's just the beginning. Have a seat." Oh, boy. "Please."

He flicks his eyes across the chattering crowd and frowns, but then he waves his black-robes into place. They all find seats in the last row, a dark bracket at the back of the assembly. Behind them, Corvina stands.

I grab hold of Deckle's elbow as he passes. "Is he coming?"

"I told him," he says, nodding. "But he already knew. Word travels fast in the Unbroken Spine."

Kat is here, sitting up front, way off to the side, talking quietly with Mat and Ashley. She's wearing her houndstooth blazer again. There's a green scarf around her neck, and she's cut her hair since the last time I saw her; now it stops just below her ears.

We are no longer dating. There has been no formal declaration, but it's an objective truth, like the atomic weight of carbon or the share price of GOOG. That didn't stop me from pestering her and extracting a promise to attend. She, of all people, has to see this.

People are shifting in their seats and the vegan oat cookies are almost gone, but I have to wait. Lapin leans forward and asks me, "Are you going to New York? To work at the library, perhaps?"

"Um, no, definitely not," I say flatly. "Not interested."

She frowns and clasps her hands together. "I'm supposed to go, but I don't think I want to." She looks up at me. She looks lost. "I miss the store. And I miss—"

Ajax Penumbra.

He slips in through Pygmalion's front door like a wandering ghost, fully buttoned into his dark peacoat, the collar turned up over the thin gray scarf around his neck. He searches the room, and when he sees the crowd in the back, full of the fellowship—black-robes and all—his eyes widen.

I sprint over to him. "Mr. Penumbra! You came!"

He's half-turned away, and he puts a bony hand up around his neck. He won't look at me. His blue eyes are glued to the floor. "My boy, I am sorry," he says softly. "I should not have vanished so— ah. It was simply . . ." He lets out a whispering sigh. "I was embarrassed."

"Mr. Penumbra, please. Don't worry about it."

"I was so sure it would work," he says, "but it did not. And there you were, and your friends, and all my students. I feel like such an old fool."

Poor Penumbra. I'm imagining him holed up somewhere, grappling with the guilt of having cheered the fellowship forward to failure on Google's green lawns. Weighing his own faith and wondering what could possibly come next. He'd placed a big bet—his biggest ever—and lost. But he didn't place that bet alone.

"Come on, Mr. Penumbra." I step back toward my setup and wave him along. "Come sit down. We're all fools—all except for one of us. Come and see."

Everything is ready. There's a presentation waiting to start on my laptop. I realize that the big reveal really ought to happen in a smoky parlor, with the sleuth holding his nervous audience spellbound using only his voice and his powers of deduction. Me, I prefer bookstores, and I prefer slides.

So I power up the projector and take my position, the blank light burning my eyes. I clasp my hands behind my back, square my shoulders, and squint out into the assembled crowd. Then I click the remote and begin:

SLIDE 1

If you were going to make a message last, how would you do it? Would you carve it into stone? Etch it into gold?

Would you make your message so potent that people couldn't resist passing it on? Would you build a religion around it, maybe get people's souls involved? Would you, perhaps, establish a secret society?

Or would you do what Gerritszoon did?

## SLIDE 2

Griffo Gerritszoon was born the son of a barley grower in northern Germany in the middle of the fifteenth century. The elder Gerritszoon was not rich, but thanks to his good reputation and well-established piety, he was able to snag his son an apprenticeship with the local goldsmith. This was a great gig back in the fifteenth century; as long as he didn't screw it up, the younger Gerritszoon was basically set for life.

He screwed it up.

He was a religious kid, and the goldsmith's trade turned him off. He spent all day melting old baubles down to make new ones—and he knew his own work was going to suffer the same fate. Everything he believed told him: This is not important. There is no gold in the city of God.

So he did what he was told, and he learned the craft—he was really good at it, too—but when he turned sixteen, he said so long and left the goldsmith behind. He left Germany altogether, in fact. He went on a pilgrimage.

## SLIDE 3

I know this because Aldus Manutius knew it, and he wrote it down. He wrote it down in his *codex vitae*—which I have decoded.

(There are gasps from the audience. Corvina is still standing at the back and his face is tight, his mouth a deep grimace, his dark mustache pulled down around it. Other faces are blank, waiting. I glance over at Kat. She's wearing a serious look, as if she's worried that something might have short-circuited in my brain.)

Let me get this out of the way: There's no secret formula in this book. There's no magic incantation. If there truly is a secret to immortality, it's not here.

(Corvina makes his choice. He spins and stalks up the aisle past HISTORY and SELF-HELP toward the front door. He passes Penumbra, who's standing off to one side, leaning on a short shelf for support. He watches Corvina pass, then turns back toward me, cups his hands around his mouth, and calls out, "Keep going, my boy!")

## SLIDE 4

Really, Manutius's *codex vitae* is just what it claims to be: it's a book about his life. As a work of history, it's a treasure. But it's the part about Gerritszoon that I want to focus on.

I used Google to translate this from Latin, so bear with me if I get some of the details wrong.

Young Gerritszoon wandered through the Holy Land, doing metalwork to make a bit of money here and there. Manutius says he was meeting up with mystics—Kabbalists, Gnostics, and Sufis alike—and trying to figure out what to do with his life. He was also hearing rumors, through the goldsmiths' grapevine, of some pretty interesting stuff happening up in Venice.

This is a map of Gerritszoon's journey, as well as I can reconstruct it. He meandered around the Mediterranean—down through Constantinople, into Jerusalem, across to Egypt, back up through Greece, over to Italy.

Venice is where he met Aldus Manutius.

SLIDE 5

It was at Manutius's printing house that Gerritszoon found his place in the world. Printing called on all of his skills as a metalsmith, but it bent them to new purposes. Printing wasn't baubles and bracelets—it was words and ideas. Also, this was basically the internet of its day; it was exciting.

And just like the internet today, printing in the fifteenth century was all problems, all the time: How do you store the ink? How do you mix the metal? How do you mold the type? The answers changed every six months. In every great city of Europe, there were a dozen printing houses all trying to figure it out first. In Venice, the greatest of those printing houses belonged to Aldus Manutius, and that's where Gerritszoon went to work.

Manutius recognized his talent immediately. He also says he recognized his spirit; he saw that Gerritszoon was a searcher, too. So he hired him, and they worked together for years. They became best friends. There was no one Manutius trusted more than Gerritszoon, and no one Gerritszoon respected more than Manutius.

SLIDE 6

So finally, after a few decades, after inventing a new industry and printing hundreds of volumes that we still think of as, like, the most beautiful books ever made, both of these guys were getting old. They decided to collaborate on a great final project, one that was going to take everything they'd experienced, everything they'd learned, and package it up for posterity.

Manutius wrote his *codex vitae*, and in it, he was honest: He explained how things really worked in Venice. He explained the shady deals he'd struck to secure his exclusive license to print the classics; he explained how all his rivals had tried to shut him down; he explained how he'd shut a few of them down instead. Precisely because he was so honest, and because if it was released immediately it would damage the business he was passing on to his son, he wanted to encrypt it. But how?

At the same time, Gerritszoon was cutting a typeface, his best ever—a bold new design that would sustain Manutius's printing house after he was gone. He hit a home run, because those are the shapes that now bear his name. But in the process, he did something unexpected.

Aldus Manutius died in 1515, leaving behind a very revealing memoir. At this point, according to the lore of the Unbroken Spine, Manutius entrusted Gerritszoon with the key to this encrypted history. But something got lost in translation over five hundred years.

Gerritszoon didn't *get* the key.

Gerritszoon *is* the key.


SLIDE 7


Here's a picture of one of the Gerritszoon punches: the *X*.

Here it is closer.

And closer still.

Here it is through my friend Mat's magnifying glass. Do you see the tiny notches in the edge of the letter? They look like the teeth of a gear, don't they?—or the teeth of a key.

(There's a loud, rattling gasp. It's Tyndall. I can always count on him to get excited.)

Those tiny notches are not accidents, and they are not random. There are notches like that on all the punches, and all the molds made from the punches, and every piece of Gerritszoon type ever made. Now, I had to go to Nevada to figure this out; I had to hear Clark Moffat's voice on tape to really get it. But if I'd known what I was looking for, I could have opened up my laptop, typed out some text in Gerritszoon, and blown it up 3,000 percent. The notches are in the computer version, too. Down in their library, the Unbroken Spine doesn't deign to use computers . . . but up above, the Festina Lente Company hired some very diligent digitizers.

That's the code, right there. Those tiny notches.

Nobody in the fellowship's five-hundred-year history thought to look this closely. Neither did any of Google's code-breakers. We were looking at digitized text in a different typeface entirely. We were looking at the sequence, not the shape.

The code is both complicated and simple. Complicated because an uppercase *F* is different from a lowercase *f*. Complicated because the ligature *ff* isn't two lowercase *f*'s—it's a completely different punch. Gerritszoon has tons of alternate glyphs—three *P*'s, two *C*'s, a truly epic *Q*—and those all mean something different. To crack this code, you need to think typographically.

But after that, it's simple, because all you have to do is count the notches, which I did: carefully, under a magnifying glass, at my kitchen table, no data centers required. This is the kind of code you learn in a comic book: one number corresponds to one letter. It's a simple substitution, and you can use it to decode Manutius's *codex vitae* in no time.

SLIDE 8

You can also do something else. When you lay the punches out in order—the same order they'd use in a case in a fifteenth-century print shop—you get another message. It's a message from Gerritszoon himself. His final words for the world have been hiding in plain sight for five hundred years.

It's nothing spooky, nothing mystical. It's just a message from a man who lived a long time ago. But here's the part that is spooky: look around you.

(Everybody does. Lapin cranes her neck. She looks worried.)

See the signs on the shelves—where it says HISTORY and ANTHROPOLOGY and TEEN PARA-NORMAL ROMANCE? I noticed it earlier: those signs are all set in Gerritszoon.

The iPhone comes loaded with Gerritszoon. Every new Microsoft Word document defaults to Gerritszoon. *The Guardian* sets headlines in

Gerritszoon; so do *Le Monde* and the *Hindustan Times*. The *Encyclopædia Britannica* used to be set in Gerritszoon; Wikipedia just switched last month. Think of the term papers, the curriculum vitae, the syllabi. Think of the résumés, the job offers, the resignation letters. The contracts and lawsuits. The condolences.

It's everywhere around us. You see Gerritszoon every day. It's been here all this time, staring us in the face for five hundred years. All of it—the novels, the newspapers, the new documents—it's all been a carrier wave for this secret message, hidden in the colophon.

Gerritszoon figured it out: the key to immortality.

(Tyndall jumps up out of his seat, howling, "But what is it?" He tugs at his hair. "What is the message?")

Well, it's in Latin. The Google translation is rough. Keep in mind that Aldus Manutius was born with a different name: he was Teobaldo, and his friends all called him that.

So here it is. Here's Gerritszoon's message to eternity.

SLIDE 9

*Thank you, Teobaldo*
*You are my greatest friend*
*This has been the key to everything*

# FELLOWSHIP

THE SHOW IS OVER and the audience is clearing out. Tyndall and Lapin are lined up for coffee in Pygmalion's tiny café. Neel is still pitching Tabitha on the transcendent beauty of boobs in sweaters. Mat and Ashley are talking animatedly with Igor and the Japanese duo, all of them walking slowly toward the front door.

Kat is sitting alone, nibbling the very last vegan oat cookie. Her face is drawn. I wonder what she thinks of Gerritszoon's immortal words.

"Sorry," she says, shaking her head. "It's not good enough." Her eyes are dark and downcast. "He was so talented, and he still died."

"Everybody dies—"

"This is enough for you? He left us a note, Clay. *He left us a note.*" She shouts it, and an oat crumb comes shooting off her lips. Oliver Grone glances over from the ANTHROPOLOGY shelves, eyebrows raised. Kat looks down at her shoes. Quietly, she says, "Don't call that immortality."

"But what if this is the best part of him?" I say. I'm composing this theory in real-time: "What if, you know—what if hanging out with Griffo Gerritszoon wasn't always that great? What if he was weird and dreamy? What if the best part of him was the shapes he could make with metal?

That part of him really is immortal. It's as immortal as anything's going to get."

She shakes her head, sighs, and leans into me a little, pushing the last bits of the cookie into her mouth. I found the old knowledge, the OK, that we'd been looking for, but she doesn't like what it has to say. Kat Potente will keep searching.

After a moment, she pulls back, takes a sharp breath, and lifts herself up. "Thanks for inviting me," she says. "See you around." She shrugs on her blazer, waves goodbye, and heads for the door.

Now Penumbra calls me over.

"It is amazing," he cries, and he is himself again, with his bright eyes and wide smile. "All this time, we were playing Gerritszoon's game. My boy, we had his letters on the front of the store!"

"Clark Moffat figured this out," I tell him. "I have no idea how, but he did. And then I guess he just . . . decided to play along. Keep the puzzle going." Until someone found it all waiting in his books.

Penumbra nods. "Clark was brilliant. He was always off on his own, following his intuition wherever it led him." He pauses, cocks his head, then smiles. "You would have liked him."

"So you're not disappointed?"

Penumbra's eyes go wide. "Disappointed?

Impossible. It is not what I expected, but what did I expect? What did any of us expect? I will tell you that I did *not* expect to know the truth in my lifetime. It is a gift beyond measure, and I am grateful to Griffo Gerritszoon, and to you, my boy."

Now Deckle approaches. He's beaming, almost bouncing. "You did it!" he says, clapping me on the shoulders. "You found them! I knew you could—I knew it—but I had no idea how far it would go." Behind him, the black-robes are all chattering to one another. They look excited. Deckle glances around. "Can I touch them?"

"They're all yours," I tell him. I haul the Gerritszoon punches in their cardboard ark out from under a chair in the front row. "You'll have to officially buy them from Con-U, but I have the forms, and I don't think—"

Deckle holds up a hand. "Not a problem. Trust me—not a problem." One of the New York black-robes comes over and the rest all follow. They bend over the box, oohing and aahing like there's an infant inside.

"So it was you who set him on this path, Edgar?" Penumbra says, arching an eyebrow.

"It occurred to me, sir," Deckle says, "that I had at my disposal a rare talent." A pause, a smile, and then: "You do know how to pick the right clerks."

Penumbra snorts and grins at that. Deckle says, "This is a triumph. We'll make fresh type, reprint some of the old books. Corvina can't argue with that."

Penumbra darkens at the mention of the First Reader—his old friend.

"What about him?" I ask. "He—uh. He seemed upset."

Penumbra's face is serious. "You must look after him, Edgar. As old as he is, Marcus has little experience with disappointment. For as firm as he seems, he is fragile. I worry about him, Edgar. Truly."

Deckle nods. "We'll take care of him. We have to figure out what's next."

"Well," I say, "I've got something for you to start with." I bend down and lift a second cardboard box out from under the chairs. This one is brand-new, and it has fresh plastic tape in a wide X across the top. I tear the tape and fold back the flaps, and inside, the box is full of books: shrink-wrapped bundles of paperbacks packed tight. I poke a hole in the plastic and slide one out. It's just plain blue and on the front it says MANVTIVS in tall white capitals.

"This is for you," I say, handing it to Deckle. "A hundred copies of the decoded book. Original Latin. I figured you guys would want to translate it yourselves."

Penumbra laughs and says to me, "And now you are a publisher as well, my boy?"

"Print on demand, Mr. Penumbra," I say. "Two bucks each."

. . .

Deckle and his black-robes ferry their treasures—one old box, one new—to their rented van outside. Pygmalion's gray-haired manager watches cautiously from the café as they sweep out of the store, singing a happy carol in Greek.

Penumbra has a contemplative look on his face. "My only regret," he says, "is that Marcus will certainly burn my *codex vitae*. Like the Founder's, it was a kind of history, and I am sad to see it go."

Now I get to blow his mind a second time. "When I was down in the library," I say, "I scanned more than Manutius." I dig into my pocket, pull out a blue USB drive, and press it into his long fingers. "It's not as nice as the real thing, but the words are all here."

Penumbra holds it up high. The plastic glints in the bookstore's light, and there's a wondering half smile playing on his lips. "My boy," he breathes, "you are full of surprises." Then he arches an eyebrow. "And I could print this for just two dollars?"

"Absolutely."

Penumbra wraps a thin arm around my shoulders, leans in close, and says quietly, "This city of ours—it has taken me too long to realize it, but we are in the Venice of this world. *The Venice.*" His eyes widen, then press shut, and he shakes his head. "Just like the Founder himself."

I'm not sure where he's going with this.

"What I have finally come to understand," Penumbra says, "is that we must think like Manutius. Fedorov has money, and so does your friend—the funny one." We're looking out across the bookstore together now. "So what do you say we find a patron or two . . . and start again?"

I can't believe it.

"I must admit," Penumbra says, shaking his head, "I am in awe of Griffo Gerritszoon. His achievement is inimitable. But I have more than a little time left, my boy"—he winks—"and there are still so many mysteries to solve. Are you with me?"

Mr. Penumbra. You have no idea.

# EPILOGUE

SO WHAT'S GOING to happen after that?

Neel Shah, dungeon master, will succeed in his quest to sell his company to Google. Kat will make a pitch to the PM, and they'll go for it. They will acquire Anatomix, rebrand it Google Body, and release a new version of the software that anybody can download for free. The boobs will still be the best part.

After that, Neel will finally be rich beyond measure, and he will come into the fullness of his patronage. First, the Neel Shah Foundation for Women in the Arts will get an endowment, an office, and an executive director: Tabitha Trudeau. She will fill the firehouse floor with drawings, paintings, textiles, and tapestries, all the work of female artists, all scavenged from Con-U, and then she will begin to give out grants. Big ones.

Next, Neel will lure Mat Mittelbrand away from ILM, and together they will start a production company that uses pixels, polygons, knives, *and* glue. Neel will buy the movie rights to *The Dragon-Song Chronicles*. After the Anatomix acquisition, he will immediately hire Igor back from Google and install him as lead programmer at Half-Blood Studios. He will be planning a trilogy in 3-D. Mat will direct.

Kat will climb the ranks of the PM. First she'll bring Google the decoded memoir of Aldus Manutius, which will become the cornerstone of a new Lost Books project. *The New York Times* will blog about it. Next, the acquisition of Anatomix and the popularity of Google Body will give her even more momentum. She'll have her picture printed in *Wired*, a whole glossy half page, standing under the huge data visualization screens, hands on her hips, blazer hanging loosely over her bright red BAM! T-shirt.

I will realize then that she never stopped wearing it after all.

Oliver Grone will complete his doctorate in archaeology. He will find a job immediately, and not with a museum, but with the company that operates the Accession Table. He will be given the task of recategorizing every marble artifact made before 200 B.C., and he will be in heaven.

I'll ask Kat out on a date, and she will accept. We'll go see Moon Suicide play live, and instead of talking about frozen heads, we'll just dance. I will discover that Kat is a terrible dancer. On the steps in front of her apartment, she'll kiss me once, light on the lips, and then disappear into the dark doorway. I'll walk home and send her a text message along the way. The message will consist of a single value, one that I have deduced on my own after a long struggle with a geometry textbook: *25,000 miles.*

• • •

There will be an organizational fracture at the base of the Unbroken Spine. Back in New York, the First Reader will threaten doom and disappointment for any more who disobey. To make his point, he will, in fact, burn Penumbra's *codex vitae*—and that will be a terrible miscalculation. The black-robes will be appalled, and finally, they will vote. All of the bound will gather in their bookish barrow and raise their hands one by one, and Corvina will be stripped of his position. He will remain CEO of the Festina Lente Company—where profits are up, way up—but down below, there will be a new First Reader.

It will be Edgar Deckle.

Maurice Tyndall will travel to New York to begin writing his *codex vitae*, and I will suggest that he petition to replace Deckle as the guardian of the Reading Room. That office could use a little life.

Even though its vessel will be destroyed, the contents of Penumbra's *codex vitae* will be safe, and I will offer to help him publish it.

He will demur: "Perhaps someday, but not yet. Let it remain secret for now. After all, my boy"— his blue eyes will narrow and twinkle—"you might be surprised at what you find there."

Together, Penumbra and I will establish a new fellowship—actually, a little company. We'll talk

Neel into investing some of his Google-gotten gains, and it will turn out that Fedorov has millions in HP stock, so he'll chip in some of that, too.

Penumbra and I will sit and talk many times about what sort of enterprise might suit us best. Another bookstore? No. Some kind of publishing company? No. Penumbra will admit that he is happiest as a guide and a coach, not a scholar or a code-breaker. I will admit that I just want an excuse to put all my favorite people in a room together. So we'll form a consultancy: a special-ops squad for companies operating at the intersection of books and technology, trying to solve the mysteries that gather in the shadows of digital shelves. Kat will supply our first contract: designing the marginalia system for Google's prototype e-reader, which is thin and light, with a skin that's not plastic but cloth, like a hardcover book.

After that, we'll have to make it on our own, and Penumbra will be an absolute pro in pitch meetings. He'll put on a dark tweed suit and polish up his glasses, wobble into conference rooms at Apple and Amazon, look around the table, and say quietly, "What do you seek in this engagement?" His blue eyes, his jostling grin, and (frankly) his advanced age will leave them stunned, charmed, and utterly sold.

We'll have a narrow office down on sun-blasted

Valencia Street, wedged between a taqueria and a scooter repair shop, furnished with big wooden desks from a flea market and long green shelves from IKEA. The shelves will be lined with Penumbra's favorites, all rescued from the store: first editions of Borges and Hammett, airbrushed editions of Asimov and Heinlein, five different biographies of Richard Feynman. Every few weeks, we'll cart the books out into the sunlight and hold a pop-up sidewalk sale, announced on Twitter at the last minute.

It won't only be me and Penumbra at those big desks. Rosemary Lapin will join us as employee number one. I'll teach her Ruby, and she will build our website. Then we'll poach Jad away from Google, and I'll put Grumble on retainer, too.

We'll call the company Penumbra, just Penumbra, and the logo, designed by me, will be set—of course—in Gerritszoon.

But what about Mr. Penumbra's 24-Hour Bookstore? For three months, it will stand empty with a FOR LEASE sign in the windows, because nobody will know what to do with that tall, skinny space. Then, finally, someone will figure it out.

Ashley Adams will show up at the Telegraph Hill Credit Union's small business office dressed in carbon and cream, carrying a letter of recommendation from the bank's oldest living client. She will describe her vision with the polish and poise of a PR professional.

It will be her last act as a PR professional.

Ashley will dismantle the shelves, refinish the floor, put in new lights, and transform the bookstore into a climbing gym. The break room will become a locker room; the short shelves up front will become a row of iMacs where climbers can get online (still via *bootynet*). Where the front desk once sat, there will be a shiny white counter where North Face (a.k.a. Daphne) will get a new gig making kale shakes and risotto balls. The walls up front will be a riot of color: bright murals painted by Mat, all based on zoomed-in details from the bookstore. If you know what to look for, you'll see them: a line of letters, a row of spines, a bright curving bell.

Back where the Waybacklist once rose, Mat will direct a team of young artists in the construction of an enormous climbing wall. It will be a mottled field of green and gray dotted with glowing gold LEDs and traced with branching lines of blue, and the handholds for climbers will be sturdy white-capped mountains. Mat will build not merely a city this time, but a whole continent, a civilization tipped on its side. And here, too, if you know what to look for—if you know how to draw the lines between the handholds—you might just see a face peering out of the wall.

I will buy a membership and start climbing again.

● ● ●

And finally, I will write down everything that happened. I'll copy some of it from the logbook, find more in old emails and text messages, and reconstitute the rest from memory. I'll get Penumbra to look it over, then find a publisher and set it out for sale in all the places you find books these days: big Barnes & Nobles, bright Pygmalion, the quiet little store built into the Kindle.

You will hold this book in your hands, and learn all the things I learned, right along with me:

There is no immortality that is not built on friendship and work done with care. All the secrets in the world worth knowing are hiding in plain sight. It takes forty-one seconds to climb a ladder three stories tall. It's not easy to imagine the year 3012, but that doesn't mean you shouldn't try. We have new capabilities now— strange powers we're still getting used to. The mountains are a message from Aldrag the Wyrm-Father. Your life must be an open city, with all sorts of ways to wander in.

After that, the book will fade, the way all books fade in your mind. But I hope you will remember this:

A man walking fast down a dark lonely street. Quick steps and hard breathing, all wonder and need. A bell above a door and the tinkle it makes. A clerk and a ladder and warm golden light, and then: the right book exactly, at exactly the right time.

**Center Point Large Print**
600 Brooks Road / PO Box 1
Thorndike ME 04986-0001 USA

(207) 568-3717

**US & Canada:**
**1 800 929-9108**
**www.centerpointlargeprint.com**

1|13
WA